Dead On

Book Nine
The Irish End Games

Susan Kiernan-Lewis

Susan Kiernan-Lewis

Dead On

San Marco Press/Atlanta
Copyright 2017

Other books by Susan Kiernan-Lewis:

Free Falling
Going Gone
Heading Home
Blind Sided
Rising Tides
Cold Comfort
Never Never
Wit's End
White Out (Summer 2017)
Murder in the South of France
Murder à la Carte
Murder in Provence
Murder in Paris
Murder in Aix
Murder in Nice
Murder in the Latin Quarter
Murder in the Abbey
Murder in the Bistro
Murder in Cannes
Swept Away
Carried Away
Stolen Away
Reckless
Shameless
Breathless
Heartless
Hopeless

1

How could Mike be gone? How could he have just vanished?

Sarah sat by the midday fire and gazed into the flames. A sea of tents surrounded her with the hulking ruin of the castle—once their refuge—looming over it all.

The people who were her friends and family, they too surrounded her—each with the worried expression of people who feared the worst.

It had only been six days since the bombing of the castle and the debris was still considerable inside the fortress and out. The tent encampment where they now lived looked like a refugee village.

Children darted between the tents playing games—oblivious to the terrors that lay just beyond the perimeter of their world.

Sarah looked at Mike's shoes on the ground.

Was he really somewhere out in the wilderness with no shoes?

Did he beam up into a space ship while they all slept?

Sarah shook the thoughts from her mind. They'd plagued her over and over all morning—the same ones. The same useless, agonizing questions. And she was no closer to the answers.

"Sarah, love?"

Sarah dragged her eyes away from the shoes to see her sister-in-law Fiona coming over to sit next to her. Fiona held the hands of two small children, Ciara and Siobhan who both looked at Sarah with wide, uncomprehending eyes.

Sarah couldn't bring herself to smile—not even for Siobhan—but she reached for her and the child slipped into her arms.

"Mommy has to go," Sarah whispered into her hair.

"Don't want you to," Siobhan whispered back.

Sarah nodded but willed herself to feel nothing. Not to feel the loss of the man who should have awakened by her side this morning or the loss of the sweet child who Sarah would soon hand off to another to care for.

She steeled her heart to all of it.

"Be a good girl, Shivvy," she said and looked into Fiona's eyes.

Fiona's face was thin and pinched. Even before the Crisis, she'd had a hard look to her. But after eight years of too many months of near starvation and hard work in all weather, as well as the loss of children and a beloved husband, she looked ten years older than her age.

Fiona sighed. "Sure, where could he have gone?"

Sarah didn't answer. She knew it wasn't a real question.

No shoes. No weapon. No jacket.

The breeze off the ocean slipped in cold and sharp and found its way down Sarah's collar. She kissed her daughter and stood up, shivering as she took a step away from the fire.

It was early autumn—too cold for living in tents. But with a destroyed castle and most of their food supplies buried beneath the rubble, the tents were a godsend.

Sarah surveyed the damaged castle. It was hard to believe it could be rebuilt. Huge chunks of stone and mortar lay scattered in the moat they'd worked so hard to make viable. The castle tower—twenty feet tall and the main access to the catwalk where their defensive archers lined up—lay in rubble on the ground.

As she looked at it now, Sarah was startled to realize that with Mike gone, a part of her was ready to walk away from all of it and start over somewhere else.

She thought back to the last week as if it were a terrible dream. They'd beaten back the invaders but at a terrible cost. Their home had been pulled down around their ears, and too many people they'd needed—people they'd loved—were gone in a shower of blood and bone.

Sarah ran a hand across her face and her shoulder began to throb. The wound from the arrow was shallow, thank God, but it still made her every movement above the waist stiff and painful.

"Are ye ready, Sarah?" Fiona asked quietly.

When Sarah turned to look at her, she saw that nearly the whole rest of the castle population had gathered around the fire.

There were fewer than a hundred now, and at least half of them children. Sarah saw Terry Donaghue and his wife Jill standing closest to her. She'd spoken to Terry earlier—after he and the others had given up searching the castle grounds for Mike.

She had to go. They knew it. Nobody could argue with the sense of it.

Well, her son John had, but only because he wanted to go too. In the end, Sarah knew he understood why she needed him to stay. There was little Siobhan and Matt and Mac to take care of.

As Sarah looked for John in the crowd, she knew it was more than that. She caught his eye where he stood in the second row of people and he nodded solemnly to her.

John was the natural leader for their group. She'd known it for a while now, had recognized it just last week as she'd watched him and Mike work together to begin the rebuilding of their community.

No, she needed him here, as much as she hated the thought of separating from him once more. And maybe, just maybe, it would be safer here than out on the road.

Sarah cleared her throat.

"You'll all have heard that we've lost Mike," she said. There were a few titters from the crowd at the way she'd phrased it. "I'm going out in bit while any tracks are still possible to read. I've asked Terry Donaghue and my son John Woodson to be in charge while I'm gone."

"Where's Himself got to?" a voice called out.

"Well, that's what I'm going to find out," Sarah said, trying to sound sane and calm. "Gavin Donovan will accompany me. But I'm asking for two more volunteers. I expect to be gone a day, maybe two."

"What if you don't find him in a day or two?" Liddy O'Malley called out.

Liddy and her sister Mary had both been widowed during the assault on the castle a few days earlier. Liddy still had a young toddler to focus her energies. Her sister Mary was childless.

"I will go on alone," Sarah said, "and send the rest back."

Sarah could see Gavin's young wife Sophia nearby. Sophia was Italian and breathtakingly beautiful. She held their baby Maggie in her arms and nodded when Sarah's gaze found her. Sophia knew Gavin had to go and search for his father. She wouldn't dream of stopping him. But Gavin had only recently returned from an ill-fated hunting trip and Sarah knew how hard it was for Sophia to let him go again so soon.

The crowd began murmuring among themselves and John emerged from the interior. He was tall and dark headed like his father David. Like everyone after the Crisis, John was lean and hard-muscled. Although not yet eighteen, he had the wisdom and seasoned look in his eye of a man much older.

What he had seen and done in the past eight years was not the province of childhood.

The seven-year-old twins Mac and Matt trailed after John. They'd been orphaned as babies and then lost their only other living relative during the recent battle. Mike and Sarah had hoped to adopt them, but for now they followed John around like stunned ducklings—not at all sure of the world or their place in it.

John gave his mother's arm a squeeze when he reached her and picked up his half-sister Siobhan, who wrapped her arms around his neck.

"I'll go," a voice called from the crowd.

"Robbie, no!" Nuala blurted out.

Nuala had been standing with her fiancé and her three small boys. Sarah could tell by the look on her face that Robbie's volunteering was the last thing Nuala expected.

Sarah directed her attention to Robbie. He had come to the castle with his brother Frank the year before as part of an earlier assault on the castle by the Provisional Irish Army. They had defected just in time to help defeat the assault. After fighting valiantly for the castle on two separate occasions, Frank had recently died from an infected toenail.

Robbie had become a valuable member of the castle community. He had fallen in love with Nuala—the woman Mike called the heart and soul of their group. Sarah had been glad they'd found each other. Nuala deserved to be happy if anyone did.

Nuala looked at Sarah and wordlessly apologized for her outburst. She'd just been caught by surprise.

You don't need to apologize to me, Sarah thought as she smiled tiredly back at Nuala. *I better than anyone know how much all of this sucks.*

"I'd be glad to have you, Robbie," Sarah said.

"I volunteer, too," a young woman's voice called out. Within seconds, Regan Murdoch strode to where Sarah stood with John.

This was a surprise and Sarah wasn't sure it was a good one.

"Really?" Sarah asked.

Regan was the leader of the team of female archers responsible for protecting the castle. The girls—many of them still in their teens—were not given to obeying orders or following rules. Until Regan took over leading them, even Mike had been at a loss to control them.

"It's *Mike*," Regan said, her voice cracking. Her wiry red hair flew untethered and free around her scowling face. "So I'm *in*."

Sarah nodded. It was true that without a parapet to shoot from, the only arrows being shot around the castle would be the ones directed at the nightly visits from the local wolves. And for that, the girls didn't need their master sergeant.

Sarah looked at Terry and he gave her a thumbs up signal. Terry was the one who forged the arrowheads and was in charge of the apprentice program to fashion the bows and the arrow shafts. She'd seen him with the girl archers on many occasions and he did seem to manage to keep them in line. Just.

"Fine," Sarah said. "Good. And thank you, Regan. You too, Robbie. Gavin's in charge of our supplies. See him if you need something extra. We'll bring a wagon, too." She didn't need to say that the wagon would be needed if Mike was hurt.

Or worse.

"We'll leave at the top of the hour," she said.

As the crowd began to break up, a few people came up to Sarah to pat her hand and give words of encouragement. She had the uncomfortable feeling that she was being treated as a widow in a receiving line.

Mike wasn't dead. By God, she knew he wasn't! And whatever happened to him she'd find out. Or die trying.

※ ※ ※ ※ ※

Moments later, as the crowd dispersed, Sarah sank into a seated position by the fire. She knew she should be checking her own supplies, her weapons, and her drugs. She was still hurting from her wounds of the week before.

Up until this morning, she'd been using a cane to maneuver around the camp. Although she'd recently transitioned from opiates to ibuprofen to handle the worst of her discomfort, to be ready for whatever she might find on the road she needed a baseline supply.

She was tired. The stress of realizing Mike was gone combined with her injuries had innervated her. She stared into the fire, letting the blessed numbness take her for just a moment.

"Are you sure you're up for this, Mom?" John asked as he handed Siobhan off to one of the camp women who helped Nuala with the nursery.

"It doesn't matter. I have to go."

John sat down next to her. He nudged Mike's shoes with the toe of his boot.

"I was surprised about Robbie volunteering," he said. "Nuala wasn't happy about it."

"He wants to do what he can to help," Sarah said. She knew the feeling. As Americans—and representing the country that basically started this whole mess—she and John both knew how it felt when you began on the wrong foot.

You were constantly trying to put it right.

Even losing his brother hadn't made everybody in the castle forget that Robbie had started out on the wrong side.

Although winning Nuala's heart had gone a long way to helping.

Fiona held out a bowl of steaming stew but Sarah waved it away.

"Take it, Sarah," Fiona said with frustration. "Sure it's likely to be the last hot thing you eat for awhile."

"I wonder what *Mike's* eating," Sarah said, but she took the bowl.

"You'll find out soon enough, so you will."

Sarah appreciated Fiona's confident words, even though she knew much of what she said was bravado. Fiona knew better than anyone how quickly you could lose a loved one.

"Are you in pain, Mom?" John narrowed his eyes.

"I'm fine, sweetheart," Sarah said tiredly. She just wanted to *go*. Tired or not, in pain or not, she wanted to get on the road. She looked up to see Mary O'Malley striding toward her.

God, now what?

"A word, if you please, Sarah," Mary said.

It was true Mary had lost her husband the week before but she'd been a problem for everyone for many weeks before that. And while Sarah was sympathetic to Mary's loss, she was also wary of the woman and her troublemaking.

"I'm not in charge of castle business at the moment," Sarah said tightly. "You'll need to talk to Terry."

"I want to come with you," Mary said.

"Sure you must be fecking joking," Fiona blurted.

Mary gave her a sideways look but addressed Sarah.

"I'm not at-tall," she said. "If ye leave me here, Sarah, the archer bitches will kill me, sure as shite."

Sarah groaned. "They won't kill you," she said wearily.

"Come to that," Fiona said, "they might."

Not long ago, Mary had betrayed the castle by destroying all of the arrows the archers had stockpiled. When the invaders attacked last week, they were defenseless. Because of Mary.

It was only because Mike intervened that Mary had not been taken out and hung when her crime was revealed. In any case, no one had forgiven her.

"I'm looking for people who can *help* me," Sarah said dryly, "Not slow me down or make me want to shoot them along the way."

"I'll cook for ye," Mary said. "And help pitch the tents at night—"

"We're not using tents."

"Well, whatever it is ye do intend to use. I promise I'll be a help. Only if ye leave me here, my death will be on your head, Sarah Donovan, so it will."

Sarah groaned. "If you slow me down, I'll leave you behind. You'll have to fend for yourself against the wolves."

Mary frowned. "Will ye give me a gun in that case?"

Once they disarmed the attackers, the castle community had walked away with almost more ammunition and guns than they'd ever had before. Mary, because she was considered unstable, had not been allowed near the firearms.

"Sure," Sarah said.

"You're not seriously going to bring her?" John asked.

Mary looked at him and gave him a disparaging look from head to toe. "Is it crazy you think I am, then?"

"Well, yeah," John said. "For starters."

Mary swiveled on her heel to face him but Sarah held up her hand.

"Stop," Sarah said. "If you're coming, go to Gavin and see that there's extra food. If you're not ready to leave in thirty minutes, I'll go without you."

Mary gave a last dismissive look at Fiona and John and then left the cook fire.

"That's a mistake," Fiona said.

2

John left his mother and Fiona by the fire and found his way to where the drawbridge spanned the moat. The watchtower where both Kevin and Davey O'Malley had perished was now just a crumbling monument to the battle.

John hadn't been part of the crew to recover the human remains from all the many explosions of that battle but it had only been six days ago. He supposed they would find bone fragments for months going forward—certainly during the whole rebuilding process.

Time, he thought. *Time will heal the wounds*. He thought of Cassie and his heart flinched. He would never forget her, he vowed. He would never allow the pain to totally leave. After all, in a way, the pain of having lost her was all he had left of her.

"Oy, John, is that you, mate?" Gavin called out to him as John neared where his step-brother stood with the horses. Sophia was standing beside Gavin. John was sorry if he was interrupting any last sweet goodbyes.

"Yeah, it's me," John said. "Sorry, Sophia."

"It is fine, *cara*," Sophia said. "My husband is just going out for the errand, *si*? He will be back in nothing time."

"No time," John corrected.

"*Si*. No time." Sophia raised up on her tiptoes and kissed Gavin on the mouth before turning and walking away.

"This really sucks, man," John said as he walked to the wagon.

Gavin had put a stack of blankets, guns, an extra saddle, and several boxes of dried food in the back next to a box of bandages and bottles of medicine. Fiona was known for her herbal remedies and the camp used her daily to mend scratches, bites and stings.

But in addition to the needles and threads and thick bandages, John saw that Gavin had also packed a small bottle of morphine. No herbal salves for this quest, John thought. Gavin was planning for the worst.

Or nearly the worst.

"Tell me about it," Gavin said.

"You okay?"

"Why wouldn't I be?" Gavin said. "I know the auld man's fine, ye ken? I feel it in me bones. We'll find him. No worries."

John couldn't help but think that every time they turned around they were trying to track someone down who'd either been taken by force or wandered off or just wasn't where they should be.

And in today's world, if you didn't keep your eye on them, you'd lose them for sure.

"What I wouldn't give for a tracker, ye know?" Gavin said with a grin.

Gavin had thick wavy red hair and a pale complexion to match. John recalled the time when he'd hit the road to find Gavin a few years ago. Gavin had had a good laugh when John told him he'd asked every Irishmen he'd met if they'd seen any redheads lately.

It gave John courage to remember that time now. It reminded him that there had been a time when he didn't know if he'd ever see Gavin again—someone John considered a brother in every sense of the word—and yet here he was in the flesh. No worries, mate.

And so would Mike be. John had to believe it.

"Did you hear Crazy Mary's coming too, aye?" Gavin said while shaking his head as he secured the harness on the horse hitched to the wagon.

"I was there when she made her pitch to my mom."

"I'll bet that was pretty. Did ye hear who else?"

John frowned. "Another volunteer?"

"I'll bet ye can guess, boyo," Gavin said as he handed the lead reins for two of the horses to John.

"Oh, don't tell me. Jordie?"

Ever since he'd come to the castle, Jordie Barrett had made a bad name for himself at just about every turn. He'd only been allowed in at all because he was the brother of one of the better archers.

Since he'd arrived, he'd helped one of the twins break his arm, accidentally set all the castle horses free, been accused of rape (which was the reason for the devastating attack on the castle), and been instrumental in the unintentional killing of one of the young women in the castle.

Cassie.

John knew Jordie wasn't a bad guy. But neither did he have a good head on his shoulders. If something was going to go wrong, Jordie would help it go as wrong as it could.

He was the last person John wanted on this trip with his mother.

"Does my mother know?"

"I think it's a secret. Jordie asked me to make room for him and said he'll meet us on the road. You know how crazy his old mother is."

Gavin looked back at the horses to see if he'd forgotten anything. He was rubbing his hands together over and over again. John could see the stress and apprehension pinging off him.

He's worried about his dad. Underneath all the confidence and bravado, he's afraid.

Gavin looked back at John. "We sure could use a little bit of that magic island of your dad's about now," he said.

John grimaced. His father's visit last month had been a shock on many different levels. Not least of which was the fact that up until then John and his mother had believed him dead.

But David Woodson had also come back with a fantastic story of a secret society dedicated to preserving all the knowledge of the world through a post-apocalyptic repository.

The way his father had described it, where he lived had electricity, computers, telecommunications and every luxury of the pre-EMP crisis world. It was truly a fantastic story but one that John didn't doubt for a minute.

"Yeah," John said, turning to lead the horses toward his mother. "You're telling me."

❧❧❧❧❧

Sarah adjusted her stirrup leathers from where she sat in the saddle. It wasn't yet two o'clock but the Irish autumn was creeping up on them and she knew they'd be riding in the dark in just a few hours.

She hated losing the time but one thing Mike had taught her was the importance of preparation. She'd sacrificed a few hours to be ready for whatever was waiting for her on the road.

Please God let it be Mike, she thought.

Let him be off to the side of the road or tucked away in the copse of trees that lined the road leading away from the castle. Let his disappearance not have anything to do with David's group or, God forbid, David himself.

Let me not be put in a situation where I have to kill my own child's father.

She had thought over and over about the possibility that Mike's disappearance had something to do with David.

One thing she knew with certainty: Mike had not left on his own.

What sane person would leave with no shoes and no jacket?

She also couldn't believe that any of the typical blackguards and desperadoes roaming the countryside would have had the finesse to lift a man virtually from his bed without raising a single dog's bark. Or the notice of his sleeping wife.

No, this wasn't magic or space ships. And it wasn't bandits.

"Ready, Sarah?" Gavin asked softly.

She looked over at him. Sophia was standing beside Gavin's horse which he had already mounted. Sarah knew Gavin was edgy. And while they hadn't talked about it, she was sure he was thinking the same thing she was—*somehow David Woodson was behind this.*

John held Siobhan up to Sarah one last time and she kissed her daughter. She hated the fact that she didn't relish the moment.

But either it was the last time she saw Siobhan in this lifetime—in which case, a single kiss was way too little—or Sarah would be back in a day or two with or without Mike—in which case she would always wonder if she'd taken too much time to get on the road.

Regan and Robbie were on their horses and Mary sat in the driver's seat of the wagon as they began to leave.

"God speed, all of ye," Fiona called. Sarah tried not to see the strain and fear in her sister-in-law's eyes.

"We'll be back," Sarah said. "Everyone here stay safe in the meantime." Her eyes fell on John and he nodded.

Everyone knew how quickly trouble could come. And although they had bows, arrows and guns, they were also sitting out in the open with not even a stone wall or a bush to hide behind.

Please keep them safe, Sarah prayed as she turned her horse toward the road.

Susan Kiernan-Lewis

3

Even Sarah could read the tracks leading from the castle encampment. Three sets of shoe prints—one set deeper than the others which indicated that the man was either a big man or was carrying something heavy.

Because Gavin was the better tracker, Sarah sent Robbie and Regan to ride point with the wagon down the drive that led away from the castle. They would meet up with them on the main road if the tracking led to nothing.

She and Gavin would ride across the patch of forest that bordered the southern edge of the castle away from the sea.

There was no way Mike could have been spirited away from the middle of the camp without being seen unless he'd been taken out by way of one of the IRA tunnels scattered about the area. The only problem with that theory, of course, was that —except for one of the tunnels—nobody knew where any of the others were.

That one tunnel was the one that David had tried to take John down the day the castle was attacked. In the course of that attack the tunnel had been destroyed. Were there other tunnels nearby?

Sarah and Gavin spent the first two hours alternately walking and riding near a bridle path that switch-backed through a forest of native spruce.

She felt the terrain lifting as they inched their way along. In the break of trees to the east she could look down and see the undulating road that Robbie, Regan and the wagon were taking.

They'd lost the tracks nearly a mile back. Sarah had hoped they'd pick them up again but that wasn't happening yet. It looked like Mike had simply vanished into thin air.

Except of course he hadn't.

Gavin knelt on the path and touched the ground. Then he stood up and looked over at her, shaking his head.

"This is getting us nowhere," he said as he slapped his baseball cap against his jeans.

Sarah fought down the feeling of frustration that was hemming her in on all sides. If they couldn't pick up the tracks again…

"Let's go back to where we last saw the tracks," she said, turning her horse in the direction they'd come.

"Sarah, this is hopeless," Gavin called out. "You know it is. He's in one of those bleeding tunnels!"

Sarah bit her lip. She knew he was right. But a part of her had hoped, no, *needed* to believe that he might be here—off in the bushes, maybe injured but above ground—with a perfectly reasonable explanation for it all.

A raindrop hit the top of her head. She'd smelled the coming rain this morning. You didn't live in Ireland a week before you figured out the sky and what it meant to do.

She'd hoped the rain might hold off until dark when they'd have to give up tracking anyway. But maybe Gavin was right. Maybe it was just as well.

She turned and saw that he'd remounted but wasn't moving. If they turned east they would hit a stretch of open country that would lead them to what used to be the N72. Now it was just an empty highway with grass and weeds scattered about the buckled cement and nothing but abandoned cars that had either been dragged to the side or left on the road.

The cars had long since been stripped of anything valuable, down to the wires, the tires, the petrol, the upholstered seats. The N72 was also where they were to meet up with the others.

The rain came down hard now. Five years earlier Sarah would've marveled at how getting wet didn't bother her any more. She would've noted how she didn't run for shelter or fuss over getting her clothes wet. A lot had happened in five years.

Except for completely erasing any chance of finding Mike's trail, she just didn't give a damn about the weather.

"The tunnels could be anywhere," Sarah said, pointing her horse eastward at the same time Gavin did. "How the hell are we supposed to find them?"

"You're sure John doesn't know?" Gavin asked.

Gavin knew that if David had told anyone it would be John.

"I already asked him," Sarah said. "He said he only knew of the one."

As they rode in single file across a pasture, the brown and brittle grasses crunched noisily under their horses' hooves.

Since they couldn't find where the tracks led to they would have to find the tunnel that was used to take Mike out. And that meant David *had* to be involved. Because if he wasn't, well, then she was officially out of theories.

"Didn't John say there was a network of tunnels near Killarney?" Gavin asked.

Of course Gavin knew the answer to that. David had publicly commented in the castle on more than one occasion about a network of tunnels that his group used in the area. Except, since David was publicly commenting about it, the information was probably a lie.

"First let's meet up with the others," Sarah said.

She had a vague idea of which direction to take, but she was hesitant to reveal it to Gavin. She wasn't sure if there would be any network of tunnels near the place and in any case it would be too late to search for them today.

They'd have to camp tonight and start scouring the area at first light.

Once they'd exhausted any hope of finding a tunnel, Sarah's only hope for quick answers would be officially over. If the tunnels couldn't be found, then the only remaining lead was a comment Sarah had overhead from David to John—a comment she was sure she hadn't been meant to hear—that might possibly take them to the location of David's compound.

But if she was left with trying to find that, they were all truly screwed.

It took them close to an hour to make their way to the main road where Robbie and Reagan and the wagon were waiting. With the sky darkening by the minute, Sarah felt a gnawing anxiety about the time they'd lost following Mike's tracks. But she knew she'd had to try the easy way first.

As usual with life in Ireland after the bomb—the easy way was also the hard as hell way.

She and Gavin trotted up to the wagon. Regan and Robbie were on foot and letting their horses graze, although both had their hands resting on their revolvers. It was the extra person in the wagon that made Sarah frown.

Sarah turned to Gavin. "Did you know about this?"

Immediately Jordie handed Gavin a canteen but Gavin waved it away.

"No joy, Missus?" Robbie called out brightly. The rain poured off his hat, creating a downward spout off its brim.

Ignoring Sarah's question, Gavin said, "Robbie, you and Regan mount up. We're heading to Killarney and we'd like to get there before nightfall."

"Killarney?" Mary said. "What's in Killarney?"

"That's where we kill you, Mary," Regan said as she swung up into her saddle.

"Sarah!" Mary yelped. "Did you hear what she said?"

"Aw, lass," Gavin said, spurring his horse up beside Regan, "do ye have to tease the daft cow?"

"Sarah!" Mary said indignantly, standing up in the wagon with her hands on her hips.

"All of you shut up," Sarah said. "Jordie, what the hell are you doing here?"

Jordie held out the canteen to Sarah, his eyes hopeful.

"Just wanting to be helpful," he said.

Sarah didn't have the energy for this drama. She tightened her legs around her horse and moved away from the wagon and toward the horizon.

Riding to Killarney felt counterintuitive to her. It was so far from where Mike had been grabbed. It just didn't make sense that David's people would drag Mike all the way through the woods and half way down the N72 before they accessed one of their secret conduits.

"Robbie, bring up the rear, please," Sarah called over her shoulder. "And everyone, put it in gear. We'll never make it by nightfall at this pace." She dug her heels into her horse and felt him gather his muscles under her. Even in the rain, it was clear he would be happy to launch into a gallop down the slippery highway. A part of Sarah would like nothing better.

But breaking her head open on the highway was not the way to get Mike back.

As she rode, she tried to imagine a single reason why David might have taken Mike.

Besides, if David hadn't done it, she was back to alien spaceships and she really wasn't ready to go there just yet.

She tried to push her thoughts away and focus on the ride. Three of the five horses were shod but Robbie and Regan's horses weren't so they rode on the softer verge of the road, one on each side, Regan in front of the wagon and Robbie behind.

Regardless of their mission, not for a minute did any of them think they were safe from bandits. Sarah watched Gavin as he scanned the horizon and every clump of bush and tree they passed. They'd all learned the hard way that staying vigilant was their only defense against a surprise attack.

Like most of Ireland, this part of the country was low lying and relatively flat but they were heading for the hills in the south.

Or at least that's what he'd led them to believe.

Technically Killarney included the beginning of a mountain range but nothing compared to anything in Europe or the States. The peaks where they were headed were a range of glacier-carved sandstone with plenty of places to hide and a labyrinth of hidden underground passageways.

The area had been particularly popular for tunneling with the IRA decades earlier and it seemed that David's group had taken advantage of that.

The rain had stopped and at first Sarah didn't even notice. The air was cool but the weak rays of the late afternoon sun filtered through the fringe of pines that lined the roadway. Sarah had never gone this far south before. Even Gavin and Robbie on their hunting expeditions tended to go north from the castle or east toward the midlands.

Every mile they rode seemed to confirm to Sarah that Mike could not possibly have been taken this far. She entertained the possibility that the men who'd taken him from the camp might have carried him past the first large copse of trees that bordered the drive.

A bicycle with a flat bed in back would have been silent enough to get him away before anyone in the camp could hear. Then a waiting Jeep along the access road to the highway could have then taken him the rest of the way.

The rest of the way where?

Was this madness? Was this Sarah's usual *do something even if it's stupid* method of problem-solving?

But what else could she do? She couldn't just go back to her tent without Mike and begin life without him. She just couldn't! What would she tell Siobhan one day when she was older when she asked where her father was?

Oh, he disappeared one morning so we just carried on.

Sarah pushed her shoulders back resolutely and tightened her muscles as if in readiness.

No. It wasn't impossible and it wasn't magic. She would find him. She *had* to find him.

She turned her head and noticed that Regan had slowed down enough to converse with Jordie and Mary. Sarah couldn't imagine in what world *that* was a good idea. Mary's voice quickly became shrill.

"Hold up!" Sarah shouted and the wagon stopped. Gavin looked over his shoulder and frowned and Sarah felt a brief ripple of relief.

If there was anybody in a bigger hurry than her, it was Gavin.

They'd been traveling for a good two hours and Sarah could see the sun was dropping quickly. They hadn't made it to Killarney but this would have to do.

"Gavin, you and Regan look for a place to camp," Sarah said. She glanced at Robbie but he knew what to do. He'd moved his horse up onto the road by the wagon. His rifle was out of its scabbard and across his knee.

His eyes searched the trees bordering the road for anything that moved.

⚜ ⚜ ⚜ ⚜ ⚜

John was ready for a break. His foot was killing him and he didn't think he'd had a moment's peace since this morning. After dropping off the twins for the afternoon with Nuala he couldn't believe how much lighter he felt.

Man, they're relentless, he thought. He was fairly sure he'd never been like that as a kid—constantly asking questions and always bugging adults.

He felt a sliver of remorse thinking about Matt and Mac's grandfather Artemus. They'd lost him less than two weeks ago. John upbraided himself for not being more patient with them.

True, they didn't look that cut up about losing their grandfather but they were kids. And they were orphans. It was hard to tell exactly *what* they were feeling right now.

Ever since the castle fell John had felt a loss he couldn't put his finger on. It was a sense of loss that went beyond losing just mortar and brick. It was true he'd recently lost Cassie and had to say goodbye to his father but the loss John was feeling was something altogether different.

He glanced around the tent city that had sprouted up on the castle lawn since the castle's fall.

This wasn't "camping out" no matter how much it delighted Mac and Matt to think so. Not when John knew that the lack of walls meant there was nothing standing between them and the wolves, the rain, the snow that was coming, and the wicked people out there who were just waiting to take everything they had.

"There you are, lad," Fiona said as she emerged from her tent. "Sure ye have a serious look on your face. Worried about your mam, are ye? Walk with me."

John took comfort in Fiona's no-nonsense approach to life. Forget that your world just got pulled down around your ears! Buck up and get on with it!

It was true that Fiona could be abrupt and she didn't shy away from telling you the truth when you needed to hear it—

even if it hurt your feelings. John had long wondered if that was an Irish thing or just a Fiona thing.

He followed her. "Just thinking about stuff," he said.

"Go on with ye!" she said with a laugh. "Now why would ye be doing that? No good can come of it." She put a hand out to stop him, a frown on her face. "Are ye hurt, lad?"

"It's no big deal," John said. "I cut the bottom of my foot. Was hoping you had something I could put on it to numb it or something."

While the Catholic nuns of Our Lady of Perpetual Sorrow operated the castle clinic with what few real medicines they still had, most people in the community came to Fiona for their everyday scrapes and aches.

She was the recognized master of whatever salves and teas you needed to get through a life without antibiotics or ibuprofen.

"Let me see," Fiona said, leading John to the cook fire in front of a line of tents. He settled down on a log and peeled off his sock and shoe. The cut wasn't deep but it looked angry and red.

"When did you do this?" Fiona asked as she held his foot in her hand and examined the cut.

"Yesterday. You got some of your magic goo?"

"Making up a new batch right now, as a matter of fact," Fiona said as she reached for a jar sitting on the stones next to a boiling cauldron hanging over the fire. The jar's contents were still steaming.

"Were you surprised to see Regan volunteer to go with Mom to find Mike?" John asked.

"Sure no," Fiona said as she dipped a tongue depressor into the unguent to coat it. "You know Regan. Life gets boring for her in a minute, so it does. And then, of course she loves Mike."

Fiona spread the salve liberally over the cut on the bottom of John's foot. It was warm from the fire but felt soothing. He couldn't detect any of the ingredients in the salve by smell but he knew it contained calendula and arnica as well as beeswax.

"What do you think happened to Mike?" John asked.

Fiona glanced at him. "Your mother thinks it was your own da took him."

"I told her that was crazy," John said, shifting uncomfortably. "She just can't seem to think anything good of him."

"Aye, well." Fiona put John's foot on a stone. "Can ye leave your sock off for a bit?"

"I guess if I have to," John said.

"Give it fifteen minutes. Then put your sock back on but don't rub it off. Mind you, it'll be messy."

"Thanks, Fi. Not sure what any of us would do without you."

"Go on with ye now," Fi said brusquely but John could tell she was pleased.

Suddenly Darby, Terry and Jill's youngest boy, ran up to them. Darby was only ten but he'd already landed on a dramatic style of dress—even in post-apocalyptic Ireland. He wasn't into electronics like his older brother Tommy but instead worked as an apprentice to become the clothes maker for the camp's clothing needs.

"Oy, John!" Darby said, breathlessly. "Me da says yer to come straightaway!"

"Why?" John said, pulling on his sock and shoe. "What's going on?"

"A stranger's come," Darby said, his eyes blinking with burgeoning unease.

Susan Kiernan-Lewis

4

It started to rain again.

Robbie and Regan tried to build a fire while Mary handed out sandwiches. Sarah hadn't been sure she was comfortable with them making a fire. It would attract attention and not the good kind—which was the main reason she'd insisted on bringing cold food.

After they unharnessed the horse, Gavin and Jordie stretched tarps across the back of the wagon. Sarah and Mary would sleep inside the back of the wagon under the tarp while the men and Regan slept underneath the wagon itself. Even so they all knew they'd wake up soaked and poorly rested.

But they weren't here for a campout.

If they were successful, they'd have Mike in the back of the wagon before end of day tomorrow and back at the castle campground before daybreak. Plenty of time for everybody to get warm and dry *then*.

Sarah huddled with the rest of them under the wagon and watched the rain create muddy rivulets in the ground around them. With the sun gone, the temperature had fallen sharply.

She hated to use the blankets Gavin brought before she crawled in the back to bed down. If she used them now, they'd be wet for the rest of the night.

"Do you mind?" Mary said sharply to Regan. "That's your second sandwich!"

"Who are you to monitor me dinner, ye old hag?" Regan said.

"Sarah! Do we have enough food for some of us to eat more than their share?" Mary said waspishly but she was looking at Regan as she spoke.

Before Sarah could tell them both to shut up for the thousandth time, Robbie pulled something out of his backpack and tossed it to Regan.

"Oy," Reagan said, looking at the item which turned out to be a large roll of duct tape. "What's this for?"

"Don't ye know?" Robbie said good-naturedly. "It's a miracle product, so it is. Applied properly, it can provide hours of golden silence."

Regan looked at the roll of tape and then at Robbie and then burst out laughing.

"Sure, you're a wit, ye auld gobshite!" she said, tossing the tape in the air and catching it. "I finally get what Nuala sees in you!"

Gavin and Jordie laughed and even Sarah smiled.

"What is it you're saying?" Mary said, the shrillness of her tone reaching new peaks.

"He's saying," Regan said, "I might tape yer gob shut to give us all some peace."

"You wouldn't dare!" Mary squeaked. "Sarah!"

"Sure, stop it now, Regan," Gavin said. "You'll not be doing that on my watch."

"On *her* side are ye, Gavin?" Regan said.

"Not at-tall," Gavin said. "We might need that duct tape, is all. Ye'll not be wasting it."

Another laugh rippled through the group.

"All right," Sarah said. "Everyone settle down, please. Noise carries, you know."

Instantly the group hushed and only the sound of the rain hitting the leaves filled the small clearing that Regan and Gavin had found for them to bed down in.

As Sarah began to drift off to sleep, her thoughts were centered on only one thing: Mike.

Often if she woke in the middle of the night, she would feel his arm draped across her hip or his body contoured to hers. Sometimes she thought that those were the moments—when the whole terrible world was momentarily asleep—that she felt closer to a perfect life than she ever had before with all her electronics and convenience mechanisms. Feeling Mike's arm around her, the slow and steady hum of his breathing, the satisfaction of knowing he was there for her—was like nothing she'd ever experienced before.

And once you've had the real thing, there was no going back to living without it.

To imagine that you would find the love of your life and that together you might have all the things you really needed— only not electricity and gas-powered vehicles—well, it was a concept too absurdly wonderful for Sarah to wrap her head around.

She had to find him. There was nothing else for it. If he was in the world, she needed to be with him.

No matter what it took.

※※※※※

Lorcan McCree was a tall man and barrel-chested. At first glance John thought people probably took him for the jolly sort.

It wasn't until the second and third glance that you really saw it.

Something very unfunny was right beneath the surface.

John had been embarrassed when Terry insisted that the table be brought out to the center of what had once been the castle courtyard. Even in the days since the attack, a lot of the rubble had already been cleared—or at least shoved to one side.

Once the sun had gone down—if you didn't look around too closely—it almost felt like this was the way things were supposed to look.

McCree sat to John's right. Fiona had insisted on this, saying it was an honor for their guest. But because of his age, John only felt awkward and out of place. His mother had put him in charge along with Terry Dongahue but when push came to shove—or when the first visitor came to call—Terry had quickly abdicated.

John hated to see the women bustling about serving them like they were royalty but he knew if they didn't, there would only be chaos instead of a hot meal. He tried to imagine Mike setting up a big dinner table like he was Henry the Eighth just to impress some passing guy.

The image wouldn't gel.

"So ye had a bit of a strammish now, did ye?" McCree said as he tore a chunk of bread apart and then spread a dollop of freshly churned butter on it. He didn't shove the food in his mouth like a starving man might. John knew how rare their castle community was for maintaining the little extra luxuries. If McCree had had fresh bread and butter in the last seven years, John would be very surprised.

John wasn't exactly sure who McCree had directed his question at—it definitely wasn't at him—but he knew the table would feel it was his place to answer the man, regardless of how he was evidently viewed by him.

"Two weeks ago, this was a castle with its walls intact," John said, shaking his head at Nuala as she came over to pour water into his cup. "We lost a couple of good men and all our defenses. As you see."

"So you've managed to survive this long without any leadership at all?"

McCree turned to look at John with a condescending expression on his face. But before John could respond, young Darby ran over to his father and spoke quietly to him. Terry hurriedly excused himself.

John witnessed the look on McCree's face as he watched Darby and his own expression hardened. Darby was different from the other boys. He was a hard-working, cheerful child and a beloved member of the community.

Watching an outsider rate and dismiss him—as he ate the food of that same community—set off alarm bells in John.

"May I ask how you came to be wandering the countryside?" John asked.

McCree turned to look at him, his eyes cold and appraising.

"I've had a misfortune," McCree said. "As so many of us have during these terrible times."

"Lost your family?" John pressed.

"Indeed I have," McCree said, reaching for a chicken leg.

John wasn't sure on whose order it was that the castle killed the fatted calf—or in their case, chicken—for this dude but it rankled that it had been done without his approval. He could see that McCree was good-looking. He probably had held a decent job before the bomb dropped.

No doubt a profession of some kind. He definitely seemed to have the gift of gab—something all Irishmen admired.

John wasn't sure exactly why it was he didn't like this guy. Maybe because he felt defenseless, sitting here among the bricks and broken boards of his home—with nary a truly responsible adult within a day's ride—and this veritable wolf sniffing around the hen house.

"I have to say Mr. Donaghue seems more of a shopkeeper than a leader of a tribe," McCree said.

"He leads with me," John said, annoyed that the man was getting to him. He shouldn't bother explaining anything. *Let the guy eat his one hot meal and then show him the door.*

If they had a door.

"With you, does he?" McCree laughed. "What are you? Seventeen?"

Don't correct him, John fumed. *It doesn't matter what he thinks.*

"What this community needs is a *man,*" McCree said. "Anyone can see it lacks leadership."

"It has leadership," John said, wishing he'd bitten his tongue.

Just get through the stupid meal!

"All I see are women," McCree said as Fiona slipped into Terry's empty seat. He turned and smiled at her. "As pleasant as that is."

To John's horror, Fiona blushed and hid a smile.

"It's true we are largely a matriarchal community," John said, raising an eyebrow at Fiona who ignored him.

The stranger laughed and waved a hand at the pile of rubble next to the table.

"How's that working for you?" he said.

Susan Kiernan-Lewis

5

Fiona was up early the next morning. She wanted to make a cup of tea for Mr. McCree before he left on his trip south. Her hands shook as she dressed and she realized with amazement that it was due to the prospect of seeing him again.

Dinner last night had been the first time in months—maybe years—that she had felt so alive. Honestly, she hadn't felt it for many months before Declan died and when she went to bed last night she surprised herself by realizing that Mr. McCree had awakened something in her.

Try as she might to brush it off or pretend it was nothing, she couldn't escape the strength of her feelings. Even if Lorcan McCree did leave today as he said he would, Fiona was glad for the one night of conversation and laughter that he'd brought to the camp.

The one night that reminded Fiona she was a woman. With a heart still yearning to love and be loved.

Ciara made a low moan from her pallet. "Why do I have to get up?" the child whined. "It's raining!"

"You want to go to Missus O'Connell's, don't you? And play with Darcie?"

"Darcie bites," Ciara whined. "And she's a baby. Besides, Damian won't play with me."

"Well, I'll talk with Missus O'Connell about that. Get dressed, luv."

Grumbling, Ciara pulled on her clothes while Fiona found a mirror and pinched some color into her cheeks.

She'd been surprised at John last night. He'd been downright rude to Lorcan and there'd been no call for such behavior at all. She assumed it had to do with his worry over his mother. Sure that was understandable.

And wasn't Fiona herself beside herself with worry over Mike gone the good Lord knows where?

But it doesn't mean we stop living. Or giving comfort to a stranger.

Fiona paused in the opening of her tent and watched the rain come down. Lorcan's eyes were green where Declan's were brown, almost black. But the way he'd looked at her last night —as if she was the only one in the room—was the same way Dec used to look at her.

She'd forgotten how grand that felt.

⁂⁂⁂⁂⁂

The next morning Sarah woke up stiff and cold. She wasn't sure if the worldwide EMPs had completely derailed global warming or what but it definitely felt like every Irish autumn since she'd been in the country had gotten shorter and colder.

On top of that, last night had been a wet one too. She glanced at Mary who was awake but not moving.

The rest of them were already up. From under the wagon tarp, Sarah could see Regan had a small fire going. Now that Sarah saw it she realized that this was what woke her: the smell of burning hickory and a pan of boiling coffee.

Jordie appeared as Sarah threw back the tarp. He had an armful of kindling that Regan must have sent him for. Gavin and Robbie were nowhere to be seen.

"Let's go, Mary," Sarah said, straightening out her legs and stifling a groan as she did. "I don't want Regan doing work you could be doing."

"Why is *she* so special?" Mary said sourly as she pulled her blanket tighter around her shoulders.

"She just is. Now get up."

Sarah lifted herself out of the wagon and nodded to Regan.

"You sleep okay?" Sarah asked. She knew Regan would have taken turns on the night watch with Gavin and Robbie. Nobody would've trusted Jordie with a watch.

"Like a fecking log," Regan said, pouring coffee into a mug. "Need to find a bush before breckie?"

Sarah accepted the cup of coffee as Mary climbed out of the wagon behind her.

"I'm good. Where are the guys?"

"Robbie thought he saw something in the woods he wanted to check out and Gavin is watering the horses."

Sarah turned to Jordie. "Go help Gavin," she said.

He jogged toward the road.

Regan stood and rubbed her hands against her jeans. Sarah remembered a time when Regan only wore dresses and more makeup than any girl should ever own. It occurred to her that in some ways Regan had changed more since the Crisis than anybody Sarah had met.

With what she's been through, that's hardly a surprise.

"Can I ask ye, Sarah, what your plans are now that we've buggered the tracks?" Regan asked, pouring herself a cup of coffee. She was looking over Sarah's shoulder as Mary lumbered off into the woods for a private spot. "Are we really off to find John's da?"

Sarah took a long sip of the hot coffee before answering. It was boiled beyond what most people would recognize as coffee but then there were a lot of things people wouldn't recognize these days.

"I don't know what else to do," Sarah said. "When Mike and I set out to find John and Gavin a couple of years back, we literally drove from village to village and knocked on doors asking who'd seen them."

"Seems like a long shot."

"And yet, we found people who'd seen them. At least they'd seen John. It just takes one person to set you down the right road."

"Except we're not doing that this time."

A squeal came to them from the woods where Mary had gone to relieve herself. Both Regan and Sarah turned in that direction. There were so many things to go wrong in this new world, it never paid to relax your guard.

Sarah had a very vivid memory of a walk in the woods two years ago that ended up with her on the business end of a Bengal tiger that had been released from a city zoo.

Anything could happen these days.

Mary came hurrying out of the bushes, a scowl on her face and Robbie a few steps behind her with a sheepish look on his face.

"Bloody tosser!" Mary said, as she hurried to the fire.

"I said I was sorry!" Robbie said, looking at Sarah with a shrug. "I didn't see her squatting there."

"Do ye mind shutting yer gob?" Mary said. She looked around the campfire as if expecting breakfast to be laid out. "There's only coffee?"

"Unless you've got the scones and rashers under your petticoat," Regan said.

"We need to get on the road any way," Sarah said. "We still have jerky. We can eat as we ride."

She noticed that Mary struggled not to respond. She held her hands out to the fire as Regan began kicking dirt on it to put it out.

A few minutes later, Jordie and Gavin were back with the horses. They quickly tacked up and put the bedding and food supplies in the wagon. The sky looked like more rain and as the temperature continued to drop Sarah wasn't at all sure any of them were dressed warmly enough.

She'd planned on leaving Robbie and Gavin back with the wagon and taking Regan with her to get better mileage under them today but she knew she couldn't leave Gavin behind. Mike was his father.

And while he looked to be all business at the moment, Sarah knew well enough that he was as anxious as she was.

She swung into the saddle and signaled for Robbie and Regan to stay with the wagon.

"Gavin and I'll go on ahead," she said. "We'll leave signs if we get too far away from you."

After all, the whole point of the wagon was in case they needed it for Mike. If they continued to travel at the rate that the wagon went, they'd never find him.

Not in time at least.

Regan and Robbie nodded solemnly and turned to flank the wagon as they pulled out onto the road.

Gavin rode up next to Sarah.

"I saw a group down by the creek when I was watering the horses," he said.

Sarah frowned. "How many?"

"Maybe six? Mostly women and kids. They looked fair to starving."

Sarah sighed. They couldn't save everyone. Not nowadays. And especially not today. It began to rain harder.

"Do you think we can find him?" Gavin asked.

"Who? Your father?"

Gavin wiped the rain from his face. "No, David Woodson."

Sarah turned to look at him. Gavin was smart. Smarter than his father gave him credit for. She knew Gavin tended to be a little sloppy on the details and he never really thought before he leapt.

Mike was always in a constant state of mild irritation with Gavin, hoping he'd morph into leadership material a little faster than he clearly was.

She also knew that Mike had started to see John in that leadership role and it bothered him. Not because he didn't love and respect John. But because John was eight years younger than Gavin.

And because when John lapped him Gavin would take it for the slight it was.

"I thought I told you we were looking for tunnels," Sarah said, looking away.

"Aye, ye did."

They rode in silence for a few moments. The road was flat but rocky. In the eight years since the first bombs had exploded over the Irish Sea and ended life as the world had known it, the highways had split and crumbled and fought against going back to nature. In this stretch of the country, nature was clearly winning.

Sarah tried to imagine that Mike had come this way—had somehow been carried this way. She tried to get a sense of how it must have been, bringing him down this road—at night—and for what possible reason. And when she thought of her big capable husband reduced to an unconscious hulk of blood and tissue as he surely must have been, it was all she could do not to break down and cry.

"Sarah?"

Sarah shook herself out of her thoughts.

"We're going to his island of magical thinking, aren't we?" Gavin asked.

"Don't call it that. They're a group of paramilitary nutcakes living in an underground shelter somewhere. That's all."

"Aye. With electricity and computers and hot and cold running water. So we're going there?"

"I don't know," Sarah said as she tightened her legs around her mount, urging him forward at a quicker pace. "I'm not sure I know *what* I'm doing."

"So you know where it is? His place?"

"No," Sarah admitted. "Not really."

"But you have some idea. Because you've chosen the direction and ye haven't hesitated since we started out."

Maybe because I think any decision beats no decision.

And that is a damn lie if anything is.

"Sarah?"

"I don't know, Gavin!" she said in frustration. "I don't have any answers! I just know we have to do something! We have to keep moving, we have to—"

Gavin reached out and touched her arm.

"No. *Look*," he said pointing with his other hand.

She followed where he was pointing and saw them. A group of at least ten, all on foot and mostly women. Sarah knew that the breakdown of law and order in the years since the first EMP had made Ireland's vulnerable people much more vulnerable. Nowhere was that more true than with the women of Ireland.

She felt a knot constricting in her stomach as she watched them approach on foot. Horses were the most valuable commodity there was in post-EMP Ireland. You could ride them or eat them. That this group was on foot probably meant that they weren't a serious threat.

Unless they were bait.

Sarah and Gavin pulled to a stop.

"What do you want to do?" Gavin said.

This, Sarah couldn't help think. *This is why Gavin will never be a leader.*

"Let's see what they do. If they're just travelers, they'll pass us by. If they're up to something…" She rested her hand on the Glock in her holster.

Gavin carried a Remington twelve-gauge shotgun they'd taken off the castle invaders last month. He had it out of its saddle scabbard.

"Wait for it," Sarah said to him under her breath. She scanned the bushes as the group approached. They didn't look dangerous to her. But she'd been wrong before.

"Hello, there," Sarah called out. "Where are you headed?"

"Cor, is that a Yank?" one of the few men in the group said. "Is it rescued we are then? Or are ye here to drop another bomb on us?"

A few of the women in the group giggled—nervously, it seemed to Sarah—and she tightened her grip on the handle of her gun.

"I don't like this, Sarah," Gavin muttered. His horse jerked and backed up. Sarah was sure Gavin was telegraphing his unease to the animal.

"I asked you where you were headed," Sarah said more firmly.

One of the women detached from the group and approached her. The woman's hands were lifted up in an imploring gesture.

"Missus, we're starving," she said. Her eyes were large and bulging out of her face. Her clothes hung on her to underscore the truth of her plea. Sarah had no doubt they were hungry. Maybe even starving.

That didn't make them less dangerous.

"Don't come any closer," Sarah said. "No offense." She scanned the group but they only stood in the road and stared at her. Several of the women were holding small children. Most of the children looked like they were skin and bones. And they'd long since given up crying for any relief for what was wrong with them.

"Watch them," Sarah said to Gavin under her breath, "while I look to see if they're alone."

She moved her horse around the woman and peered along the gorse that lined the road. It wasn't a great spot for an ambush. There wasn't enough hedge to hide behind.

"I think they're okay," Sarah called to Gavin. She twisted around to pull open her saddlebag when the woman rushed her.

Sarah turned and aimed her gun at the woman. "Stop," she said.

The woman held up her hands and looked from Sarah's gun to the saddlebag and Sarah felt shame course through her. The woman was starving. Her children were starving. She only wanted food.

"I'm going to put my gun away," Sarah said. "But my friend will have his shotgun out and trained on the back of your head. Do you understand what I'm saying?"

The woman nodded mutely, her eyes large and resigned.

Sarah slid her pistol back in the holster and opened her saddlebag. She pulled out a large package of jerky. It was one of the foodstuffs that they had plenty of back at the castle. Dried beef or venison kept forever, travelled well, and the children could be taught to make it.

She tossed the packet to the woman who caught it and hugged it to her chest, her eyes welling with tears.

"I'm sorry it has to be like this," Sarah said.

The woman nodded and began to turn back toward her group.

"Before you go," Sarah said, "may I ask you a question?"

"Anything you like, Missus," the woman said in a strong voice, a smile on her trembling lips.

"I'm looking for someone."

The woman nodded. "Everyone is."

"I'm looking for a man, a big man. If you'd seen him, you'd remember him," Sarah said, trying to fight past the catch in her throat as she thought of Mike. "He's six feet five, with brown hair to his shoulders. Unshaven. He was wearing a red wool vest but not a jacket. His name's Michael Donovan. He…he'd have been tied up."

The woman nodded. "Sure it was himself on the road not two days since," she said.

Sarah couldn't believe what she was hearing. This woman had seen Mike? Was that possible?

"He...he might have been in a wagon," Sarah said. "His hands tied—"

"The man we saw fits your description," the woman said. "Maureen!" she called to a woman in the group who hurried over to them. Maureen looked terrified and didn't take her eyes off Gavin and his shotgun.

"Wasn't the man who gave us food yesterday a big one with brown hair?"

"With the red vest? Aye, he was."

"And his friends called him Mike."

Sarah frowned. This didn't make sense. Could his captors have taken his vest from him? But what were the chances there would be another man as big as Mike?

Named Mike?

"He...he would have been a hostage," Sarah said. "Likely barefoot and maybe not with a jacket on."

"Sure no," Maureen said as she took the package of jerky from the first woman. "This man had boots on, blue eyes and a nice smile, so he did."

She frowned at Sarah, "But he was definitely nobody's hostage."

Susan Kiernan-Lewis

6

Fiona shook the bottle of herbal syrup. It was thicker than usual and that bothered her. When you were dealing with live plants and herbs, it didn't do to allow too much variation from batch to batch.

She'd tried to sweeten this batch more than usual since the children in the camp complained of the bitter taste of the turmeric root in it.

Fiona set the bottle of syrup down. She'd watch it a little longer. If it clouded up or continued to thicken, she'd throw it out. The last thing she wanted to do was make someone sicker than when they came to her.

Nuala sat beside her with her little Darcie in her lap. Darcie was the product of a violent rape three years earlier and was a constant joy to Nuala as well as to Nuala's two young lads Dennis and Damian.

Fiona's own child Ciara, now five, played alone in the dirt with some of the nontoxic herbs that Fiona had set out to dry.

Before the castle came down, Nuala had been the camp's main child-minder. She loved children and they loved her. Since the castle had disintegrated, most families had begun tending to their own children since communal chores were at least temporarily a thing of the past.

Except for the odd night of campfire stories and songs, the community rarely came together any more.

Fiona thought that was too bad. Although some of them had gotten right under her skin, it had felt so much more like a big family when they all lived together in the castle.

Or maybe the feeling of isolation was because Mike was gone.

Fiona had gone to bed thinking of her older brother. It was Mike who'd originally brought all these families together—*and kept them together*—through fire and famine, insurrection, and invasion.

And now he was gone.

Sarah would find him, she told herself sternly. *Sarah would find him and bring him home.*

"Someone walk over your grave then, Fi?" Nuala said as she attempted to fold clean clothes with a lively toddler in lap.

Fiona picked up her chipped mug of tea, wishing she had milk to go in it. Funny how some things—no matter how long she'd been forced to live without them—she just never got used to.

The tea mug reminded her of her moment with Lorcan this morning when she'd found him to bring him his tea.

He had been genuinely delighted, his eyes lighting up with pleasure at her thoughtfulness. It had been all Fiona could do not to tell him how significant his visit to the castle was to her personally.

"Earth to Fiona," Nuala said dryly. "Are ye some place nice, I hope? Wherever it is you've gone?"

Fiona shook herself out of her reverie and sat down next to Nuala.

"I imagine you'll be planning your big day, then, eh?" Fiona said.

Nothing distracted Nuala like talk of her upcoming wedding to Robbie Murphy.

True to form, Nuala beamed at the mention of it and Fiona felt a flinch of envy to see her face shine with so much joy.

Robbie was a good lad and Nuala deserved that. Truly she did, especially after all that she'd been through.

"Sure do ye think Himself will be able to walk me down the aisle?" Nuala said.

"Such aisles as we have," Fiona said. "I'm sure Mike will be honored, so he will."

"In that case we'll do it as soon as Sarah brings him home."

That had just a nice optimistic sound to it and Fiona wondered if Nuala said it to give comfort to Fiona or because she really believed it.

"I hear there's a priest over by Caragh Bridge," Fiona said. "Not that most people bother with such things nowadays."

"Go on with you, Fiona Cooper! Do ye mean to tell me if you were to meet a man ye couldn't keep your hands off ye'd just live with him and not claim him for your own before God and the world? I don't believe it for a minute."

Fiona found herself blushing and hurriedly sipped her tea so Nuala wouldn't notice. The minute Nuala had suggested it, Fiona realized she'd been thinking of exactly that for most of the night and the morning.

Lorcan McCree.

What was the matter with her? She'd been a widow nearly two years now—longer if you counted the time that Declan had been missing and then ill for so long. Until Mr. Lorcan McCree had come striding into their encampment, Fiona could honestly say she'd never given a second thought to the idea of remarrying.

Now she couldn't stop thinking of it.

"Robbie loves your lads, doesn't he?" Fiona said, picking up the herbal syrup bottle and giving it a shake.

"Sure he's grand with them," Nuala said. "They can't wait for him to be their da. They were too young when they lost their real da."

Fiona shot a quick look at Nuala. Her friend was a garrulous sort and never short of a word in all the years that Fiona had known her. But she'd never once talked about Dennis and Damian's father. Fiona didn't even know if Nuala had married him. Or if he was still alive.

"I hope that McCree chap keeps moving," Nuala said. "Gives me the bleeding creeps."

Fiona dropped the bottle she was holding. It shattered against the rocks that lined the main fire pit and unctuous goo spread across the dirt and grass.

"Cor!" Nuala said. "Is it supposed to smell like that?"

Little Darcie wrinkled her nose and scrambled off Nuala's lap. She ran over to Ciara and dropped to her knees to play.

"No, it's gone off," Fiona said, grabbing up a rag to wipe up the mess. "Why don't you like him?"

"Who? McCree?"

"He was full of such stories last night that I thought everyone enjoyed what he had to say."

"Did ye notice he had stories but no news?" Nuala said. "What's the point of feeding a stranger at your table if they can't tell you information you didn't already know?"

Fiona crossed her arms and glared at Nuala.

"Why, Nuala O'Connell! That is *not* the only reason we feed strangers who come to our door!"

"Well, sorry to disappoint ye, Fiona," Nuala said standing up and holding her hand out to Darcie. "But food's short enough and you know that well enough. I didn't trust him and I'll tell you right now that neither did John nor Terry neither!"

"Why! I…" Fiona sputtered. "I can't imagine what you're on about. You're all seeing monsters behind every tree, so ye are!"

"Maybe that's because there *are* monsters behind every tree," Nuala said grimly as she scooped Darcie up in her arms. "As ye well know."

❄❖❄❖❄❖❄

That first full day Sarah and Gavin crossed a stretch of open country and made their way to the entrance of a broad valley they'd never seen before.

As they waited for the others to catch up, Sarah finally let herself think about what the starving women had told her. She'd spent most of the day pushing their words away—denying them —and trying to imagine where David's compound might be from here.

She knew it was near Ballingeary on the other side of the Killarney National Park. She'd overheard that much from the conversation between John and David. Ballingeary would have been an hour's drive by car in the old days. Ninety kilometers. Sixteen hours by foot. Fourteen hours on horseback. All things being equal.

Which of course nowadays they never were.

Sarah had to admit the starving woman who claimed to have seen Mike didn't sound like she was lying. *Why would she lie?* What possible motive could she have had?

But if she wasn't lying…how was it possible that Mike could be voluntarily traveling this way—not in handcuffs or bound hand and foot but…willingly?

Sarah tried to picture the image of Mike handing out food to the starving group. Smiling, his blue eyes flashing. And all of it was so believable, she could see it. Right down to the thanks he'd refuse to hear for it.

They weren't lying.

Dear God. The women had seen Mike a single day after he'd left barefoot and bareheaded from Sarah's bedside. They'd seen him with a smile on his face and a goal in his heart.

How in God's name was that possible?

"The valley's our best bet for bedding down tonight," Gavin said solemnly.

Sarah turned to look at him. She knew he had been processing the woman's words too. They'd ridden in single file most of the day, eliminating any chance at conversation. Sarah hadn't wanted to talk about it. Maybe Gavin hadn't either.

Sarah lifted up on her toes in her stirrups and twisted in the saddle to survey their position. The temperature had dropped even further and with the rain that had pelted them nearly nonstop since the morning, they were both wet and shivering.

They'd left markers every few miles for the others to find them and Sarah was sure—barring an ambush or rock slide—that the wagon and Regan and Robbie would be on within a few hours.

The light was already beginning to fade. The upside of her and Gavin riding ahead was that it allowed both of them to feel as if they were fast on Mike's trail—true or not, and probably not. The downside was that they had to stop to bed down for the night well before dark or the wagon would never find them.

"There's a glade just there," Gavin said, pointing. "If we make a fire the others will find us easily even if they miss the signs we left."

But so can anyone else, Sarah thought. But she only nodded and began to move down into the valley.

Susan Kiernan-Lewis

7

John stood where the castle gatehouse had been, its massive wooden door buckled into three pieces even with the iron hinges that had held it together. The portcullis which had been suspended from the gatehouse ceiling was now a tangle of jagged metal on the ground.

He wasn't sure why he kept inspecting the damage. Looking wasn't going to put it back together. Maybe because in spite of Mike's brave words, it was pretty clear that nothing was ever going to put this mess back together.

He gazed out over the garden beside what had been the entrance to the castle. Across from the main drive was the parking lot the size of a football field. In the lot were two decrepit vehicles rusting in the ocean air, their upholstery long since ripped out and used for bedding.

He smelled the aroma of cooking meat. Someone was making a stew of some kind. Just two weeks ago, that would have meant food for everyone. If someone trapped even a rabbit, it went into the communal pot. When dinner came, you lined up with your plate for the fresh baked bread and stew that belonged to everyone.

Now the community had quickly split up into a series of small campfires that families had pitched their tents in circles around—with their backs to their neighbors.

Mike had been meaning to restructure how everyone had put their tents up but hadn't gotten to it before he disappeared.

John didn't feel confident marching up to these people— eighty or so—and telling them to move their tents and put them up again in an order of his choosing. The ways things were going, he wasn't completely sure they'd do it even if Mike asked them to.

He walked over to his mother's tent which he'd taken over since she left. Siobhan was more comfortable in her own tent and it was bigger to house the two of them plus the twins. As a result, it was also a chaotic mess.

Nuala or Liddy O'Malley usually took Siobhan first thing every morning which John was grateful for. The twins had attached themselves to Terry and his boy Darby. Terry was always manufacturing arrows or something else equally fascinating to little boys.

It gave John a much needed break and the freedom to try to figure out what he was going to do.

His mother had been gone a day and a half. Some part of him believed she should have been back by now with Mike in tow. But another, bigger part of him, knew it wasn't going to be that easy.

And there was always that *other* nagging piece in the back of his mind that said his mother wouldn't be back either.

He shook off the thought as he turned the final corner to his tent. When he did he saw Darby standing there waiting for him.

John liked Darby. Everybody did. He was clever and funny. And like most smart children, he knew when to help and when to disappear.

Right now he looked as if he wanted to disappear. He stood by the opening to John's tent, his hat in his hand and dried tears visible on his cheeks.

What the hell?

"Hey, Darby," John said. The boy hadn't seen him approach and he snapped his head around at John's voice. His face crumpled and he looked about to burst into tears at the sight of John.

"John," Darby said. "I've been w-w…waiting for you."

"You want to come inside?" John opened the tent flap. Darby clearly needed a moment to pull himself together.

"Aye," Darby said and ducked inside where he settled down on the floor of the tent.

John joined him.

"Okay, so what's up?" John said. He found it hard to believe that Darby had been bullied. He was ten and while it was true he was noticeably different from the other ten-year-old boys, he was also secure and self-confident. His parents adored him as did his older brother Tommy, who had left the camp last week.

"I...when I..." Darby waved his hands and then stopped, clearly afraid to speak for fear it would trigger more tears.

"Was someone ugly to you?" John coaxed.

Darby nodded, his eyes wide with wonder that John could have known. "Aye," he said.

"Who?"

"Mr. McCree."

At first John didn't register the name. When he did, he tried to calm his quickly escalating temper.

"He didn't leave this morning?" John said.

Darby shook his head. "He's been in Mr. Donovan's library for most of the morning me dad said."

That's why I didn't see him. Too bad he didn't break his neck walking on all the rubble to get to the library.

"You had a run in with him?"

Darby looked around the tent as if to find the words.

"I...I was just doing me usual chores," he said. "He came upon me and when I...when I looked up to say hello, he..."

Darby shook his head and tears squeezed out of his eyes. He closed his mouth in a firm line.

Damn that man! John thought. *Who the hell does he think he is to come here, eat our food and insult one of our own?*

"Did you tell your da?" John said.

Darby nodded. "He said to ignore it."

"What did he say to you, Darby?" John leaned over and laid a firm hand on Darby's shoulder.

Darby took in a long shuddering breath.

"He said there was no place in our new world for abnormalities."

"In that case what is *he* doing walking around?"

Darby managed a small smile and shrugged.

"I'm sorry he was a jerk to you, Darby. He said he'd be leaving today and I'm going to remind him he needs to do just that."

Darby looked at John, his eyebrows drawn together. "Do you think he'll go?"

⁂

When the wagon arrived that evening it was much later than Sarah thought it should have taken. Regan admitted they'd had to stop a few times for various reasons and that there was a stretch of the N69 from Listowel that had been impassable for the wagon.

They'd had to dismount and lead the wagon horse down the shoulder into a steep ditch on the side of the highway before resuming their trek.

Everyone was wet and cold. Sarah could see Regan was anxious and she knew it was because she was chomping at the bit to lead the expedition. Regan had a special relationship with Mike. He had been the closest thing to a father to her since her own father was murdered four years earlier. It was surely exasperating for her to hang back with the wagon as Sarah had requested.

But Sarah knew she couldn't give in and let Regan ride with her and Gavin. The wagon was important and to leave it protected with only one guard was to court disaster. As quiet as the countryside appeared, Sarah more than anyone knew what evil could be hiding under every rock or behind every innocent looking hillock.

She and Gavin had the campfire going by the time the wagon showed up. Since Sarah had agreed to the fire there was no point in eating cold jerky—especially since they'd given away most of what they had. Sarah wasn't willing to let Gavin shoot game—not with every sound echoing up and down the valley.

Sarah's plan was to send Regan, once she arrived, into the woods to shoot a few rabbits with her bow and arrow.

Not surprisingly, Regan had already shot three large hares during the day. Mary soon had them gutted, dressed and tied to a spit over the campfire. Sarah was surprised that she'd done it without anyone asking her to.

Mary had spent most of the last year complaining about the archers and their special privileges in the castle—especially one particular archer who'd taken very special privileges with Mary's husband. It seemed that nothing had come out of Mary's mouth in months that wasn't a shrill complaint or accusation.

To see her pitching in without being asked was a relief.

After Robbie and Jordie stretched the tarp over the back of the wagon for their bed that night, everyone changed out of their wet clothes and bundled back up in dry clothes. Sarah had brought Mike's parka which she snuggled into now and left her soaked riding coat steaming by the fire.

As she shivered inside the coat, waiting to finally get warm, she wondered if Mike would even need it when they found him?

The woman on the road had said she saw the red vest that Mike was wearing when he disappeared but she said he was wearing it under a heavy wool coat.

And when Sarah had stuttered out the question about his footwear, the woman had looked at her as if she were mad and affirmed that indeed the big man was wearing boots.

None of it made sense.

Was there any way it was a case of mistaken identity? Was that something Sarah was hoping? Because a sighting of Mike was surely better than none, wasn't it? Even if it did appear that he had left her of his own free will after all?

Sarah moved closer to the fire where the rest of the group was tearing pieces of meat off the rabbit on the spit. Robbie and Gavin were sitting beside each other and talking in low voices. Sarah had noticed before that they had become close friends after Robbie's brother died.

Regan sat next to Sarah and handed her a rabbit leg. The skin was charred black but the fragrance reminded Sarah that she'd had little to eat all day.

"Did you see that lot on the road?" Regan asked. "The women and babbies?"

"We gave them our jerky," Sarah said, eating her dinner.

Jordie sat down on the other side of Sarah. She could tell he was being very careful around her as if he expected to be sent home any minute.

"We offered them ours, too," he said. "But they wouldn't take it. Said you'd already helped them."

Sarah frowned. Did that make sense to turn down food when you were traveling with a group of starving children?

"Aye," Regan said. "But we made 'em take it anyway, didn't we? Which they did fast enough."

Sarah sighed. She knew why she wanted to discredit them but it really did appear that they were on the level. They were just a group of starving people going who knows where in hopes of something better and they'd been helped out by one of the kindest men in all of Ireland—handsome and big so nobody could ever misidentify him—and Sarah just didn't want to believe it.

He left on his own accord? Without a word? A message? A note?

"Sarah?"

She looked up to see that Robbie and Gavin had taken Jordie and Regan's places. She felt a flush of irritation with herself. This was not the time for inner dialogue and woolgathering. More than ever they needed to be vigilant and keep their wits about them.

"Where did Regan go?" Sarah asked. Mary was packing up what was left of the roast rabbit.

"She had first watch," Gavin said. "And I sent Jordie to check the horses' feet and make sure they hadn't picked up any stones."

Sarah felt a pinch of warning creep over her skin.

"So is this a private meeting?" she asked the two young men

"We were just wondering if you knew where we were going," Robbie said, looking down at his athletic shoes which didn't look brand new, but also didn't look as if they'd survived eight years in post-apocalyptic Ireland. Sarah didn't fault anyone for looting—especially not when there was so little to be had anywhere. Sometimes you just didn't want to know what people had had to do to survive before they came into your world.

"Roughly," Sarah said. "Are you sure Jordie can handle the horses? You remember what happened last time."

Gavin gave Robbie a look and after a brief pause Robbie got up.

"Sure, I'll check on the lad," Robbie said and left the fire to go to the tethered horses by a line of Juniper bushes on the perimeter of their camp.

"Okay," Sarah said. "What's on your mind, Gavin?"

"I want to know if we're going to the Island of Secret Knowledge," Gavin said. "And is that where me da is?"

"It's not really an island."

"You know what I mean, Sarah."

Sarah glanced at Gavin. She'd known him since he was a teenager. She'd met him the same day she'd met Mike—and nearly shot him in the process. Three days after that she'd been responsible for Gavin being shot off his horse as they attempted to storm a bandit gypsy encampment.

She loved him like her own son.

"Before I left I asked John flat out where his dad's headquarters was," Sarah said.

Gavin scooted closer to Sarah and she could tell he was trying to get his excitement under control.

"As you can imagine, he said in no uncertain terms that his father had nothing to do with Mike's disappearance."

"Well, he would do, wouldn't he?"

Sarah stared into the fire for a moment. She saw that moment two weeks ago when she'd been walking the castle halls—*when there had been castle halls to walk*—looking for John and had come upon John and his father talking in the library. She hadn't overheard much.

But enough. She's heard David tell John that his compound was located on the other side of the Killarney National Park in Ballingeary. That wasn't a whole lot to go on since she didn't know exactly where the portal or entrance might be to the compound and Ballingeary was not a small town. She had an image of herself running around a field outside Ballingeary waving her arms hoping to show up on one of David's surveillance screens.

"I think I might know roughly where David's group is," she said carefully.

"Where?" Gavin asked breathlessly.

Sarah reached over and took Gavin's hand in hers.

"I don't want to get your hopes up," she said. "But if David *didn't* somehow—for whatever reason—take Mike, then I have to hope he can help us find him. I don't know what else to do."

Gavin's eyes probed hers.

"What do you make of what the woman we met on the road said?" he asked. "Do ye really think Da gave them food while riding *away* from Castle Henredon?"

"We have no proof it was him. There's every reason to believe that whoever took your dad also took his vest. It's possible there's another man in Ireland as big as your father and now wearing his clothes."

Gavin paled. "I hadn't thought of that."

And I wish I hadn't said anything, Sarah thought. She patted his knee and looked around. Mary had climbed into the back of the wagon to bed down for the night but nobody else was around. The silence in the valley seemed to crawl under Sarah's skin.

"Shouldn't Robbie and Jordie be back by now?" she asked in a low voice.

The moment the words were out of her mouth, the woods erupted in a series of gunshots. Sarah flung her plate to the ground and grabbed for her gun holster at her feet. She and Gavin both jumped to their feet.

A man's voice yelled from the interior of the woods and one of the horses screamed.

"Go to the woods!" Sarah shouted to Gavin. "Go!" She gave him a push and saw him scoop up his semi-automatic .22 on the ground as he ran.

Sarah ran to the wagon. She could see Mary huddled in the back under the tarp, her eyes large with terror.

"Stay put!" Sarah barked at her before wheeling around to the other side.

Where were Jordie and Robbie? Had they been shot?

She crouched behind the rear wagon wheel, her gun pointed toward the center of the camp. Whoever was out there, unless there were more than three, she should be able to pick them off one by one. She licked her lips and waited, her eyes darting around the camp.

The dying fire made shadows jump and elongate eerily, adding movement where there was none. She strained to listen.

Suddenly, she saw the bushes move and she tensed and braced her gun hand on her knee, taking careful aim.

A figure stumbled out of the bushes. From where Sarah crouched in the shadows, she could see blood seeping out of the wound in the front of the figure's parka.

Sarah watched in horror as the figure staggered to the fire and then fell to her knees and then her face.

It was Regan.

Susan Kiernan-Lewis

8

Sarah didn't have time to react to what she'd just seen. Whoever was attacking them wouldn't come into the clearing. They must know she was waiting to shoot at them.

Forcing herself not to look at Regan's body, Sarah climbed to her feet, then turned and bolted into the woods behind the wagon. Not caring about the branches that tore at her clothes or clawed at her face, she pushed into the woods, jumping over fallen logs only barely visible in the moonlight.

She had to think!

She saw a thick tangle of hawthorn ahead and crept into it. As soon as she was reasonably well hidden, she allowed herself to think.

Ambushed. Had they been lying in wait for anybody to come along?

Bandits. Likely their intention was to murder everyone and take the guns and horses. Sarah took in a long breath and let it out as quietly as possible.

Where was the rest of her group?

She cringed at the thought of Regan lying face down by the campfire. Shot before she'd been able to raise the alarm.

Robbie and Jordie were with the horses.

Mary was hiding in the wagon.

Gavin was somewhere in the woods. Gavin—who without anyone to tell him what to do—would likely just stay in the woods indefinitely. Or do something crazy.

Think, Sarah, think!

As she was trying to decide what to do, a single gunshot exploded in the air from the direction of camp. The sound of men's laughter followed. How many? Did they shoot someone? Did they finish off Regan or did they find Mary?

Sarah's finger itched against the trigger. How she longed to storm back to camp with guns blazing!

But how many were there? They must know that some of the group had escaped into the woods. Why weren't they searching the woods? Were they waiting for morning?

Sarah heard a sound twenty yards away from her. She tensed and instantly got into a crouching position, her gun raised.

Could it be Gavin? Who else would be attempting stealth? The bandits clearly didn't care about secrecy at this point.

Men's voices drifted back to her from the campsite. And then a woman's scream.

Mary.

Sarah got to her feet.

To hell with this.

She hadn't gone ten paces toward the camp when she heard their voices coming closer. They were in the woods now. Mary must have told them that Sarah and Gavin had fled there. Sarah stopped, her back to a tree. She held her breath.

Let them come, she thought, her adrenaline raging.

The rain had started again and for that Sarah was grateful. It would camouflage any noise she might make as she got into position. The men were talking, unmindful of how their voices carried, or that anyone might hear them or be able to pinpoint their location.

Good, she thought. *Be arrogant and stupid. Be that way right up to the moment I shoot you in the face.*

She held perfectly still and waited. Another terrified scream from Mary sent a tremor of fury up her arms and she raised her Glock to chest level. Through the branches and the dark leaves, the moonlight flickered over the wet foliage.

And then she saw them.

Two shadows moving deeper into the woods. Toward her.

They'd stopped talking. They held their rifles out and ready.

The shadows were closer now, less than twenty yards away. They moved silently, relentlessly. Sarah held her gun and braced her elbows against the tree behind her. She felt herself hyperventilating, her chest heaving with every breath. She was sure they could hear her gasping. She tried to slow her breathing.

Then the figures were swallowed up in the gloom of the woods. All she heard was the sound of the rain rattling the leaves overhead.

And then the crunch of footsteps near her.

Without waiting, she pulled the trigger, once, twice, three times. Her ears rang with the onslaught of the noise and a lone man's startled cry.

She'd hit one. The second one was still there. Near.

Somewhere.

There was no point in secrecy now. Sarah needed to get back to the camp. They wouldn't expect that. Besides, Mary was there and still alive.

Sarah turned and slammed into a wall of black pain that shut off all her senses.

All noise and feeling instantly snuffed out.

Susan Kiernan-Lewis

9

The campfires of all the families twinkled in the evening as John wound his way through the maze of tents. Most people had already made their evening meal and were tucking in for the night.

He passed Eliza Barrett's tent and saw she was sitting outside with Liddy O'Malley. Mrs. Barrett was nervously shredding a piece of cloth in her hands as she talked. While Mrs. O'Malley was a new widow—and she'd dearly loved her husband—Eliza Barrett was the kind of person who worried about everything at top volume no matter how inconsequential it was.

John had sensed a new level of unease in the community since Jordie and Mrs. Barrett come several months before. Mrs. Barrett's constant and unrelenting worry over Jordie's safety was generally considered nuclear even for motherly concern. And it tended to be contagious.

It was typical that Liddy O'Malley was at Eliza Barrett's tent comforting *her*—when *she* was the one who'd actually experienced a significant loss. Jordie might be a lazy screwup, but he wasn't likely to get himself killed by running into burning buildings or taking risks.

As John passed through the encampment, many people looked up and nodded at him in greeting. Oddly, many others totally ignored him.

If he wasn't on a mission he might stop to think about why that was. This confrontation with McCree would be the first real test of John's leadership at the camp.

McCree should never have been given a bed for the night, let alone a meal. And John knew he should have assigned someone to watch him during the time he was with them.

What if he's a serial rapist? Or he's here to steal our food reserves? Or worse, our guns?

No, letting the guy wander around without a chaperone was a serious breach of castle rules and one John was sure Mike would never have made.

He felt the Colt single action army revolver in his holster.

Would it come to that? Or would the guy leave peacefully?

"Oy! John!" a woman's voice called out.

John didn't break stride but turned to see the head archer Aibreann standing between two tents, her toddler Bill in her arms.

"A word, Chief?" she said.

The ring of five tents where the archers lived was on the ocean side of where the west wall of the castle used to be. There was no strategic reason why the archers had set up camp there except perhaps an unconscious preference to be near the place where they'd once ruled.

That, and the fact that because of their unruly natures and generally disobedient habits they weren't the most popular members of the community. In any case, it worked out for all that they were situated both figuratively and literally on the fringe of the community.

"Kinda in a hurry here, Aibreann," John said. "Can it wait?"

"That it cannot," Aibreann said as she hurried to match his stride. Like all the archers, Aibreann was the embodiment of the young Amazon warrior. Lean, tan and virtually fearless, before the castle fell the community had depended on Aibreann and her archer band for their very lives.

Now that there was no place to shoot their arrows from, not so much.

"What's the problem?" John said, slowing his gait to accommodate her.

"It's Kyla," Aibreann said, shifting the baby to her other hip. "It's a right balls-up and no mistake."

John blew out a breath of frustration and wished Regan were here to sort this out. She was the archer's leader and a take-no-prisoners one at that.

The archers were a wild group with little to no regard for rules or other people's feelings and it took a strong kickass leader to make them tow the line.

Regan was undeniably that leader but Regan wasn't here.

"Look, Aibreann," John said, "I don't know why you can't keep your girls in line. You're not doing anyone any favors by—"

"Oy, ye fecking eejit," Aibreann said, stopping and forcing John to do the same.

He turned and regarded her, his hands on his hips.

She scowled at him.

"Sure it's not Kyla I'm talking about," Aibreann said. "It's that tosser what waltzed into camp yesterday. Whom ye *allowed* to waltz into camp yesterday."

John rubbed a hand across his face. "Tell me what happened."

꧁ꕥ꧂ꕥ꧁ꕥ꧂ꕥ꧁ꕥ

Fifteen minutes later, John entered through the broken archway of the castle. Lanterns had been set up in the courtyard which he found strange—and troubling.

Why waste fuel in the middle of the night? Except for the clinic and the relatively undamaged section of the castle that was used by Terry for his workshop, there was no need for illumination in this section.

He paused at what had once been the castle entrance and listened. Because the interior walls had been mostly blown away, it was easy to hear voices and to tell where they were coming from.

Mindful of where he put his foot in the rubble, John picked his way across the courtyard to the first set of stone stairs that led to the second floor—now open to the elements. A section of the stairs was gone but John had long legs and easily jumped the gap.

There was no reason for anyone to be up here at this time of the evening, he thought.

Unless it's a private meeting. And there's *really* no reason for that.

He followed the sound of the voices down the open hallway to where Mike had had his study. The room had once been the most elegantly furnished room in the castle—with thick Oriental rugs, heavy drapes and massive floor to ceiling bookcases crammed full of leather-bound books looted from a nearby mansion.

In the days since the explosion had taken down the walls, many of the books were now sodden and unreadable. The carpet was spongy with rainwater and mud.

As John rounded the first corner of the hallway he saw people standing in the hall peering into it.

A warning fissure flared in his gut.

It was definitely a secret meeting. But mostly it looked like it was just secret from *him.*

John pushed his way through the crowd to stand in the doorway of Mike's study. There at the massive oak desk that John and Gavin had personally dragged into place two years before sat Lorcan McCree, his hands steepled on the desktop as he gazed out at the people in the room. Everyone in the room was male.

That's quite an interesting statement for a community that's eighty per cent female.

"And why do the wee bitches eat first?" a tall thin man, Riley O'Meara was saying. John remembered when O'Meara first came to the community. He'd begged Mike to take him and his wife in and their three sons.

"Why do any of them?" Danny McGoldrick chimed in. A big man with bushy eyebrows, he was the husband of one of Mike's cousins. A quiet man, he'd been with the community for nearly the whole seven years—from Donovan's Lot to Ameriland and finally Henredon's Castle. "They keep the best cuts for themselves and only hand off their rejects!"

"Steady on, gents," McCree said. "Seems we have a visitor."

"What's going on here?" John said, consciously working to keep his voice calm and authoritative. He knew most of the community still saw him as a kid.

"What's *going on*, lad," McGoldrick said derisively, "is the adults are sorting out a problem."

"You're not in charge here, McGoldrick," John said, walking to where McCree sat. "What do you think you're doing, McCree?"

"I'm filling a need, lad," McCree said easily, waving his hands to encompass the group of men.

John noticed Terry stood in the far corner as if he were trying to be invisible.

Was it possible he was with this group?

"Looks to me like you're the one causing a problem," John said. "One we didn't have before you came."

"Ah now that's where you're wrong, lad," McCree said. "You've had this problem for a very long time. Am I right, lads?"

The group of men concurred loudly.

"We're treated second class!" one man shouted.

"We do all the work and get none of the goods!"

"Those bitch archers rule this place, so they do!"

John turned on the last man who spoke. Riley O'Meara.

"If you don't like it, O'Meara, you can clear out. No one's putting a gun to your head to make you stay."

"Aw, it's always the same! Complain just a bit and they threaten to toss you out! It's an oligarchy, so it is!"

"Nay, Riley," McCree said. "Even worse than that. It's a fecking *matriarchy*. The lad admitted as much to me last night."

"*Whatever* we are is none of your business," John said. "It's time for you to go."

"At night?" McGoldrick said. "With the wolves everywhere near? What would your mother say?"

A few of the men laughed and John forced himself to tamp down the anger that was bubbling up inside him.

"We've invited Mr. McCree to stay for as long as he likes," O'Meara said.

"That's not your place to do," John said.

"Says who?" O'Meara shot back.

John was tempted to move his shoulder back to remind O'Meara that he was armed. He decided once he did that he might be pushed to actually use it and there were more of them than he had bullets.

"Says the charter of this community that you and everybody here agreed to when you joined," John said.

"We're rewriting the charter, boyo," McGoldrick said with a grin. The rest of the men in the room agreed with murmurs and shouts.

McCree stood up.

"These are men, here!" he shouted. "Men who are tired of being led by women!"

The group cheered.

"Men who are tired of one set of women eating first and eating best!"

The group cheered louder.

"Are these lasses better than you?" McCree asked the assembled group.

"Nay! They're *lasses*!"

"How can ye stay civilized if you allow *women* to rule you? It's abnormal! It's not right!"

John raised his voice until everyone turned to hear him.

"This is not the way we operate," he said. "And you all know it. Now if you have a specific grievance—"

"*I* have a grievance!" McGoldrick shouted. "About that bitch archer who stole and roasted one of the community pigs in the woods without telling anyone!"

The whole room erupted in indignant shouts and it was several moments before John could be heard again.

Aibreann had told him that Kyla had indeed killed a piglet and the archers had roasted it and eaten it among themselves. It was a serious rule infraction and the archers all knew it.

"If it's true," John said, "she'll be punished."

"What do you mean *if it's true*?" one of the other men yelled out. John recognized him as Durgan Fegan, the father of one of the boys that Matt and Mac played with. "Of course they'll deny it. And you'll believe them."

"Their leader has already owned it," John said. "But as you well know, we've established a separate military tribunal for the archers."

John knew this was probably not the best time to remind the men that the archers were not held to the same laws as the rest of the castle community.

"Bugger the tribunal!" O'Meary shouted. "We want justice!"

"Aye! Justice!" the men shouted. "Burn the bitches! We don't need them any more!"

John saw that things were getting out of hand but he had an even bigger problem. Aibreann had said that Kyla had been dragged off this afternoon. This group wasn't just letting off steam, they were taking things into their own hands. Should he demand that she be released? Or would that just make them dig in deeper?

"Sure, are ye to let this lass eat bacon while your children go hungry?" McCree said.

"Nay!" the crowd roared.

"And then when she's caught red-handed, there's no consequence for her crime? Is that the way of it?"

"Nay!" the men said, their voices thick with anger and outrage. "No more!"

John glanced at Terry and saw that he stood now with his shoulders sagging and his eyes on his feet.

"We're men! And we'll have justice by God!" said McCree. "The archer will be tried at noon tomorrow by a tribunal of our making."

The men cheered.

"After which time, she and her crime will be presented to the community as an example that no one is above the rules set for all."

"Hear! Hear!" the men cheered.

"An example to be made at sundown tomorrow night," McCree said. "By the removal of her right hand."

Susan Kiernan-Lewis

10

Sarah floated up to consciousness aware of only two things —men's voices and a staggering agony reverberating in her head. She opened her eyes and saw that it was morning. She was lying on her side by the campfire which was out and cold.

"Sarah?" Mary said softly. "Are ye awake, lass?"

Sarah's hands were tied behind her and when she moved a searing pain erupted in her shoulder forcing her to stop. She saw a knee beside her—Gavin or Jordie's—and ten feet away, a booted foot from the body that lay where it had fallen hours before.

Regan.

"Oy! The bitch is awake, Laith," a man's voice said.

Seconds later, Sarah felt rough hands grab her and pull her to a seated position. She cried out at the agony exploding in her shoulder from having slept on it all night with her arms behind her back.

The man squatted in front of her, his face near hers. He was thin, his beard thick except for a few bare spots. His long dark hair was pulled back into a ponytail.

"So yer awake, are ye?" he said, blasting her with a jet of foul breath. She must have grimaced because he laughed at her reaction.

She turned her head to confirm that Gavin was beside her. His face was bloodied and one eye was swollen shut. Next to him was Jordie. His eyes, wide and terrified, were red-rimmed as if he'd spent the night weeping.

She couldn't see Robbie and a terrible feeling filled her. They'd killed him. Dear God, how would she tell Nuala?

"I'll be needing your attention, Missus," the man said. "I'm Laith Killoran and this is me mate, Bran Griffin. Say hello to the lady, Bran."

"Screw you, Missus," Bran said as he came nearer. He was heavyset which was unusual these days. He had coarse red hair and a full beard. "Which I fully intend to." He laughed at his own wit. He held a rifle and it was a moment before Sarah recognized it. Up until last night, she had last seen it in Robbie's hands.

Her eyes searched both men for any sign of the damage she'd done last night. She could well have killed the one she'd shot. For some reason, she thought she'd only wounded him. But there could be no other explanation for why neither Killoran or Griffin showed any wounds. Unless they had some kind of protective vests on?

"You know your own party, of course," Killoran continued, "but you'll not have met the lovely Moira."

He waved a hand to a woman sitting on the other side of Mary. Also redheaded, Moira looked like she was in her late twenties. Blood streaked both cheeks, one eye was blackened, and the other shone out with pure liquid terror on everything happening around her.

"We found Miss Moira on the road, so we did," Killoran said. "And enticed her to accompany us. Didn't we, luv?"

"What do you want?" Sarah blurted out. "Our rifles? Our horses? Take them and go."

Killoran blinked and then rocked back on his heels and laughed.

"Do ye hear this lass?" he said. "Tied up, beaten with nary a hope of escape or mercy, and still giving orders!" He looked at Gavin. "I feel for ye, mate, I truly do. Must be the Yank in her."

He turned back to Sarah and reached over to finger the buttons of her parka.

"What I want you'll be happy to know, Missus, is something that's yours to give." He patted Sarah's cheek and she flinched with each touch.

"Now, mind your manners and I might untie you." He nodded at Mary, and Sarah realized that Mary was not bound.

Griffin came to the cold fire and dropped a pack on the ground. Sarah saw Mary's fingers tremble as she opened it and drew out a chunk of raw bacon, a frying pan and a packet of eggs.

Several of the eggs were broken, the yellow yolk dripping from Mary's fingers. She worked quickly to get the fire started again and set the frying pan over the embers.

"We'll be here awhile," Killoran said. He walked over to where the horses were now tied closer to the camp. He ran a hand down the legs of Sarah's gelding and then patted its flank. "Might as well be comfortable."

༈༺༈༺༈༺༈༺

As the aroma of Mary cooking breakfast floated around the camp, Sarah tried not to look at Regan's body off to the side. It had all happened so fast. It was unbelievable that the girl was gone.

Regan had always been so full of life. And while it was true she was tortured and largely unhappy, everybody loved her.

It's because of me she's dead, Sarah thought dully. *Mike will never get over this.*

Sarah looked at the rest of the members of her group. Jordie was working hard to be invisible and Sarah would do him the favor of not reminding these ruthless men that he was alive. She turned to Gavin who sat near the woman Moira.

"How did they catch you?" Sarah asked in a low voice.

"I...I couldn't go very far," he said.

Sarah understood. Not with Mary screaming the way she'd been. Neither of them could truly escape with the thought of her being hurt back at the camp.

"Have they said anything about what they want?" she asked.

He shook his head.

"Regan's dead," he said bitterly, his eyes going to where her body lay. "I can't believe it. I'd give anything to have five minutes with these bastards and me hands untied."

"Maybe Robbie made it out," Sarah said. "Maybe he's gone for help."

"What would help look like?" Gavin said. "A posse from the castle? Led by an eighteen-year-old boy?" He shook his head. "Besides, Robbie wouldn't leave us."

"You think they killed him," Sarah said quietly.

"They're monsters and no mistake," Moira said, her lips trembling as she spoke.

"Where are your people?" Sarah asked.

"Gone," Moira said, a tear streaking down her cheek. "Either dead or run off. Me husband…" She shook her head and pressed her lips closed in a firm line.

Sarah knew that feeling. Talking about the horrors wouldn't help. Talking about them only made you relive them.

"I shot one of them," Sarah said.

Gavin jerked his head up. "You did? Did you kill him?"

Sarah shrugged and glanced at the two men as they sat by the fire wolfing down food and talking amongst themselves.

"I must have. You don't see him, do you?"

A noise from the bushes made all of them start. Griffin and Killoran dropped their plates and stood up. Griffin raised his rifle.

"Show yourself!" he shouted.

Sarah felt as if the group was collectively holding its breath as the bushes parted and Robbie stepped forward, his hands in the air in a gesture of peace. Both Griffin and Killoran lowered their weapons and went back to their breakfast.

Confused, Sarah looked at Gavin and then back at Robbie who refused to look at them. He went to stand by the fire. It was then that Sarah noticed he was armed.

And that he was wounded.

11

John knew confronting McCree last night would have been a mistake. After breaking into the meeting in Mike's den, John had made his way back to Nuala's tent to pick up Siobhan and the twins. But Nuala had insisted he not wake the children and so he had gone to his mother's tent where he spent the night alone.

Usually, one of the camp women would have brought him a cup of tea and a bun of some kind. This morning, John woke to find nothing outside his tent except a cold ring of stones where a fire should have been.

Aside from that the world looked for all intents and purposes as if nothing had changed.

But John and every other male in the community knew something fundamentally *had* changed.

Had he really buggered everything up in just the two short days his mother and Mike had been gone?

He felt a stab of indigestion burning in his gut.

Quickly he pulled himself together. First thing he needed to do was talk to Terry to see where he stood. John hadn't really been able to tell last night. But between John's knowledge of the man and the fact that McCree threatened Terry's son Darby John was pretty sure he knew where Terry's loyalties lay.

Then he needed to find where they were keeping Kyla.

But before *that* he needed to revisit the archers' camp. They were armed and they were pissed off.

Never a good combination.

On the way to the archers' campsite, he swung by Nuala's tent to see that she was feeding fresh baked bread to her three along with Siobhan and Matt and Mac. The six children were huddled around the small fire in front of the tent.

"Hey, Nuala," John said as both twins attacked him and tried to climb him in greeting. "Sorry I left you in the lurch last night."

"Not at-tall, young John," Nuala said, smiling tiredly at him. "Is something going on?"

"You might say that. That guy McCree is becoming a problem."

"What do you mean? A problem how?"

"You see Fiona this morning?" John asked.

"I'm expecting her to drop off Ciara any time now."

"I noticed that Bill was with Aibreann yesterday."

When Aibreann gave birth to Bill—another product of rape—she'd gratefully given him up to Fiona who'd recently lost a baby.

You didn't have to have eyes to see that Aibreann had changed her mind—and Fiona wasn't happy about it.

"More and more, it seems," Nuala said as she directed the girls back into the tent to get dressed.

"Fiona was there last night," John said. "I think she's under this guy's spell or something."

Nuala didn't answer but went over to the fire to stir a pot of oatmeal.

"Do you know something, Nuala?" John asked.

"Sure, no, not at-tall," Nuala said. "Fiona's been through a lot, so she has."

"Yeah, haven't we all."

"Will ye have some porridge before ye go, John?"

John shook his head. "I've already eaten," he lied.

"Let us come with ye, John!" Matt crowed. "We'll behave. Promise!"

"None of that!" Nuala said sharply. "John has camp business to be about and doesn't need you lot tripping about his feet. Now here are the lasses so you lot go in and get dressed. Go on, now!"

The boys left with some grumbling just as Fiona showed up holding Ciara's hand.

"Oh!" she said when she saw John. "I didn't expect to see you here."

Fiona looked guilty. There was no other description for it. She hurriedly kissed Ciara's face and the girl went to kneel down next to Siobhan and Darcie who were eating their oatmeal from heavy ceramic bowls.

Before John had a chance to respond, Terry's wife Jill and Darby arrived. Jill was carrying a large basket of freshly baked bread.

"We're here," Jill sang out cheerfully. If anybody had less reason to be cheerful it was probably Jill. Not yet forty, she looked sixty.

She'd lost her husband twice, said goodbye to her oldest boy two weeks ago for God knew how long—possibly forever —and was now in the unenviable position of needing to stand between her ten-year-old son and a man who would make an example of him and his "differences."

John faced Fiona.

"Tell me you're not in on this," he said.

Fiona crossed her arms and looked away.

"Fiona?" Nuala said.

"Darby," Jill said. "Take the children to the beach, will you? There's a good lad."

"Cor, all seven of them?" Darby said.

"I'm sure you can handle it," Nuala said smiling. "They look up to you, Darby."

The boys emerged from the tent and when they saw Darby immediately set on him, cheering and wrapping their arms around him until he was able to shuffle all the children away from the tent and toward the beach.

Fiona turned to John. "Look, John—" she began.

"No, Fi, *you* look," John said hotly. "This is against every rule and law we have. And who gave that guy McCree the right to rabble rouse or make any decisions about our community?"

"I don't know, John. But the people obviously want to hear what he has to say."

"And you, Fi?" Nuala said pointedly. "Do *you* want to hear what he has to say?"

Fiona ignored her.

John turned to Nuala. "Kyla caught a piglet yesterday and killed it. She and the archers roasted it."

Nuala shrugged. "Sure I don't see how that's any different from what everyone else has been doing these last few days."

"Exactly," Jill said. "It's just an excuse to go after the archers."

"That's not true!" Fiona said. "The archers did it because they know nobody will call them to task!"

"So O'Meara and a few of the men took Kyla," John said to both Jill and Nuala, "and McCree says he'll lop off her hand for her crime."

Nuala looked at Fiona with a stunned look on her face.

"Surely no," she said. "Fi? Did ye know this?"

"How is this any different from all those times in the past when Mike had to deal with miscreants?" Fiona said. "Or is it because Kyla's a woman? Lorcan says there's a law for men and one for women in this community. And it's not fair."

"Mike would never agree to something so barbaric," Jill said.

Fiona turned on her. "But he has! Many times!"

"For people caught stealing horses or weapons," John said. "And then he only ever ordered whipping or exile. Never dismemberment."

Fiona stood with her arms crossed and stared John down.

"You know as well as I do that exile is the same as a death sentence," she said. "And Mike and Sarah have both handed those out pretty freely. Remember Ava? Or Archie? Or even poor Aideen?"

"Aideen and Archie were given choices and they *chose* to go," John said. "And when Archie returned he was met with open arms. As for Ava, she was a friggin' cannibal, as you well know, Aunt Fiona. Would you really feel comfortable with her in the next tent to you and Ciara?"

"What Kyla did was wrong and she needs to be punished," Fiona said flatly.

"But that's not what's happening!" John said fiercely. "Don't you see? She's being attacked because the archers have always enjoyed special privileges. *That's* her real crime."

Fiona shook her head. "Nay, John. She stole food. These times call for strong laws. We shouldn't have rules for one and not for all."

"So will you go?" Nuala asked, her mouth open in stunned disbelief.

"Go?" Fiona asked.

"To see them chop off her hand? Will you set Ciara on a high stool so she can get a good view? Thank God we don't have to worry about wee Bill being forced to witness such a thing. He's safely back with Aibreann."

Fiona's lips curled. She clenched her fists and for a moment John she would strike Nuala but in the end, she just turned on her heel and stomped away.

John turned to Jill. "You knew about this?"

"Aye. Terry told me last night."

"He's not with them, right?"

"Acht, John! How can ye even ask such a thing?"

"Okay, yeah, I know. Sorry."

"There was no point in him speaking out last night. Surely you learned that for yourself?"

Nuala wiped her hands on her jeans and stood up.

"Enough," she said firmly. "Let's go find Kyla."

Susan Kiernan-Lewis

12

Every time she looked at Robbie Sarah felt sick.

So *he* was the one she'd shot. *He* was the one who'd come after her in the woods, who'd hunted her like prey. And now *he* was the one who shared his breakfast with these bastards who'd killed Regan and likely intended to kill them as well.

She just couldn't make the pieces fit. Not Robbie. Not Nuala's Robbie. It didn't make sense.

Sarah looked at Gavin and saw he was every bit as stunned as she was.

Or was he? Gavin looked furious. But did he look astonished?

"Why is he doing this?" Sarah asked.

Gavin looked at her, his eyes wide. But Gavin was a bad liar. He knew something. He looked away from her.

"I have no idea," he said.

"Did you know he might do this?"

This time Gavin looked at Sarah with genuine horror.

"Sure ye can say that to me, Sarah? Me?" He face was flushed red with indignation and anger.

"He's *your* friend," Sarah pointed out. "So tell me. Why is he doing this?"

Killoran approached them and squatted again in front of Sarah. Robbie stood behind Killoran and looked at his feet.

"Does Nuala know you're doing this, Robbie?" Sarah spat out. "How are you going to explain my dead body to her?"

Killoran grabbed Sarah's chin and jerked her face toward him.

"Ye'll not be upsetting the hired help now, lass," he said. His voice was light but the steel in his eyes made Sarah shiver involuntarily. "Robbie's only doing what he thinks is best for everyone. Isn't that right, Robbie?"

"Aye," Robbie said, still not looking up.

"Shite, what a poof," Griffin said, sneering at Robbie.

"Shirrup, Bran," Killoran said, still looking at Sarah. "Would ye care to guess what we want from ye, Missus?"

"I have no idea," Sarah said.

"They want the tunnel," Gavin said, his voice full of malice and disgust. "They want the tunnel that leads to David Woodson's so-called island."

Killoran flicked his eyes toward Gavin for a moment, his smile never wavering.

"The lad's got it in one," Killoran said.

They were looking for David's group—which they'll have learned all about from Robbie. Sarah looked at Robbie.

"How do you know these men?" she asked.

"We were in the army together," Killoran said easily. "We mostly scattered after our attempt to take Henrendon last year but Bran and me we didn't go far. We ran into young Robbie here at last month's market in Kilderry, didn't we, boyo?"

Robbie's face hardened but he didn't respond.

"How did you know where we were?" Sarah said.

"Word travels fast when the American woman from the castle and a small armed group go on the road."

"You're lying. Who told you?" Her eyes went to Robbie. Could he be involved in Mike's disappearance too? How else would Killoran have known she would be on the road?

"I don't know how to get to any tunnel," Sarah said.

"Well, that's just it, Missus," Killoran said. "Seems our friend Robbie here thinks in fact you do."

"He's wrong. I have no idea where it is."

"Oh, see, here's me thinking you're lying," Killoran said. "Robbie?"

Robbie finally lifted his head.

"I know you know where it is," Robbie said sullenly. "The whole castle knows you know! A place where there's light and warmth and nobody's hungry? A place like it was before? You know exactly how to get there."

"Except I don't," Sarah said.

"Well," Killoran said, standing up, "let's just say it'll be a bit too bad for you and your friends if that's true."

✵✵✵✵✵✵

Killoran and his crew broke camp within the hour. Muffled thunder rolled through the basin, shaking the pines. Weak sunlight dappled the needled floor of the forest as they moved southeast toward Killarney.

Sarah and Gavin's horses were tied to the back of the wagon which Mary drove. Sarah and Moira sat beside her.

Moira and Mary were unbound since, like most men, their captors did not consider them a threat.

Jordie and Gavin, with their hands tied behind them, walked on each side the wagon.

Killoran rode in front and Griffin brought up the rear. Robbie rode alongside the wagon nearest to Gavin.

Sarah's mind whirled as she tried to think what to do. Somehow Robbie knew to head toward the Killarney National Park. Either he'd overheard Sarah talking to Gavin or he'd gotten that much from John.

Once they arrived at the park, Killoran would amp up the pressure on Sarah to tell him exactly *where* in the national park to find the tunnel that was the compound entrance.

She didn't bother getting eye contact with Robbie. Like most zealots he believed he was doing bad things for all the right reasons. Sarah knew she only stood a chance of using him later if she didn't alienate him now.

Clearly Gavin wasn't on the same game plan.

"Your mates killed Regan!" Gavin snarled as he walked beside the wagon, his face a visage of fury.

"Thought you and her were done," Robbie said. But his face belied his flippant words. Sarah could tell he was upset about her death.

"You're a fecking murderer," Gavin said. "I only hope someday Nuala learns the truth of who you really are."

"I'm doing this for Nuala! For everyone!" Robbie said hotly. "How many times have I heard you say the same thing? Electricity! Hot water! Wouldn't your Sophia love that? I'm doing it for everyone."

"How about Regan? Are ye doing it for her too?"

"That…that shouldn't have happened. I hate that that happened." Robbie's face reddened. Sarah had no doubt he expected this whole plan to go off without a drop of blood being shed.

But now that things had turned out otherwise, he had to convince himself to go forward. Too much was at stake now. If he didn't go forward, Regan will have died for nothing.

"How did your mates know where we were?"

Robbie shook his head.

"Come on, ye fecking tosser! Have ye been planning this since you and your gobshite brother first came to the castle?"

"Don't talk about Frank like that!" Robbie said. "My brother would have given his life for every person in that castle, as ye well know!"

"So how did your friends know where to find us?"

Robbie shook his head again and glowered at the horizon.

"Oh, I see. They've been tracking us, haven't they?" Gavin said. "How long? Since we left the castle? Have ye just been waiting for something like this? Cor, it was *you* lot what took me da, wasn't it?"

"That's bollocks!"

"Ye wanted to get Sarah away from the castle so what better way? Grab me da and sure as shite she'll be after him. So who planned it?"

"We had nothing to do with your da's disappearance. I swear it," Robbie said.

"And your word being so valuable and all."

"I swear on me granny's grave I had nothing to do with it, nor did any of this lot. I just…when it happened…I knew she'd be leaving the castle. It's why I volunteered! So I could control the situation. I only wish you'd see how much good will come from this."

"Sure when you put it that way, maybe I do."

Robbie drew up his horse and Gavin stopped walking.

"Truly, Gavin?" Robbie said, his face hopeful and open.

"Aye, Robbie. Why not?" Gavin said. "We could all use some light and a hot shower about now, couldn't we?"

Robbie leaned over as if he would shake Gavin's hand.

Gavin grabbed Robbie's hand and pulled him half out of his saddle before spitting fully in his face.

"May *that* be a starter for ye on the hot showers, ye unholy bastard," Gavin said before turning his back and striding forward.

Susan Kiernan-Lewis

13

After splitting up from John and Jill, Nuala went to search the stables and Terry's workshop on the backside of the castle. Like John, her first logical guess would have been the dungeons.

The dungeons were one of the few places in the castle that were still intact and functional, and because of them the entire castle population except for the poor O'Malley brothers had escaped harm in the bombardment.

On the other hand, the pathway to the dungeons wasn't as easily taken as it had been before the bombing. Giant boulders of castle stone were still positioned in the courtyard making it necessary to climb over them to reach the part of the castle unaffected by the assault.

It was hard for Nuala to imagine the men subduing Kyla, who was a true warrior and would not have come along nicely. But to drag her over rocks and rubble the size of a small compact car? Nuala couldn't imagine it.

Besides the dungeons, there were less obvious places where the men might have taken Kyla. The nuns had set up a chapel in the castle's inner bailey before the bombing. It had largely been demolished along with the Sisters' sleeping cells.

But even so, Nuala had heard from the children—who she was constantly warning not to play there but who did anyway—that there were several rooms behind the ruined chapel that, if not undamaged, were at least useable.

Nuala picked her way across the courtyard mindful of how easy it was to get hurt and how tragic it had been to lose Frank, her beloved Robbie's only brother, to a mundane accident.

Their community school teacher, Frank had cut his toe on a rusty nail helping one of the women rearrange furniture and died of infection within a week.

Nuala knew that if Frank had lived and if Robbie had not gone on the expedition with Sarah to find Mike, both men would have been solidly against the likes of Lorcan McCree and whatever it was he was trying to do in the castle. She felt a rush of pleasure at the thought of Robbie. He was a gentle man and also a gentleman. In fact he reminded her of Mike Donovan.

It was nearly an impossible task to retain your humanity during these times but somehow Robbie had done it.

She heard raised voices on the other side of the rubble and recognized one of them as belonging to Darby Donaghue. She hurriedly climbed the last boulder and slid down the other side in time to see Lorcan McCree towering over Darby who stood bravely in front of the children with his face resolute but on the verge of tears.

"You spineless little bugger," McCree said as Nuala came upon them. "Wait until I—"

"Oh, hello Mrs. O'Connell!" Darby said with immense relief in his voice.

McCree spun around to see Nuala trudge the last few steps toward them. Instantly the girls ran to her. Damian, Dennis and the Morgan twins Matt and Mac stayed beside Darby. They were all glaring at McCree.

"What's happening here, please?" Nuala asked, hating how shrill her voice sounded.

Ciara tugged on Nuala's tunic.

"This man said me mum told me to come with him," she said, her voice laced with barely suppressed hysteria.

Nuala looked at McCree and narrowed her eyes.

"Oh, he did, did he?" she said.

"Fiona asked me to bring her daughter to her," McCree said, giving Darby a last look of disgust. "This rodent refused to release her to me."

"Don't speak to him like that," Nuala said, feeling her ire rise. "He is doing his job not to release the children to anyone except me or their parents. Thank you, Darby. Boys, please come with me now." She held out her hand to indicate that they should cross McCree's path to join her. All the boys hesitated. "*Now*, lads," she said.

Reluctantly, they moved toward her, each giving McCree a look of loathing and promise. Nuala shook her head. It started early with men, she noted. Each of these boys was marking Lorcan McCree as their enemy. And making sure he knew it.

She couldn't help but feel very proud of all of them.

As she ushered them away and over the boulders she turned back briefly to see McCree watching them go with a sour look on his face.

"Ye should know, Mr. McCree," she said, "that I know well the kind of man ye are. And once Fiona emerges from her fog, she will too."

McCree grinned, showing an inch of gums and teeth. But there was nothing jolly about the look in his eyes.

"You've made an enemy, Missus. Not sure you wanted to do that."

⁂

It had been a long day and John felt he had very little to show for it. He'd visited as many castle campsites as he could to talk to people about what was happening and had been welcome at none.

He'd not made it as far as the dungeons but was convinced that was where Kyla was being held. He'd tried to talk to Fiona but he watched her dodge him as he approached her tent and didn't pursue it.

He'd thought about approaching McCree but was fairly sure the time for peaceful confrontation was over. He'd yet to run into Terry but Jill had assured him that Terry was not with McCree and so John didn't bother wasting time looking for him.

Now John was at the only place in the camp he felt welcome except for Nuala's or perhaps at the line of camp beds set up by the Sisters of Our Lady of Perpetual Sorrow. He was sitting at the campfire of the archers on the far side of the community to make sure they didn't decide to do something stupid and irreversible.

Aibreann sat in front of the fire with her baby Bill in her arms. Her sister archers sat around her—Hannah, Nola, Tilly and seven others John didn't know by name.

"So what are we going to do, mate?" Aibreann asked John. "If the berks won't listen to you, I reckon we just go in and break Kyla out. I'll be buggered if we let the bastards chop her hand off. She's one of our best shots."

That almost made John smile. But he was too tired and discouraged at the moment to feel much humor in anything.

"They can't just do this, can they?" Hannah asked. She was one of the younger archers but was already considered the best.

It was because Hannah was such a good shot that her brother Jordie and their mother had been allowed into the castle.

Well, as John remembered it, *Regan* had made that decision and not given Mike any choice in the matter. John couldn't help but smile at the memory.

God, how he wished Regan were here now!

Although, truthfully, Regan had a hair-trigger temper. If John was hoping for some sane and peaceful resolution to this crisis, Regan would have been the last person he'd ask for help. On the other hand, they might be at the end of the road for sane and peaceful.

"They've got all the guns," John said. "And the people seem to want it."

"The men, you mean."

"Well, the women aren't putting up a fight about it," John said.

"Bloody typical. The women in this camp are a bunch of pathetic slags."

"I say we go in and take Kyla!" Tilly said, jumping up with her bow in hand. "I'll shoot the eye out of the first bastard who tries to stop me!"

"It's possible they're waiting for you to do exactly that," John said. "We need to *think*. There has to be another way."

"Bugger another way," Aibreann said, gazing down at her sleeping son. "Tilly's right. We can't let them do this to one of us."

Before John could mention that it was the whole *us versus them* perspective that had started this mess in the first place, he realized he'd heard a sound nearby that didn't qualify as one of the ordinary camp noises.

"Did you guys hear that?" he asked.

Suddenly, the bushes burst into noise and a flurry of flying leaves and twigs as five men rushed the camp with their rifles drawn.

Aibreann and John jumped to their feet and instantly had the barrel of a rifle jabbed into their faces.

"Don't move!" Riley O'Meara screamed from behind his rifle. "Put your bows down. Now!"

John watched in bewilderment as the men held them at gunpoint and snatched the bows out of the archers' hands.

"What do you think you're doing?" John said over the baby's wails. "This is an attack! Punishable by exile from the community!"

"This is a preemptive strike," Danny McGoldrick said as he tossed the bows onto the campfire.

"Are you insane?" John yelled as he made a move to kick the bows out of the fire. He took two steps before the butt of McGoldrick's .22 caliber rifle slammed into his head.

Susan Kiernan-Lewis

14

Sarah let the rain pound down on her head. She glanced at the backs of Griffin and Killoran. The pair had only had one horse between them when they'd attacked but now they were both mounted. Griffin was on Regan's horse.

Just thinking of Regan made Sarah want to scream or cry or both. That these monsters could end Regan's life without a thought—and that Robbie could allow it! Sarah knew Robbie had bitten off more than he could chew.

She knew he'd not meant for anyone to get hurt. But someone had. Someone had—real bad.

She glanced at Robbie. She saw blood seeping through his shoulder sleeve where she'd shot him. It was pretty clear it was just a bullet graze. Nothing that a tight bandage and a little luck wouldn't sort out fast enough.

That is, unless it got infected and turned septic. That was something they all lived with every day. These days a splinter or a blister could kill you.

He must be counting on getting to a fully-stocked medical facility at the end of all this.

Sarah refocused her thoughts on what they needed to do next. Mary and Moira sat solemnly, staring straight ahead, not a word between them.

That wasn't unusual for women these days. Especially women who found themselves in a bad situation. There were no more knights in shining armor lurking about ready to rescue anyone. Half the time, the knight was just waiting to take his turn…

Gavin coughed and Sarah glanced at him.

What's the plan? his expression said.

She could see he was afraid. And for good reason. He knew as well as Sarah did that once they arrived at the national park, there would be a confrontation that meant life or death for at least someone in Sarah's group.

She felt a shiver migrate across her shoulders. The rain, the dropping temperatures and her plummeting mood were doing little to help her think of a plan.

Sarah took in a long breath and tried to concentrate.

All she knew for sure was that they were riding parallel to the N70 toward the Killarney National Park. What she knew that Killoran *didn't* know was that to find David's compound, they would need to go at least ten miles further east toward Ballingeary.

Sarah also knew that giving Killoran that information would be a death sentence for all of the captives.

She glanced over at Jordie. The boy was petrified. He was probably grateful just to staying upright about now. Gavin was doing better but he'd been betrayed by someone he thought was a friend. He was on a back foot in a lot of ways right about now.

And trusting himself or feeling any kind of confidence—both of which they badly needed if they were going to fight back in any way—were not virtues in large reserves right now.

Then there was Mary and Moira.

As far as Sarah could tell, their only function beyond driving the wagon—which if push came to shove Sarah could do—was to serve as collateral. She had an image of Killoran putting a gun to Moira's head and giving Sarah two seconds to make up her mind.

When or if she hesitated, Moira would be executed. And then the gun would go to Mary's head. And then Jordie's and finally Gavin's.

Sarah felt her stomach muscles constrict and nausea swirled in her gut. She forced herself to get back to the task at hand.

Think!

Robbie was the weak link. He was basically a good guy who'd made a bad decision and who was now probably starting to doubt that the people he was with were on the same page with him. Regan's death had taken him there.

Griffin turned in the saddle to look over at Sarah. That must mean they were getting close. The time to act was coming.

Sarah noticed that both Mary and Moira had pressed in tighter on both sides of her. Everyone was cold and wet now. Moira's shoulders were shaking.

Sarah realized she wasn't just trembling with the cold. She was crying.

"They intend to kill us all," Moira said. "Sure it's as clear as day. That Bran is a sick bastard."

"Did he hurt you?" Sarah asked.

Moira wiped the tears and rain from her face. "Let's just say I'll kill him if I get a chance."

Sarah glanced at Bran and Killoran as they rode ahead. She didn't have much in her bag of tricks but something was better than waiting for them to act first. She turned to catch Gavin's eye. She raised an eyebrow and lifted her chin.

He'd have no idea what her plan was.

But at least he knew she had something.

❋ᕀ❋ᕀ❋ᕀ❋ᕀ❋ᕀ

Killoran stopped just inside the forest tree line that faced a wide brown meadow bordered on both sides by towering pine trees. He held up his hand and Mary pulled the wagon to a halt behind him.

Sarah knew this was it.

"It's okay," she said to Mary and Moira, but really more for herself. "I'm going to lead them to where I think it is."

Mary turned to look at her, her face a grimace. "Sure do you think that's wise?"

When Sarah didn't answer Mary shivered and turned away. "We're all going to die anyway," she said under her breath.

"You okay, Jordie?" Sarah called out.

"Yes, Mam," he said in a small voice.

"Follow my lead, Gavin," Sarah said as Killoran and Griffin rode back to where they were stopped.

Killoran pulled his .22 out of his holster and glanced at the two women riding with Sarah in the wagon. Before he had a chance to make whatever grandstand threat he was about to make, Sarah spoke hurriedly, "I'll take you. I think I know where it is from here."

Killoran hesitated as if she'd spoiled his moment but he grinned.

"And by 'it,' Missus, you mean…?"

"One of the tunnels. One that hopefully leads to the compound. I think I know where a tunnel is. Not too far from here."

Killoran looked at Robbie and nodded.

"Everybody out of the wagon, please," Killoran said.

Sarah felt her stomach lurch. Killoran could play this one of a hundred ways. And killing everyone but her was still a very viable way.

"Gavin," Robbie said as he dismounted, "you and Jordie go stand in the ditch."

"Not even bothering to dig our graves, Robbie?" Gavin said and Jordie gave an involuntary squeak.

"Nobody's killing anybody," Killoran said, "unless you force us to. Now get in the fecking ditch."

Jordie scurried around the back of the wagon and both he and Gavin stepped into the ditch. Then they stood and looked at the men watching them.

Mary and Moira had already climbed down from the wagon but Sarah stayed where she was. It would have been impossible to manage with her hands tied behind her back anyway.

Griffin jumped on the wagon and sawed through her bonds, shaving a layer of skin off the back of her hand in the process.

Sarah groaned as she pulled her arms back in front of her —the first time in several hours. She joined the other women on the ground by the wagon.

"How far is it?" Killoran asked.

"Maybe a mile."

"She's lying, Laith," Griffin said. "You can tell by her eyes. She has no idea where the fecking tunnel is."

Sarah turned to look at Griffin. "I know more than you do."

Killoran walked to the back of the wagon where he pulled the reins of one of the horses and handed it to Sarah.

"You and I will ride on ahead. Your friends will come in the wagon. Ye do know why I want them along, do ye not?"

"I know."

"That's grand. Mount up. Bran, stay back with this lot. Robbie, ride with me and the Missus."

"Nay!" Griffin said. "Sure why should I stay back? I want to see the tunnel too!"

"And so ye will, me boyo," Killoran said. "But it's only you I trust not to let this lot run off and escape, ye ken? No offense, Robbie, but they did used to be your mates just a few hours ago."

Robbie blushed furiously and remounted his horse, turning its neck sharply away from the group in the road.

"And Bran, lad," Killoran said as he remounted. "Try not to kill any of them unless you really must, aye?"

Griffin snorted in bad humor and mounted his horse.

Killoran turned to Sarah. "Missus? After you."

The next hour was agony. Not only did Sarah need to go slow enough that Griffin and her group weren't too far behind them, but she had to try and look like she knew where she was going. On top of that, and if at all possible, she had to somehow find a bloody tunnel!

The good news was that John had told her that this area was a honeycomb of IRA tunnels. The bad news, of course, was that the openings were likely so overgrown it would take a lot more than an afternoon hack on horseback to find one.

On top of that of course was the fact that it was inconceivable that, should she find one, it would lead to anything except a den of irritable badgers.

Plus she was keenly aware that like most plans that relied solely on a stalling tactic, this one only worked if the waiting provided a chance of rescue at the end of it.

As far as Sarah knew, her plan was only slightly better than the alternative which was to refuse to tell or insist she didn't know and watch her party be murdered one by one.

Sarah appreciated that Killoran didn't attempt to engage her in conversation. Once they'd crossed the meadow, he was busy looking around the woods for any possible tunnel entrance. Sarah decided they had less than an hour of daylight left.

If she could stall just one more hour—by continuing to say she thought they were close—she'd buy herself another evening to come at this nightmare from another angle. If she could stall long enough for one more camp out, she might be able to get to Robbie.

It was her only hope.

That or find a friggin' tunnel.

The woods were scattered over terrain that alternated between steep climbs and rain-filled gullies. She knew there were dozens of tunnels somewhere around these woods!

The IRA combatants of the last century had relied on them to escape from the English by disappearing while they were being chased, but also used them as hideouts to plan and assemble their bombs when cottages and crofts proved too dangerous.

Sarah stopped and pointed to the ground.

"It's boggy here," she said. "Can we dismount and go on foot?" That would help Griffin catch up with them. They hadn't heard a gunshot yet but that didn't mean they wouldn't any minute.

"Have you ever been here yourself?"

Sarah hesitated. The best lies were always those laced with bits of truth. But when dealing with crazy people, that might not always be a plus.

"No," she said finally. "I was only told how to get here."

"And this looks familiar to you?" he asked as he dismounted.

She nodded and knelt to feel the spongy texture of the forest floor.

"I know it's on the far side of the meadow by the entrance to the park. This is exactly as it was described to me."

"Get on with it then," he said coldly, the smiling villain's facade gone.

It did occur to Sarah that Killoran might suspect she was hoping for darkness to push the search off another night. But there was little she could do about that.

She pulled her horse behind her and stepped toward a stone protrusion in the path. The terrain here resembled the North Carolina mountains where her family vacationed when she was a child.

"I think I see something," she said in a voice of feigned excitement. As she approached what looked like a wall of ivy and privet, she felt the ground begin to slope downward.

She felt a lightness in her chest as she looked around her. There were rocks and boulders of all sizes off to one side. They looked as if someone had strategically placed them there.

Even Killoran could see this was different from the bushes and pine trees they'd passed before now.

"Is this it?" he asked, grinning widely.

Sarah leaned back against her horse to steady herself as she inched down the slope. The horse balked and so Sarah dropped the reins and found herself rocking forward, her hands slapping against a thick blackthorn to stop herself from falling.

If she hadn't slid down the slope, she would never have seen it.

A hole. Half in the ground and half in the rock wall hidden behind the greenery.

She'd found a tunnel.

Susan Kiernan-Lewis

15

Griffin, Robbie and Killoran stood and stared into the hole. Robbie scratched his head and glanced at Sarah as if he was trying to decide whether this was some kind of ruse. Griffin was smoking a cigarette and pulling his pistol out of his holster repeatedly in nervous agitation.

Mary and Moira sat on each side of Jordie on a rotting log. They had their arms looped through his in a gesture of comfort and support.

Sarah and Gavin were leaning against a large granite boulder.

"This is your plan?" Gavin said in a hoarse whisper, his eyes on the men at the opening to the tunnel.

"I don't know what it is," Sarah said. It occurred to her that she'd pretty much assumed she would lead them a merry chase until it got dark and then use the extra time to overpower them. Somehow.

Finding the tunnel put a different spin on things and at the moment she wasn't exactly sure how to make it work for them.

"Once Killoran goes into the tunnel," Sarah said, "we have a chance to overpower Griffin. Robbie won't shoot us."

"I wouldn't be too sure of that," Gavin said. "But in any case, he'll never leave you up here while he goes down."

"He doesn't have to. If I can just get him to go down *first* —" she said.

"I'm telling ye, he'll never fall for that."

"Well, I'll just have to wing it, I guess," she said in frustration.

Griffin turned to look at her and noticed her conference with Gavin. He made a face.

"Oy!" he said, "move away from him."

Sarah shifted down the rock face.

"This isn't going to work, Sarah," Gavin said.

"It has to. It's all I've got."

"You could tell them where the real portal is."

Sarah turned to look at Gavin.

"You know I don't know where any portal is."

"I know that's what you say."

"You think I'm lying?"

Gavin shrugged. His face was impassive as he watched the men make up their minds about how they were going to handle going into the tunnel.

Sarah fought to control her nervousness. More than any single one thing, emotions leading to panic and bad decisions were her worst enemy right now. Getting angry at Gavin or thinking he was somehow responsible for Robbie's treachery was not going to help her stay calm and keep a cool head, which was absolutely necessary if they were going to live to see another day.

Clouds sailed overhead in the dimming twilight sky. Wisps of fog had gathered at the base of the wall over the tunnel, giving it an eerie veiled appearance.

Sarah knew that *whatever* was down there wasn't hot chocolate and electric blankets no matter what these imbeciles believed. It would be dark and wet and very likely lethal if a viper or an antique bomb was hidden in it.

She rubbed a hand across her face, feeling the exhaustion of the day. Her continual dissembling was weighing her down. To think she imagined that night would bring a respite or chance at a miracle.

Instead, it now looked like things were going to go worse really fast—only in the dark.

"Oy! Missus!" Killoran yelled.

Sarah eased herself into a standing position.

"Why don't you make the sniveling gobshite go down first?" Griffin said to Killoran, pointing at Jordie.

"I reckon he'd get lost down there," Killoran said with a grin as he watched Sarah pick her way toward him.

Sarah now understood his intention. He was going to make her go down that filthy hole first. If only he had been too excited to let anyone go down first but himself, she would have had time to work on Robbie and maybe overpower Griffin.

This way, there wasn't a single person in her group who would take the initiative or do anything but wait for the worst to happen.

"After you, Milady," Killoran said, pointing to the hole.

"Sure you're a bloody coward to make her go down that filthy bog!" Gavin called out.

Sarah appreciated his effort, ineffectual and useless as it was

"Shirrup, ya fecking bugger!" Griffin yelled back at Gavin. "Murphy, ye eejit! Mind he's tied up proper!"

Robbie edged away from the hole and worked his way back to Gavin.

"Help us, Robbie," Sarah whispered to him as he passed. He blinked but gave no other indication that he'd heard her.

Sarah went to stand by the gaping hole. Killoran had pulled away the largest tendrils of snaking ivy and vines. The tunnel loomed dark and ominous and Sarah felt her stomach buck as her heartbeat raced.

She glanced at Killoran and he grinned at her. She didn't dare drop her eyes to his hip where his holster was. If he caught her looking at his weapon, he'd be on guard. As it was, he probably wouldn't expect her to try anything.

"Give her the candle, Bran," Killoran said.

Behind him Griffin reached out and handed Sarah a stubby lit candle.

"I'm praying for ye, Sarah!" Mary called out.

"Aye! And me!" Moira echoed.

"God speed, Missus," Jordie said in a soft voice.

Sarah wiped her hands on her jeans. She stepped up to the tunnel and tried to remember how she'd felt when she was a child playing in the North Carolina mountains. Then the caves had been like so many natural playhouses. She tried to remember how she'd felt and channel that sense of confidence and lack of fear now.

Dear God. There was no way out of this.

"I'm not a hundred per cent sure this is one of them that leads to the…compound," she said breathlessly.

"Then we'll find out in short order," Killoran said impatiently.

Sarah dropped to her knees and crawled through the passageway. She could feel the tangle of roots scraping her shoulders and neck as she pushed herself down the tunnel.

She willed herself not to think of what she was doing or what snakes or other creeping things might be inside the tunnel. She tried to think that if this truly was an old IRA tunnel, there would probably be furniture in it. If the tunnel was collapsed, well, she'd find that out too.

Her stomach clenched as the channel deepened, allowing her to stand up, although by stooping. The candle flame made the sides of the tunnel flicker and move. Sarah felt like her insides were quivering. Her mind raced as she walked—as slowly as she dared.

"Are ye there yet, Missus?" Killoran called.

That's when she saw that the tunnel jogged off to one side in a sharp turn. She held her breath and hurried to the corner. Around it she saw a clearing. Empty and a dead-end.

"This is it," she called up, hearing how shaky her voice sounded. "I'm pretty sure."

Howls of delight erupted between Killoran and Griffin. Sarah disappeared around the corner, her hand that held the candle shaking.

Once Killoran entered the tunnel she had two things going for her: the fact that she controlled the lighting in the tunnel.

And the fact that Killoran was just arrogant enough to believe she was no threat to him.

Sarah would need to use both.

16

"Where are you?" Killoran called out. The flickering of his own candle told Sarah he was about to reach the corner where she hid.

She held the large rock she'd found on the ground and waited until he was about to turn the corner before extinguishing her own candle. She knew this was her only shot.

The second Killoran appeared with one hand holding the candle and the other his pistol, Sarah flung the rock she was holding.

Immediately she heard a sickening *thump* sound as the rock slammed into him. She also heard the sound of his gun falling to the ground—skidding into the darkness—as he dropped his candle.

Killoran gave a roar, "You bitch!"

She hadn't knocked him out! She crouched in the dark, scuttling further back into the tunnel and desperately combing the dirt floor. Her fingers found another rock and she threw it. She heard it crash into the rocky part of the tunnel wall.

She missed.

She grabbed up a handful of smaller rocks and flung them in Killoran's direction, one after another. Each either pinged or thudded against the walls in the dark. She heard him moving toward her and she flattened herself against the tunnel embankment, trying to silence her panicked breathing.

She dropped to her knees to find another rock, her heart pounding in her chest like a jackhammer, her fingers frantically raking the dirt floor of the tunnel.

"You'll pay for this," Killoran rasped.

Sarah felt a large heavy stone cut into her palm.

She closed her eyes to try to picture in her mind where Killoran must be standing in the dark. She pulled back her arm a split second before she heard his breathing as he bent over, probably searching for his gun.

She corrected her aim to allow for his lowered head and threw the rock with all her strength.

His scream of rage and startled pain told her she'd guessed right.

※※※※※

The sound of Killoran's howl made Gavin jump to his feet. Robbie stood next to him, having checked the strength of Gavin's bonds only moments before. Now Robbie was focused on the scream that had come from the tunnel.

It only took a moment for Gavin to reach over and wrench the rifle from his hands.

Robbie gave a startled yelp as Gavin pointed the gun at him with his hands tied.

Griffin turned to look at them both with a startled look on his face.

"Drop your gun," Gavin said, jabbing the gun barrel in Robbie's direction. "Or I'll shoot him."

"Go on with you!" Griffin said with a guffaw. "Is that the truth, then? Sure, no, ye wouldn't."

"I'm not kidding!" Gavin said. Robbie backed away with his hands in the air.

"Here's what's going to happen now, me boyo," Griffin said, his red beard glinting in the fading daylight. "You'll be handing that rifle nice and proper back to its rightful owner."

Griffin stepped over to the women and grabbed Jordie by the collar and flung him to the ground in front of him.

"Don't you do it!" Gavin yelled, his eyes wide with fear at the sight of Jordie cowering on the ground.

"Don't do what?" Griffin said, pointing his rifle at Jordie's head. "This?"

He pulled the trigger. The sound of the gunshot echoed around the clearing as Jordie's head vanished in a sudden puff of red mist.

Mary and Moira screamed. The smoke from the gun's discharge circled the devastation of the bloody body splayed on the grass and the leaves. Mary dropped to her knees by Jordie's body, her hands to her face in horror as a disbelieving keening erupted from her lips.

Griffin stepped up to her and placed the rifle barrel against the back of her head.

"So you'll be handing the rifle over *now*," he said to Gavin.

The rifle sagged in Gavin's hands as he stared at Jordie's body, a splattered red chunk where his head had been.

For a moment nobody moved. Only Mary's heartbroken wails filled the air between them.

Robbie didn't reach for the rifle, but stood staring, his mouth open at Jordie's body on the ground.

"Jaysus, Bran!" he said in an anguished voice.

"Take the fecking rifle, ye bastard," Griffin said before yelling over his shoulder, "Laith! Are ye all right, mate?"

Robbie took the gun from Gavin whose eyes were riveted to the body before him.

Griffin unlocked the bolt on his rifle, sending the spent cartridge flying, then dropped another in the breech and slammed the bolt closed before grabbing Mary by the hair and jerking her head back.

"I'll be needing ye to shirrup, Missus," he said, "so I can hear meself think." He flung her forward. She lay on the ground, sobbing quietly.

"Laith! Are ye alive?" Griffin called.

Gavin couldn't keep pace with what was happening. He couldn't understand how Jordie could be dead and the rifle that he'd felt in his hands just moments before was back to being pointed at his chest.

Griffin went to the entrance of the tunnel.

Even from where Gavin stood, he could hear someone scrambling to get out of the tunnel. Griffin stepped back and lifted his rifle, pointing it at the opening.

"If it's the bitch through that opening first," he said, breathing heavily, "she dies and everyone else right behind her."

"Don't come out, Sarah!" Gavin screamed.

Griffin swiveled to face him, his gun aimed at Gavin's face…

…just as Sarah emerged from the tunnel.

17

"Don't shoot, Bran!" Killoran yelled from behind Sarah. "I'm alive, ye tosser!"

Sarah felt his hand thrust her forward and she grabbed for a branch by the opening and pulled herself the rest of the way up. The first thing she saw was the body lying on the leaves and Mary huddled beside it, her shoulders rocking and quaking.

Griffin kept his aim on her as Sarah crawled all of the way out of the tunnel. She picked out Gavin and felt her heart squeeze with relief. She staggered to her feet and went to Mary who fell into her arms.

"Bloody hell, man!" Griffin said. "What the feck happened? We heard ye yell!"

"Bugger it," Killoran said as he hoisted himself out of the hole. His left eye was swelling shut and a line of blood dribbled from a gash over his other eye. "The bitch attacked me with rocks. I dropped me gun. It took me a moment to find it."

Griffin turned to look at Sarah who was holding Mary. Sarah was careful not to get eye contact with him.

"What happened here?" Killoran said pointing to Jordie's body. "Aw, bugger it, Bran. I'm only gone five minutes and ye murder one of the hostages?"

"The bastard got Robbie's gun from him!" Griffin said. "What was I supposed to do?"

Killoran looked at Robbie and shook his head. "Is that the right of it, Robbie? A man *with his hands tied* got the drop on you?"

"I don't know why we have him," Griffin said, looking at Robbie. "He's worse than a lass."

"Nay, Bran, no harm done," Killoran said, kicking Jordie's shoe with the toe of his boot.

"Ye want me to teach her, Laith?" Griffin said glaring at Sarah. "I'll make sure she never raises a hand to you again."

Sarah could see that Griffin was hungering to be let off the chain. If Killoran was single-minded and Robbie was determined about finding the compound, then Griffin was just insane.

"No worries, mate," Killoran said. He walked to Sarah and backhanded her hard across the face. The pain exploded in her lips and jaw as she fell backward to the ground.

Mary screamed and the sound quickly faded into a meek sob.

Sarah felt Killoran grab her jacket and pull her back to her feet.

"Ye'll not be trying any more tricks again, will ye, Missus?" Killoran said.

Robbie looked at Sarah and dragged a hand across his face. Her whole face felt on fire. She could tell her lip was already swelling from Killoran's blow.

Robbie put a hand on Killoran's chest.

"What Bran did was *not* in the plan!" he said. "First Regan and now Jordie? The lad weren't doing a thing! He was just pissing himself trying to stay alive and do what he was told!"

"Sometimes we have to go off plan, Robbie," Killoran said brushing Robbie's hand away. "Remember what we're about here, son."

"Don't call me that!" Robbie said. "We're not in the army now, Laith! You don't outrank me!"

Sarah knew that the more Killoran and Griffin ragged Robbie, the greater chance she had of pulling him back over to her side.

Not that she'd ever forgive him. With Regan and Jordie both dead. There could be no hope of that no matter what Robbie did now. But he didn't need to know that.

Killoran turned to Sarah and grabbed her upper arm and twisted it until Sarah thought she would cry out. She bit her lip rather than give him the satisfaction.

"Now, Missus, I believe you were mistaken about that tunnel and sure we all make mistakes, isn't that the truth?"

"The bitch tricked you, Laith!" Griffin said. "She knew all along that weren't the right tunnel."

"That's possible," Killoran said. "But then all these tunnels look alike, do they not? Mayhaps I haven't done all I could to help her remember correctly."

Sarah felt a tightening in her chest at what was to come.

"So before we call it a day, I'll be asking ye, Robbie, to place the barrel of your rifle to the head of young Donovan there while I help the missus with her memory issues."

Sarah felt her stomach tighten and the nausea well up in her throat.

"Don't do it, Sarah!" Gavin shouted. "They'll kill us anyway! Tell 'em bugger all!"

Griffin strode to Gavin and slammed the butt of his rifle into Gavin's stomach. Moira and Mary both screamed. Gavin sagged to his knees, his head slumped forward.

Griffin shoved his rifle into Robbie's arms, nearly knocking Robbie's own rifle to the ground. Griffin grabbed Gavin by the hair and jerked his face upward before driving his fist into his face.

Gavin's eyes rolled into the back of his head as the blood gushed down his face.

"Stop it!" Sarah said to Killoran. "Stop it, please!"

"Sure ye know the very words that will get me to put a stop to it, Missus," Killoran said, his face grim as he watched Griffin punch Gavin in the face again and again.

"I...I think I might know of another place," Sarah said. Gavin was still conscious but only barely. His features were barely visible through the blood pouring down his face.

"Oh aye?" Killoran said. "Bran, lad!"

Griffin dropped his grip on Gavin's hair and Gavin fell to the ground. Bran turned to look at Killoran. Sarah could see he didn't want to stop. She could see the look in his eye. He wanted to beat Gavin to death and he was well on his way to doing it. She felt a spurt of agony. If she ever saw Mike again, would she have to tell him how she witnessed his only child beaten to death before her eyes?

"Do ye have yer combat knife, lad?" Killoran said conversationally.

Griffin looked confused for a moment. Then he reached for his sheath on his belt and pulled out a wicked looking blade, easily eight inches long. His eyes lit up in acknowledgement and he turned back to Gavin.

"What the feck, Laith?" Robbie burst out. "I'll have no part of this!"

"Fine," Killoran said casually. "You can bugger off then. We'll think of you when we're in the hot tub watching porn on cable, won't we, Bran?"

Griffin laughed. "Aye, while you, ye sorry bugger, are eating your own shoelaces to keep from starving to death."

Killoran turned to Sarah.

"Now, lass, do ye *think* ye know of a another place or do ye *know* because it'll matter a mite to your stepson as to how many fingers I have Bran chop off."

"You're a monster!" Mary screamed where she stood, one arm around Moira.

"I'm confident," Sarah said, her eyes on Gavin where he lay on the ground. "I *know* exactly where the tunnel is."

"She's lying," Griffin said as he knelt by Gavin and grabbed one of his hands. "This'll be more effective if he's awake when I do it." He drew back his hand and backhanded Gavin.

Gavin twitched and groaned. Sarah watched his eyes flutter open.

"For the love of God," she said. "I'm not lying. I'm telling you I *know* where it is."

"I thought you said *this* was the tunnel," Killoran said, frowning. "So was Bran right? Were you trying to trick us before?"

"I…I…" Sarah had no idea which way to go. If she told the truth or lied they were all likely going to be tortured and killed before it was over.

"One finger!" Killoran bellowed to Griffin. "Then throw it to me, Bran!"

"No!" Robbie yelled and he pressed the barrel of his rifle against Griffin's chest. "Back off!"

Griffin held up both hands but didn't look at Robbie.

"Are ye sure ye want to be doing this, ye mad bastard?" Bran asked quietly.

"She doesn't know where the damn tunnel is!" Robbie shouted, his posture rigid and trembling. "For God's sake, if she knew, she'd have told ye!"

"If ye have a suggestion, Robbie," Killoran said dryly, "I'd get on with it. I truly do think Bran is going to murder ye if ye drag this on much longer."

Robbie wet his lips and moved the gun away from Griffin's chest.

"She doesn't know," he said. "But I know who does. We all know who does."

"Robbie, no!" Sarah said before she knew the words were coming out of her mouth.

"Her lad, John, back at the castle," Robbie said, his eyes finally meeting Sarah's and holding them, the sadness and finality coming to her as loudly as if he shouted them out.

"John Woodson is the only one who knows where the tunnel is."

Susan Kiernan-Lewis

18

John blew out a breath and groaned.

"Move slowly, lad," Fiona said softly.

He opened his eyes. He was in Fiona's tent lying on her bed pallet. By the glimmer of light through the flap of the tent, he could tell it was late afternoon. Instantly, he jerked to a sitting position and immediately regretted it as pain shot up through his neck into his skull.

"You'll not be wanting to jump around," Fiona said. "Ye've had quite a crack on the head."

"Where are they?" John said, struggling to his feet. "What did they do with the archers?"

"John, please, I'm that sure you've been concussed so ye should be lying flat."

"Answer me, Fiona! I know you know!"

Fiona stood between John and the tent opening. She held a wet cloth in her hand and from the scent of berries and herbs that seemed to fill the tent interior, she'd been applying a salve to his head. He put his hand to the back of his head and felt the lump.

"Try to understand," Fiona said. "The archers were going to do something mad and you know it!"

The hell of it was John knew Fiona was right. Just before they were attacked, Aibreann and her crew were ready to take up arms and bust Kyla out. For sure someone would have gotten hurt. He felt the back of his head again. *Gotten hurt worse.*

"Where are they?" he asked evenly.

"They've been put with Kyla—just until the punishment's been dealt out and then they'll be released, sure they will."

"I can't believe you, of all people, Fi." John shook his head and was instantly sorry he did. "That you would be okay with this kind of barbarism. I don't even know you any more."

"Sure I don't know any of us any more," Fiona said. "After what we've all been through it's a wonder there's any civility left in any of us."

"This is wrong what McCree is planning on doing. It's wrong and it's evil."

"It's for the good of the community. And it's done now."

John snapped his head around. "What are you talking about?"

"The trial. It was held an hour ago."

"Wait don't tell me," he said sarcastically. "Kyla was found guilty."

"She admitted to killing and roasting the pig!"

"And who spoke on her behalf? I know it wasn't you!"

"She spoke on her own behalf! She said she did it and there's an end to it. She wasn't even sorry!"

"Half the people in this community are cooking and eating food they don't share any more!"

"Yes, but they're not stealing it first."

"She's twenty-one years old, Fi. You'd maim her for life for one stupid pig?"

"It's for the good of the community," Fiona repeated and turned away.

"It doesn't worry you that this guy can waltz in here and imprison nine people before chopping the hand off a tenth? That doesn't bother you?"

"No! We need leadership! We need direction! I'm sorry, John, but as clever as you are, you're just a lad and we need men to lead us, so we do."

"Is that what McCree told you?"

"It's what I know. What are you doing?" She watched him as he tied his shoes and looked around for his gun.

"I'm leaving. Where's my gun?"

"John, please lie low. If not for your injury, then for my sake. It'll all be over in an hour and then we can go back to—"

"We're not going back to shit, Fiona! Where's my stupid gun?"

She crossed her arms. "They took it. It was hard enough to convince Lorcan that you wouldn't interfere. He wanted to put you in the dungeon with the rest of them!"

"Yeah, well, thanks, Auntie," John said, pushing past her to emerge from the tent. "You're a real peach."

"Don't make me out a liar, John Woodson!" Fiona said shrilly as John strode away. "I said you'd be no trouble!"

Her words rang in his head as he hurried toward Gavin and Sophia's tent. Gavin had a pistol that he probably brought with him but a rifle he probably hadn't.

What has happened to everyone? he thought angrily, as he made his way through the tent settlement, dodging people as they moved toward the center of the castle courtyard where the punishment would take place.

Do they really want to see this happen? Did I ever know these people at all?

Realizing he had no time to find Terry or Nuala or anyone else to try to figure out what they could do to stop this disaster from happening, John went directly to Gavin's tent.

The only thing he knew for certain was that whatever happened next was up to him to stop.

🎄🎄🎄🎄🎄

Fiona moved in the opposite direction that John had gone.

He was such a hot head and sure she had never seen this side of him before!

What did he think? That Aibreann and her lot would just sit back and watch the show? *Of course* they had to be jailed! That was only sensible.

But something else niggled at her, like a sharp pebble chafing under a saddle pad. Something that John had said.

Kyla was only twenty-one.

Fiona remembered what *she'd* been like at twenty-one. While she'd never been silly, she'd made mistakes. Plenty of them. Thanks be to God she'd also done them in a time where there weren't very serious consequences for those mistakes.

Killing and roasting a piglet didn't seem like that terrible an infraction—at least during any other time. And as serious as it was now—*and it was serious, make no mistake!*—but to lose a hand…

She slowed as she approached Mike and Sarah's tent. It was the nicest, the biggest and had the best placement in the camp. Situated on a rise overlooking the entire camp, it was protected from the wind by the walls of the castle still standing and provided a direct sightline down the main drive.

Lorcan had moved in right after they'd brought John unconscious to Fiona's tent.

These were harsh times but this was appropriate! It was right that Lorcan have the best tent! He was pulling them all out of the quagmire of indecision and weak leadership that had plagued them since they moved to the castle.

In fact, as hard as it was for Fiona to hear it, Lorcan had explained to her how Mike's handling of both assaults on the castle had, in effect, been the ruin of all of them.

Aye, it had been a painful thing to hear but Lorcan had praised her for being able to recognize the truth when she heard it—even when it was unpleasant.

She stopped at the entrance to Lorcan's tent. Two men stood outside—Riley O'Meara and Sean Dolan who was a distant cousin to both herself and Mike. They looked at her with open derision, something she had never experienced from either of them before.

"If you're looking for Himself, Fiona," Sean said, "he's got his hands full, so he has at the moment."

"I'll speak to him, even so, Sean Dolan," Fiona said. "Lorcan! A word, if you please."

Lorcan came to the entrance of the tent. His hair was thick and dark and he looked almost mythical the way he was outlined in the opening. Smiling at her with his teeth white and straight, he could have been George Clooney's body double.

"Oh, that's grand, lass," he said, opening the tent flap to allow her inside.

As she passed, both Jimmy and Ryan sniggered. She heard Ryan make a rude sexual comment and she blushed to her roots.

When she entered, she saw a knife on the floor by the footlocker where Sarah used to keep her books. Fiona wondered if that was the knife Lorcan would use.

Lorcan sat on the thick bedding and patted a space beside him.

"What is it, Fi?" he asked. "Something is troubling ye, lass?"

Fiona sat next to him, feeling her heart hammering in her chest to be seated so close. She knew her face was flushed and she was amazed and delighted at the pleasant fluttering sensation she felt in her stomach.

He took her hand in his and held it on his lap. Fiona felt the tingling start in her fingertips and shoot up her arm to her breasts. She licked her lips.

"About Kyla," she said. "I wanted to ask ye about Kyla."

"Aye, lass?" he said softly, his eyes on her mouth. "Ask me then."

"I…do ye…do we have to do this?"

He smiled into her eyes then and brought his hand to her cheek.

"Jaysus, you're a beauty, Fiona," he said in a throaty whisper. "Just the sight of ye melts me down to me core, so it does."

"I…really?" Fiona said as he bent her gently down onto the pallet, her lips vibrating with need and expectation.

"I've never met the like of ye before, *leanbha*," he murmured as he lowered his face to gaze at her.

As his lips gently touched hers, Fiona felt her very soul explode within her as she hungrily gave herself up to the immenseness of the moment.

Then she felt his hand between her legs and heard the coarse laughter rise up outside the tent.

Susan Kiernan-Lewis

19

Low dark clouds scudded across the treetops as Killoran's group set up camp by an old wagon trail that had been carved through the meadow probably centuries before. Even in the dark Sarah could see the mountain peaks to the south. The night had fully arrived now. There was a waning moon.

Nobody had flashlights, of course, which reminded Sarah as always that this was how their ancestors must have traveled a hundred years ago—by the moon or not at all.

She sat on the cold ground, her hands tied in front of her. Killoran had moved them back to the meadow. Because he and Griffin were both ex-army, the camp was sufficient if not exactly comfortable. And because they were the predators and not the prey, there was a blazing fire for warmth.

They'd left Jordie's body where he'd fallen and every time Sarah thought of him, she wanted to weep. She remembered how much trouble he'd had ever since he'd arrived at Henredon Castle and how hard he'd tried to fit in and be worthy.

His mother will lose her damn mind.

Mary and Moira prepared another bacon and egg meal which Killoran felt no need to share with Sarah or Gavin. Gavin had walked from the tunnel entrance without too much problem so Sarah had hopes he'd suffered no internal injuries from Griffin's brutal beating.

She watched Robbie as he sat with his rifle in his arms. He wasn't eating. Every now and again, she caught him looking at her as if he was hoping for some sort of silent forgiveness for what he'd done.

As soon as he'd said that John was the one who knew where the compound was, Killoran and Griffin made immediate plans to return to Herendon Castle and get the information out of him.

Sarah was pretty sure if she had a chance in this lifetime to kill Robbie for his betrayal, she would take it without hesitation. Up to now she'd never killed except to save her life or the life of a loved one.

This was the first time she knew she could kill purely for vengeance.

She swallowed down the knowledge and turned her attention to her hands in her lap.

"Sarah?" Gavin shifted next to her and groaned when he did.

"Hey, Gavin," she said. "How are you doing?"

"Pretty sure he busted a couple of ribs. Otherwise, I'm grand, so I am."

Just like his father, Sarah couldn't help but think with a sharp pinch in her heart. *Always making light of something that would have a normal person in intensive care.*

"Can I ask ye something?"

A roar of laughter erupted between Killoran and Griffin on the other side of the fire. They were in good spirits. They could clearly see the way ahead of them now—and the prize at the end of the road. Her son. Her boy, John.

She turned to Gavin. "I hope you're not looking for answers," she said. "I'm fresh out."

Gavin didn't speak for a moment and when he did, his eyes were on the fire not Sarah.

"I reckon I know why this lot—or anybody—would want to have electricity and all that again. And maybe I even understand why they might kill to have it."

Sarah waited.

"But what's the point of the island in the first place? Sure I never really understood that and John could never explain it to me."

Sarah felt the exhaustion and weariness of her day seep into her shoulders. Her jaw throbbed from where Killoran had hit her. She'd been a fool to think she could have stopped him by throwing rocks. All she did was anger him and prove to him that she was not to be trusted.

"When something happens like what happened to us," she said slowly, now also staring into the fire and trying to will away the exhaustion and the hopelessness that she felt coursing through her, "there's an innate need to save what you have."

"You mean like food."

"No, it's bigger than that. When everything else is falling apart around you, people naturally want to stockpile the things we as humans have learned from our time on earth."

"What's more important than food? Without it we die."

"Knowledge is more important. Without it we die as a race. What my crazy ex-husband and his crazy friends are trying to do is admirable in a very real way. It's just that he's working on a global level while the rest of us are still just trying not to starve to death."

"Sure it's easy not to worry about starving to death when you have a fully stocked refrigerator," Robbie said, joining them.

Sarah bit back her first reaction and she nudged Gavin with her foot to make sure he did the same. As satisfying as it might be right now to spit in Robbie's eye, he was still their only hope for getting away from Killoran and Griffin.

"That is true," Sarah said mildly. "They have all the comforts we enjoyed before the first EMP changed our lives forever. But what they are trying to do is bigger than food or security—even though they have all that."

"What's bigger than those things?" Robbie asked with a frown.

"Well, safe-guarding the knowledge of the world," Sarah said. "Keeping what we've discovered about the planets, about science, about medicine, even literature. These are the things that we need to survive as a species."

"Literature? Sure, no," Gavin said.

"Absolutely," Sarah said. "Or else what's it all for?"

In the silence that followed, there was only the sound of the fire snapping and cracking. Sarah saw Killoran on the other side of the fire watching her.

"What will your friends do with us now?" she asked in a low voice. She was careful not to include him in their group.

"Laith will go to Henredon in the morning," Robbie said.

"And us?" she pressed.

"Ye'll not be harmed, Sarah," he said earnestly. "I swear on me mother's grave."

Sarah knew what it cost Gavin not to snort with disgust at that and she was grateful he held back.

"And John?" she asked quietly. "What are his plans for my son?"

"There was nothing else I could do!" Robbie said. "I couldn't watch the mad bastard cut pieces off Gavin, now could I?"

Gavin stared silently into the fire and Sarah forced herself to nod at Robbie.

"I know," she said. "I forgive you for that."

But I don't. Not for a minute. Not ever.

"I...I just couldn't stand it," Robbie said. "Once he'd finished with Gavin he'd just start on Mary or you. Make no mistake. There'd be no end to it."

None except taking your gun and shooting the "mad bastard" between the eyes, Sarah thought. But she held her tongue.

Killoran stood up and walked around the campfire toward them.

"No! No!" Moira cried out from the other side of Sarah. Sarah snapped her head around to see that Griffin was standing before her and Mary. Sarah started to get to her feet but Robbie put out a hand to stop her.

"Nay, Sarah," Robbie said. "There's no point. You'll just end up getting hurt."

Griffin jerked Moira to her feet and she lashed out a fist but he caught it with his hand and twisted it around her back. Mary squealed in horror and stood up, her face a mask of trepidation and fear.

"You can't let this happen, Robbie," Sarah said desperately. "If you do, you're as bad as they are!"

"Sure, take her into the woods, ye randy bastard," Killoran said. "I don't want to see yer naked white arse!" He laughed as

Griffin threw Moira kicking and screaming over his shoulder and strode toward the woods.

"You have to think of the end game, Sarah," Robbie said as Killoran joined them. "Nothing else matters."

"Don't call me by my first name, you weasel!" Sarah blurted. "I pray I live long enough to tell Nuala who you really are!"

Robbie turned away, his face red, and stepped from the fire.

"Take the first watch, *ye weasel!*" Killoran chortled. He turned to Sarah as Robbie stomped off.

"Move yer arse, boyo," he said to Gavin.

Gavin scooted away but kept his eye on both Killoran and Sarah. The sounds of Moira's screams drifted to the campfire.

"No worries," Killoran said to Sarah as he settled down beside her. "We'll not be taking liberties with yourself."

"Go to hell."

Killoran pulled out a withered notebook and handed it to Sarah.

"I know you've had quite a day, Missus. What with trying to brain me with rocks and all. So I'll be leaving ye to your beauty rest after one last request." He held out a ballpoint pen.

"You want me to write a note to my son."

"It would make things easier, so it would."

"Drop dead."

Killoran sighed.

"I said I could protect you and the other one from Bran's attentions and sure, that I can. But only if you meet me half way, aye?"

"So you're saying write the note that will lead my son to his death or risk rape by a scum ball who you'll no doubt allow to rape me anyway?"

"Ye have me word, so ye do, Missus. Not a hair'll be touched on yourself or yon matron."

"Screw you."

Killoran looked at her in surprise. "Sure ye'll have heard the not-quite-amorous moans of the other lassie, have ye not? I think we can *all* hear them. Is it *that* you'd wish on the old lady there?"

Sarah wouldn't give him the satisfaction of glancing at Mary who she knew was hearing every word of their conversation.

"You intend to kill us both anyway," Sarah said as she dropped the notebook and pen on the ground at Killoran's feet.

Killoran gathered up the notebook and pen.

"Aye, well, it was worth a try." He gave Mary an exaggerated wink and then turned to look at Gavin but his words were for Sarah.

"I'll be leaving at first light. Robbie and Bran will mind you lot until I get back."

"So your trained lunatic doesn't have orders to execute us in your absence?"

"Nay, lass not at-all. He knows ye may yet prove of worth to us. Just imagine if my *trained lunatic* as ye call him were to hold a knife to your throat in front of your son? I don't think we'll have any trouble now. Good night to ye, Missus."

Killoran walked away just as Moira burst from the woods, her shirt torn in front, and blood streaking both her cheeks. She ran to Mary who gathered her in her arms while glaring over her shoulder at Griffin as he made his way back to the fire.

"Tie the women up before you turn in," Killoran said to Griffin. "Ye don't want your last romantic conquest sneaking up in the middle of the night to put a knife in yer gut." He laughed and settled down on a blanket by the fire.

Sarah scooted closer to the fire as she watched Griffin roughly tie both Mary and Moira's hands and then glance her way. She held up her hands to remind him she was already tied. He turned toward his own blanket.

"I killed him, Sarah," Gavin said in a quiet voice. "Jordie. He died because of me."

Sarah sighed and leaned on Gavin trying to give him her strength, her body heat.

"He died because of a crazy man with a gun, Gavin."

To be honest, Sarah knew in her bones that Jordie had always been heading toward today ever since the moment the EMP had flung them all back in time.

"If you say so," Gavin said as he turned and gingerly laid himself down to sleep.

Sarah stared into the fire for a few moments longer.

Regan. Jordie.

Young people, cut down before they'd had a chance to fall in love, have a family, see twenty summers.

Senseless and mad.

Mary and Moira murmured to each other and Sarah was grateful that Mary was able to comfort the poor woman.

What a nightmare this world is we live in.

She tried to shut off her thoughts and her feelings long enough to allow sleep to come. But it was impossible. Two people, Mike and John, whom she loved more than her own life were in mortal danger. And there wasn't a damn thing she could do about it.

She thought of that moment back in Florida, a few years back when she'd gone to John's bedroom and told him they were returning to Ireland. And when she remembered the excited glitter in his eyes when she'd told him, she realized how young he'd been then.

Just a boy, not even in his teens. And she'd packed him up —knowing what was waiting for them back in Ireland—and brought him to this moment when a madman was going to find him and force him through any means necessary to betray his father.

Sarah couldn't imagine what methods Killoran would employ to get John to do such a thing. For sure it would have to be a threat against Sarah.

Betray your father to save your mother.

And Sarah was the one who'd put her dearest boy in that position. She'd packed his bags, bought his ticket and driven him right to this moment in time.

David was right. He'd accused her of putting their son in harm's way so she could be with Mike.

She squeezed her eyes shut and tried not to think of her husband. Tried not to imagine where he must be, or how he must be living if please God he was still alive.

To not voluntarily return to her was unthinkable. That he'd been prevented from doing just that was evident—regardless of what the women on the road had said.

Susan Kiernan-Lewis

As Sarah lay her head down on the hard ground, wondering if she'd ever been so close before to losing everyone and everything she'd ever loved, she let the horrors of the day and her exhaustion push her to the brink of sleep.

And then, with a prayer on her lips for Jordie and his poor mother, Sarah gave herself up to the blessed darkness.

20

Nuala was sitting in Liddy O'Malley's tent and trying to get her thoughts in order.

"Sure I don't have the stomach for such villainy," Liddy said. "This would never have happened under Mike's watch."

Nuala glanced at her two boys as they sat with the orphaned twins Mac and Matt. The boys were old enough to know something was up. Instead of their usual exuberant antics, all four of them sat solemnly and quietly—as if they were not at all sure what would happen next.

Nuala dearly wished she could have the same ignorance.

"Me and Mac ain't seen John in a whole day," Matt said quietly. "I reckon he don't want us no more."

"John is busy, lad," Nuala said. "He was put in command of the whole camp when Mr. and Mrs. Donovan left. He has important things to do."

"He's not in charge no more," Mac said. "Billy Hefferman said his da told him John's too young, so he is."

"Well, that's not for Billy Hefferman's da to decide."

Nuala caught Liddy's look.

"Is he really going to chop Kyla's hand off, Mum?" Dennis asked, his eyes fearful.

Nuala ground her teeth. At this moment she hated McCree more than she'd ever hated anything. As horrible as it was what he intended to do, the fact that she had to tell her son that she was powerless to stop such senseless depravity was a moment she'd hope she'd never see.

"I don't know, Denny lad," Nuala said as she pulled him and his brother into her arms. Mac and Matt came over too and when Ciara and Siobhan and little Darcie saw, they rushed Nuala and also threw their arms around her.

"Don't let 'em hurt Kyla, Missus O'Connell," Siobhan said. "She needs her hand." Siobhan pulled away and gazed at her own hand as if trying to imagine what it would be like to live without it.

Someone needs to murder that man, Nuala thought before she could stop herself.

She shook the thought out of her head and gave the children a last squeeze.

"Now all of you mind Missus O'Malley, aye?" Nuala said.

The children nodded and Nuala turned to Liddy.

"Make sure they don't leave the tent," Nuala said.

The minute Nuala stepped out of Liddy's tent she saw that the entire community had gathered near a makeshift stage that was erected beside the moat where the drawbridge had once been.

Mothers were dragging their children close to the stage, no doubt intending to use this gruesome example of punishment as an unspoken threat against future bad behavior. Nuala turned away in disgust.

She'd looked all morning for John and Fiona but found neither. In a group as small as theirs it could only be because neither wanted to be found.

She pushed thoughts of Fiona out of her mind. She'd heard the gossip that Fiona had slept with McCree, which was hard to believe. Worse, the way Nuala had heard the story, the coupling had been damn near public.

The Fiona that Nuala knew could never have done something like that.

It had barely been three days since McCree had come to the castle but it was pretty clear that the Fiona Nuala knew was long gone.

Nuala stared as the section of a large tree trunk was rolled onto the stage.

She shivered.

Was this really going to happen?

She looked around at her gathering neighbors—people she'd fought with against a common foe, wept with, rejoiced with. Were these people really going to let this happen?

Like everybody here, Nuala had been given a weapon to protect herself and her family. When they'd repulsed the last wave of invaders, they'd taken a significant cache of weapons. Most of the newer rifles and handguns went to those tasked with formally protecting the castle—Mike, Gavin, John, Terry, and Robbie.

The men.

Nuala had been given a .22 pistol. Mike had instructed her how to break it down, clean it and use it. With three children of her own to mind and the job of camp nanny where she was tasked with caring for several families' children while their parents worked Nuala had had no time to practice shooting the gun.

Besides, what could one gun do against McCree and his eight-man squad?

She found a place near the stage front.

Suddenly the mood of the crowd changed. Nuala craned her neck to see. The crowd parted for Aibreann who was walking with her head up and her hands tied behind her back.

What was going on? Why was Aibreann here?

Nuala watched in an awed stupor as every archer walked behind Aibreann, each bound, their faces grim and morose. Bringing up the rear was Riley O'Meara holding a rifle to the back of the last woman—Kyla—who walked woodenly, her face a mask of controlled terror.

Nuala's stomach dropped when she saw Kyla. Until that moment, it hadn't been real to her. But when she saw the young woman and realized what the men were planning to do, the base villainy of the crime cascaded over her.

"Shame on you, Riley O'Meara!" Nuala blurted out as Riley passed. "To do this to a wee lass won't make you feel any more òf a man!"

"Shirrup, Nuala," Riley snarled as he passed, but she could see she'd startled him. Up until that moment, he'd been feeling pretty good about himself.

Behind Riley came McCree himself and behind him, Fiona.

Nuala bit her tongue, hoping her expression would do all the talking, but Fiona refused to look at her. When she'd passed, Nuala watched as the other men came from the crowd to position the archers—none too gently—in a line in front of the stage so they would get the best view.

McCree and Fiona waited for the archers to take their places. A horse-drawn wagon had been pulled to the stage. Nuala hated thinking it was there to carry Kyla away after the dreadful deed was done.

Will nobody stop this?

McCree climbed on the stage and two men lifted Kyla up and shoved her next to him. The chopping block was behind them. Kyla was white and her lips trembled as she scanned the crowd.

"We're with ye, Kyla!" Aibreann shouted.

"You've got us, lass!" another archer called out.

Nuala saw Kyla's almost imperceptible nod.

McCree raised his hands. "Friends and neighbors! We are here today to address a crime that has been happening among us for far too long now."

Three of the men—McGoldrick, Sean Dolan, and Regan's on again, off again boyfriend Aodhan O'Dorchaidhe—all loudly endorsed McCree's words with shouts and cheers.

"The archers," McCree said, sweeping a hand to encompass the line of eight women standing before him, "will no longer be getting special treatment in this community."

"Hear! Hear!" a man shouted.

"In fact, after today, they'll no longer be a part of this community at all."

Nobody cheered at that and Nuala saw a few people look at each other in confusion. She knew that most people in the community resented the archers—their arrogance, their insistence that the rules didn't apply to them—but they also knew that the archers were their first and last line of defense.

Does this idiot really think eight men are enough to protect the community?

Before the bomb dropped, most of these men had worked in air-conditioned offices or under the hood of a car. By the looks on their faces, some of the women in the crowd were thinking the same thing.

Fiona was standing by the stage, her head down, her face solemn and unreadable.

Suddenly a gunshot exploded a chunk of wood at McCree's feet. Kyla yelped and jumped back.

Nuala searched the crowds to see where the shot had come from.

"Back away from her," John said loudly.

All eyes looked to where he stood—without cover—on the apex of the broken watchtower. He held his rifle to his shoulder, McCree in his cross hairs.

"We wondered when you'd show up, lad," McCree said, stepping around the bullet hole in the stage floor. He turned to the crowd and shaded his eyes.

"Can we take care of this little matter, lads?" McCree said.

Instantly four men emerged from the crowd. Two grabbed an archer each and rammed a gun barrel into their necks. Two more dropped to one knee and drew a bead on John where he stood.

"On my signal," McCree said calmly, a thin but trembling smile on his lips.

"No!" Fiona screamed.

Susan Kiernan-Lewis

21

Nuala saw the scene unfold like some terrible made-for-TV movie that should never have been made but was somehow coming to horrible vivid life right in front of her.

John held his rifle on McCree while no fewer than four rifles had him in their sights.

Nuala knew that if John succeeded in killing McCree, he would do it at the cost of his own life.

A truly terrible plan.

"That's enough!" A strong voice called out from the fringe of the crowd.

Nuala turned to see Terry and Jill Donaghue standing shoulder to shoulder on the back of the wagon as if they'd just materialized there. Man and wife held bows with arrows drawn and notched.

Both were aimed at Lorcan McCree.

"Stand down or die here today," Terry said, his eye looking down the sightline of his bowstring. His hand rock solid on the bow.

"Are you mad?" Sean Dolan yelled out. He didn't lower his gun but pivoted to point it at the couple.

"That boy you have in your sights is Mike Donovan's stepson," Terry said between his teeth. "Mike is the true leader of this community!" Terry looked around the crowd until he spotted someone he knew.

"Sean Dolan," Terry said, "Mike brought you and your wife into the fold six years ago when you were starving with no place to go! Will you be the one to tell him you shot his son? I promise if you hurt that lad, Mike will track you down to your dying day and sure you know he will."

"Mike Donovan's dead!" Riley O'Meara said.

"Maybe he is and maybe he isn't," Terry said. "But Lorcan McCree *definitely* is if any of you takes a single shot at John Woodson."

"You can't shoot us all, Donaghue!"

"No, but I'll get *you*, O'Meara. On that ye may be sure."

"Shoot any of us and I'll shoot *you*, Donaghue," McGoldrick said.

"Aye," Jill said, turning her bow and arrow until it pointed to a beautiful young girl standing in the front of the crowd. "And I'll kill your beautiful Beth with one straight to her heart. Test me if ye don't think I will."

A gasp of horror emitted from the crowd and the girl squeaked out, "Da!"

McCree raised his voice over the crowd noise. "Well sure this has gone arse over tits in a hurry," he said with a laugh, obviously trying to break the mood. "Gentlemen—and ladies— put your weapons down. They'll be no shooting of anyone today." He turned to O'Meara. "Your rifle *down*, Mr. O'Meara, if ye please."

O'Meara reluctantly lowered his gun but Terry, John and Jill kept their weapons pointed.

"Since it's clear ye don't want to belong to this community any longer," McCree said to Terry, "and because I have happy news to share and don't wish it poisoned by a wee massacre first…" He smiled at Fiona. "…I'll tell you now what I'd already intended to announce *before* young John went off half cocked."

He waved to the two men holding the archers and they began to untie them—Kyla included.

"The archers are welcome to leave unharmed if they walk away right now. That includes the lass who has already been found guilty and sentenced. I give this as a gift of mercy at the request of the woman who this day has agreed to be my wife." He turned and smiled at Fiona.

There was a smattering of confused applause from the gathered group.

Nuala's mouth fell open in shock.

"Sure I think we've all learned a powerful lesson from this," McCree said. "We've learned who wants to be with us going forward and who doesn't. Mr. Donaghue, you and your wife and son will quit the community immediately. You'll go with the archers and young Woodson tonight and never return."

"You cannot do that!" Sophia Donovan burst out of the crowd, her small daughter in her arms. "You cannot throw them out!"

McCree narrowed his eyes at her.

"Ah, it's Donovan's daughter-in-law, is it not? The Eye-talian? You're welcome to go with them, Señora. *More* than welcome."

Sophia faltered, her face white. Her child Maggie began to whimper and Sophia melted away into the crowd.

"That's what I thought," McCree said. "Anybody else?"

"Nuala!" John called as he descended the ramparts to join the others. "Nuala O'Connell!"

"Aye, John," Nuala called as she hurried toward him. "I'm here."

"Will ye mind Shivvy for me and the twins?" John asked as Nuala reached him. "I'll be back for them as soon as I can."

"If ye come back, ye'll be shot," McCree said matter of factly. "And there's no question of taking the children. They belong to the camp now."

Nuala turned back to John. "I'll mind them, John. Don't worry. They'll be fine."

John joined Terry and Jill where they stood with Darby. The archers grouped behind them, glowering at the members of the community as the men herded them through the camp and toward the main drive.

Nuala watched them go and as she turned to look at Fiona to see how she was taking all this, she saw Lorcan McCree watching *her*.

It was pretty clear that regardless of the amicable words he'd just spoken to the crowd, he was humiliated over what had happened here today. Humiliated and angry.

Very, very angry.

Susan Kiernan-Lewis

22

Nuala burst into Fiona's tent.

"Have you lost your mind?" she said. "Terry? Young *John*? Do you have a *clue* as to what Sarah will do when she gets back and sees you've thrown her child to the wolves? *Literally*?"

Fiona was stirring a jar of elderberry syrup that she carefully set on the table and wiped her hands on a towel hanging from her waist.

"John made his choice, Nuala. I tried to talk to him."

Nuala grabbed Fiona's arm and jerked her around to face her, knocking the jar to the floor of the tent. "You're his aunt, ye selfish baggage! Did ye remember that?"

Fiona tried to pull away. Her eyes looked red-rimmed as if she'd been crying.

"Of course I remember! And I'm sick about it! It kills me that he made the choices he did."

"You're really barking, do ye know that? He put himself in harm's way to save one of our own. What did *you* do?"

"I did what I could! It's because of *me* that Lorcan showed mercy to Kyla."

"Oh, aye? Is that really what ye think? Are ye so love struck ye can't see the facts in front of your face? Then let me remind you of who Sarah is to ye, Fiona. She's your sister-in-law. She's the one your brother loves above all else in this world. Am I ringing any bells yet? She's the one who was rescued from this living hell-hole and flew *back to America*, the land of running hot water and fast food restaurants while the rest of us were starving and eating shamrocks—*and she packed it all in and came back to us!*"

"I don't need you to remind—"

"But clearly ye do! And when she came back, she brought with her sugar, guns, and whiskey! She brought a generator for a refrigerator. Am I jogging your memory at all, Fi? She had a seven thousand pound truck airlifted in, as well as baby shoes, seeds, blankets and chocolate—all of it for *this* community. *Her* community. The one you've just allowed this bastard to throw her son out of."

"Nuala, no, I—"

"Shut yer gob! And on top of all that, when she'd been stolen away across the Irish Sea in handcuffs she somehow found her way back to this group and when she did she brought a little something extra with her. Do ye need me to remind you of what that was, Fiona? Because if you do, ye need only look as far as your bonny little lass since she's got his eyes, so she does."

Fiona broke into tears.

"Dear God, what have I done?"

Nuala put her arms around her. "You're lost and you're hurting," she whispered.

"It had just been so long since…since…"

"I know. I know, lass."

"I miss Declan so much. Even now I wake up and I can't believe he's not there beside me. I can't believe my time with him was so short."

"Fiona, it's nightmare hard on all of us, so it is. But we have to fix this."

"How can I ever look Sarah in the eye? She'll have every reason to hate me."

Nuala patted Fiona's arm. Ideally she would allow Fiona to digest her new realization and come back in a day's time so they could formulate a plan. But she didn't have that luxury.

Nuala knew what she told Fiona next could well be the breaking point but it couldn't be helped. If Fiona was going to break down, she'd be no use to Nuala, but if by some miracle she *could* handle the truth…well, there was no one else for Nuala to turn to.

"*Leibhan*," Nuala said soothingly. "Ye need to let that go for now. Sarah will forgive ye because that's who she is. You know that in your heart."

Fiona wiped her tears away.

"But I have something to tell ye that will be hard to hear and maybe harder to believe but—"

"I'll believe you, Nuala. I'm that ashamed it took me this long to come to me senses."

"And that's grand, Fi. But like I said, this is going to be hard to hear but it's why we have to do something, you and me, and there's only us to do it."

"Tell me."

Nuala regarded Fiona and realized she either accepted what Nuala had to tell her or she didn't. Nuala didn't have time to spoon-feed Fiona the facts.

"I'm fair certain that McCree is a pedophile," Nuala said.

Fiona looked at her as if she didn't understand the word.

"Did ye hear me, Fi? I know it's hard to believe but I have eyewitness testimony to back up me belief. Sure he's asked me twice to give Ciara to him and yesterday Sophia told me she stopped him from taking wee Mandy into his tent. I know it's terrible to think but it's true."

Fiona disentangled herself from Nuala and went to the entrance of the ten. Nuala knew Fiona was looking but not seeing the tents or hearing the sounds of the children laughing far in the distance.

She's replaying in her mind things McCree had said and done in her presence that might fit with this.

Nuala held her tongue to let her friend take as long as she needed to process the new information. And she prayed.

She prayed that when Fiona finally turned to look at her it would be with acceptance and with that fight and determination that Nuala needed for the two of them to do what was needed in the hours ahead.

Finally, Fiona turned and in her eyes Nuala saw confirmation that Fiona indeed believed her.

But Fiona's eyes held no fight or determination. Only pain and defeat.

Lorcan McCree stood in the doorway of the library. At first he'd tried to get a sense of the man whose room this had been but in the end he knew it didn't matter.

Fate had brought him to this place and all the humiliations and trials he'd endured up to now had only been preparing him for this, his final destiny.

The tent community was quiet now after the excitement of the day—after that stupid lad and his even stupider bow-wielding elders had forced his hand with the archer so that he'd been obliged to appear as if it had been his own idea all along.

Lorcan had watched the eyes of the people as the drama had unfolded. Without exception they'd turned to him—to Lorcan McCree—to help them make sense of what they were seeing. He could have told them to march their own children up to that stage to lose their hands and he was sure they would have done it.

Sheep need a shepherd. If his father had taught him nothing else he'd taught him that.

"Lorcan?" The soft mewling sound of the girl on the couch behind him pulled him out of his reverie.

It was just as well, he thought as he turned to her. *No sense going down the dark back roads of your mind.*

In the end, that always led to grief.

"Coming, darlin'," he said.

The girl wasn't yet fifteen but as eager as a whore. Lorcan appreciated her enthusiasm but like everything else, it wasn't enough.

It was never enough.

He wasn't precisely sure *why* he'd made the betrothal announcement this afternoon. He'd not even mentioned it to the idiot woman beforehand but Fiona hadn't batted an eye when he'd announced it to the world.

Absurd! That anyone could believe he would take a wife so close to his own age! He'd announced it for the dramatic emphasis. And for that alone, it had been worth it.

But now Fiona would have to go. Not only was she beginning to have certain expectations, but he could see that beneath all that girlish simpering there was a vein of willfulness that sooner or later would have to dealt with.

After all the excitement died down of thinking someone like himself could actually be attracted to her, Fiona would eventually turn back into the woman she really was.

Stubborn. Opinionated. Headstrong.

Not under any circumstances could that be allowed to happen.

Susan Kiernan-Lewis

23

It was raining again the morning Killoran left to go back to Henredon Castle. Sarah needed every ounce of her self-control not to grab a horse and race back to the castle to warn John. As she stood with Mary, Moira and Gavin under the shelter of one of big yew trees and watched Killoran ride away, her heart felt heavy.

Please don't let him hurt my boy.

After Killoran had gone, Griffin and Robbie sat in the back of the wagon and watched the hostages huddling under the tree as the rain came down.

Sarah didn't know much about these two but she knew this détente couldn't last. Griffin was insane and one thing she knew about crazy people was that they didn't do boredom well.

A cursory inspection of Moira showed that last night's assault had resulted in a black eye and a split lip. Sarah hated seeing such evidence of Griffin's crime but she was buoyed by the thought of Moira fighting back.

"How are you, Moira?" Sarah asked.

"How do ye think?" Moira said, her eyes full of venom and focused on Griffin where he sat in the wagon swinging his feet. "If he touches me again, I'll chew his throat out and no mistake."

"We'll all do what we need to do to survive," Mary said quietly.

Gavin looked bad this morning. Sarah was concerned that his beating yesterday had seriously damaged him. There was a dullness to his eye that she didn't like. His face was slack and forlorn—like he'd given up.

Sarah turned her back on Mary and Moira and lowered her voice so only Gavin could hear her. "I have an idea," she said.

He looked at her but she thought she saw more fear than interest in his eyes.

An idea was what had gotten Jordie killed.

"Maybe we should wait and see what happens," he said.

"I need you to talk to Moira."

"Whatever for?" Gavin frowned and glanced at Moira.

"Because I want to give our captors certain information but it wouldn't be believable coming from me or Mary or you."

"What wouldn't be?"

"You know we have to overpower those two, right? Are you up for that, Gavin? I'll do it myself if you're too badly injured."

Gavin straightened his back.

"What do you want me to tell her?"

⁂ ⁂ ⁂ ⁂ ⁂

Griffin had gotten louder in the last hour and it was clear for anyone to see that the relative calm of the morning wouldn't last. The rain had finally stopped and Sarah went to the fire to try to rekindle it. Gavin sidled up to Moira and Mary where they stood under the yew tree.

"Sarah has a plan," he whispered to the women.

Mary snapped her head around to look at Sarah as she knelt by the cold fire, prodding it with a stick.

"What kind of plan?"

"She's thinking she'll go ahead and tell these two where the portal is after all so they can get there before Killoran gets back."

Moira's mouth fell open.

"Sure you're not telling me she knew where it was all along? Why didn't she say so to keep Killoran from going after her son?"

"She knew he wouldn't have believed her. Even now, why would anyone believe her?"

"Sure they wouldn't," Mary said, shaking her head.

"But if this lot found the tunnel to the compound *before* Killoran returned…" Gavin said.

"How would that help us?" Mary said in frustration.

"Don't ye see? We can use the information as a bargaining tool," Gavin said. "We tell Robbie and yon maniac the very thing that Killoran wants."

Moira frowned. "I don't know."

"At the very least, we'll tell 'em they'll be heroes when Killoran returns," Gavin said. "Or if they're ready to give their leader the heave-ho, well, now they don't need him."

"And why would Sarah be wanting to give these two what they've wanted all along?" Moira said with a frown.

"Because we need to delay the inevitable as long as possible. I already overheard Griffin say he wants to use Mary here as target practice."

Mary blanched.

"We give 'em what they want," Gavin said, "then maybe they untie us or even let us go. After all, there'd be no more reason to keep us."

"That's the truth," Moira said, clearly becoming excited.

"But it's got to be you, Moira," Gavin said. "They'd think it was a trick coming from me or Mary or Sarah."

"Sure, I see that," Moira said, glancing at the wagon.

"Just tell Griffin you overheard me talking to Sarah and she admitted she knows there's a tunnel near here."

Moira caught her breath. "Is there really?"

This was the part that Sarah had been very clear about to Gavin. There was no portal that Sarah knew of, but Moira would be more believable to Griffin if she didn't have to lie.

"Turns out there is," he said.

Moira chewed her lip and looked at Griffin. "That's it then."

As Moira rubbed her palms against her pants and began to walk to the two men in the wagon, Mary turned to Gavin.

"If they get what they want," Mary said, "what's to stop them from killing all of us?"

Gavin frowned at her. He couldn't believe he hadn't thought of that.

Moira walked up to Griffin and spoke softly. Within moments, Griffin jumped down, his rifle in his hand. He pushed past Moira, knocking her down as he ran to Sarah by the fire.

"Bran, no!" Robbie called.

Griffin grabbed Sarah by one arm and flung her to the ground where he planted a boot on her chest.

She gasped for air.

"Ye knew all the time, ye lying bitch?!"

"Bran, stop!" Robbie said running to them.

Gavin's heart was pounding in his throat. The look on Sarah's face did not look faked.

She looked scared to death.

"Tell me, ye lying Yank bitch!" Griffin screamed, raising the butt of his rifle to drive down into her face. Sarah covered her face with her hands.

"Bran, stop!" Robbie said breathlessly, reaching for Griffin's arm, "If she knows, we can get there before Killoran!"

Griffin froze and the only sounds in the clearing were the muted calls of crows in the distance. Griffin lowered his weapon.

"*Screw* Killoran," Robbie said to him. "It'll be two days before he can make it back here with John. You and I'll be on our second round of pints by then! Mate, listen to me! We don't need him!"

Griffin removed his foot from Sarah's chest. Even from where he stood Gavin could see the effort this cost Griffin. He wanted to kill Sarah.

"Aye," Griffin said in a low rasp, almost reflectively. "I've missed the piss."

"Haven't we all?" Robbie said. He glanced at Gavin and it was then that Gavin knew that Robbie didn't believe a word of it. He knew Sarah and Gavin were up to something. And he was trying to help them.

Griffin walked over to Moira. He put his rifle down on the ground and pulled out his combat knife. He grabbed Moira by the hair and dragged her before him so Sarah could see him clearly.

"Take us to the tunnel," he said flatly.

Sarah licked her lips, her eyes darting from Moira's terrified face to Griffin's.

"I'm not sure I know what you—"

Moira's scream came out shrill and reedy as Griffin cut a shallow line across her throat.

"Don't hurt her!" Sarah said. Her face had gone white. "I'll tell you! Please! I'll tell you!"

Susan Kiernan-Lewis

24

Fiona knew she would find Lorcan in Mike's study. She had no idea why he was attracted to the room. The books were useless to him and the rug squished when you stepped on it. Just being in the library depressed Fiona because she was reminded of how it used to be when Mike sat in this room, hale and hearty. Drinking brandy and laughing.

Mike.

What will he say when he sees what a dog's dinner I've made of everything?

Quickly she chided herself for her selfishness. She should be focused on praying for his safe return, not worried about him taking her to task for her idiocy.

It's thanks to me that John is exiled from the community. How the hell will I ever explain that?

"Fiona?" McCree called from the study. "Is that you skulking around out there?"

Riley O'Meara was standing guard at the door, a smirk on his face.

Why was he acting like she was a whore? Did he not hear that she and Lorcan were to wed?

Blushing furiously, Fiona entered the room to see Lorcan sitting at Mike's desk. Danny McGoldrick lounged in one of the leather chairs nobody had bothered to drag down to the encampment. He didn't stand up when she entered but shook his head in disgust. Fiona came to stand in front of the desk.

"I need to talk with you, Lorcan," she said.

"I'm busy at the moment," McCree said, although it didn't look like he was doing anything as far as Fiona could see.

She looked at McGoldrick and spoke pointedly to him.

"*Alone*, if ye please," she said.

McCree raised an eyebrow to McGoldrick who took his time standing up and leaving the room. He began to pull the door closed behind him.

"In case ye need a little privacy, squire," he said to McCree with a wink.

Fiona blushed again.

How dare that man make crude insinuations! She looked at Lorcan to see if he was angry on her behalf.

He was angry. But it didn't look like it was McGoldrick he was angry with. Lorcan stood up and leaned across the desk, his face a mixture of rage and indignation. In spite of the look in his eye, Fiona thought for a moment he intended to kiss her.

"Don't ye ever come in here when I'm working," he said in a low sinister voice.

Fiona was so startled she was nearly speechless.

"I…I just…I needed to talk to you about John."

McCree's face hardened at the mention of John's name.

"He's done and gone. What is there to talk about?"

"Lorcan, my…my love," Fiona said, feeling fear creep up her arms as she looked into his hardened face. "I think you…*we* made a mistake. John is my nephew—"

The blow was unexpected, catching her on the side of the head and knocking her off her feet into the chair where McGoldrick had just been. The room went black as white stars blasted across her field of vision. She gasped at the pain ricocheting through head.

Before she could pull herself upright, she felt a terrible pressure on her scalp as McCree lifted her by her hair.

She screamed at the pain and instantly—involuntarily—clawed the air to get free. She felt her hand strike his face and he hissed in pain.

"You will regret that," he said with venom.

⁂

It was not until Nuala had gone to collect the children from Liddy's tent late that evening that she heard about Fiona.

She sat stunned while Liddy and Sophia put together a meal for the three of them and told her what they'd heard.

Fiona had been carried out of McCree's study early that afternoon and thrown into one of the dungeon cells.

"Sister Alphonse said nothing was broken but he'd beaten her something rotten."

"Holy Mother of God," Nuala whispered. "He's insane."

"My question is this," Liddy said, "if he's doing *that* to his fiancé, what's to become of the rest of us?"

"This is what I am saying too," Sophia said. "Should we stay? Should we go?" She looked at her toddler Maggie and bit her lip.

"If only we knew that Sarah was coming back," Liddy said.

"Of course she's coming back," Nuala said. "They all are. Oh, my God. Poor Fiona. *Why* is she in the dungeon? Do ye know?"

Liddy shook her head. "I heard Himself will be speaking to the camp at the main cookfire tonight. Sure I imagine he'll tell us then."

Nuala looked at the children. They had eaten earlier and were already in their sleeping bags. It was really too cramped for them all but Nuala needed to ask Liddy to keep them a while longer.

"I have to find John," Nuala said.

"Petal, what good would that do?" Liddy said, shaking her head sadly.

"I don't know. I don't know."

"He'll not be rescuing his auntie Fi if that's what you're thinking," Liddy said. "The lad was lucky to escape with his life today, so he was."

"I am being so afraid when they are pointing the guns at John," Sophia said. "I thought they are killing him."

"We all thought so," Nuala said. "Thank God for Jill and Terry."

"It's because of their lad being gay and all," Liddy said in a hoarse whisper. "They know it was Darby on the chopping block next."

Sophia reached out to squeeze Nuala's hand.

"You will see tonight what the madman intends? Please? I cannot be there. He hates me."

"He hates everyone," Nuala said. "Yes, I'll go." She turned to Liddy but before she could speak, Liddy said, "Go see what the mad bastard is up to, Nuala and don't worry about your little ones."

Nuala smiled her thanks and left the tent.

She thought she'd hidden it well, but hearing that Fiona had been beaten and thrown into the dungeon was a devastating development. If McCree didn't bother pretending any more, what hope was there for any of them?

The closer Nuala got to the main cookfire, the more people were milling about. Even so, there were far fewer than had showed up to see Kyla's hand taken off. Either the mothers were putting their young to bed or people had had enough madness and hatred for one day.

Even so, there were nearly twenty men and women seated by the fire, waiting.

Nuala decided that bringing attention to herself was not her best idea so she slipped into the shadow of a nearby tent where she could be close enough to listen without being seen.

Within seconds of settling down, McCree and his vanguard of O'Meara and McGoldrick strode to the fire where McCree's figure was backlit in a ghostly silhouette.

"Good people," he said in a loud voice. "We have a problem."

The words struck fear into Nuala's heart.

"Now I know ye all know Fiona Cooper and ye consider her a friend," he said. "I, myself, had been taken by her charm as ye well know since only today I announced my betrothal to her."

"Cold feet is it, McCree?" one of the men yelled out. The other men laughed but McCree didn't smile.

"Not at-tall," he said tightly. "But I have information that I've just learned this day…terrible information…that affects us all." He took in a long breath and Nuala noticed his audience was entranced with him. He had the gift, make no mistake, and he was using it to spin his web.

Something terrible is coming.

"Is there a family in this community who has not gone to Fiona for help with an illness or injury?"

The audience began to murmur and look at each other.

"So ye'll be stunned to learn—as I was—that the woman has been practicing witchcraft on your children with her potions and herbs."

A woman shouted out, "No!"

"It's true," McCree said, shaking his head. "Just this evening I have seen children doing terrible perverted things. Now don't ask me who as I'd like to protect the innocent. But trust me, I've seen it and it's true."

"Who?" a woman screamed. "Which children?"

"Not yours, Missus," McCree assured her. "And now ask me no more specifics. It's hard enough to have to come here tonight to tell you this." He covered his face with his hand in the picture of naked misery.

"Ye can't have any idea how heartbroken I am to learn that the woman I love…" He fought as if to compose himself.

Several women jumped to their feet. A few ran back to their tents while others just stood in place wringing their hands as if they didn't know what to do with themselves.

"I am handling this," McCree assured them. "Fiona Cooper has been incarcerated and will not have access to your children ever again. Her tent is in the process of being searched where all her vile potions are being destroyed. I assure you!"

"And what about Fiona?" one woman yelled. "What's to be done with her? Or with her poor Ciara, come to that?"

"Ciara will live with me," McCree said. "I feel it is the least I can do for the poor orphan." He waited until the crowd was quiet again. "As for her mother and in accordance with our new laws, she will be executed by the community she wronged."

Nuala watched in horror as the people in the audience sat in mute acceptance of his words.

As McCree turned away, his eye fell on Nuala. He smiled. Then he lifted his hand and formed a gun with his hand and pointed at her.

The unmistakable message: *You're next.*

Susan Kiernan-Lewis

25

Sarah led her group into the Killarney National Park just before noon. The rain continued relentlessly and came down cold like tiny needles hitting their sodden jackets. The park trails were wide enough to easily accommodate the horse and wagon. Mary drove it with Moira next to her. Everyone else was on horseback.

Although Gavin and Sarah still had their hands tied in front of them they were under no illusions. If they bolted on their horses, they stood little chance of dodging a bullet in the back.

A quarter mile from the park entrance, the trail narrowed and became more difficult to navigate due to fallen trees and thick foliage. Sarah guessed they were several thousand feet high. Tall firs and pines towered around them and the forest floor was covered with a carpet of needles.

The silence of the park was all-encompassing. Sarah shifted in her saddle. She'd slept surprisingly well last night but she was miserable now, wet and tired with stress that weakened her by the minute.

Added to that the rigors of horseback riding, and she could only imagine how much pain Gavin must be in with his broken ribs. She looked over at him but his face was stoic.

He knew what she knew: at some point, with their hands tied, they were going to have to overpower both Robbie and Griffin. Sarah had picked up on the possibility that Robbie was working for her team again but she couldn't trust t hat.

One way or another, the moment of truth would come and they had to be ready.

Unlike the last time, Sarah knew exactly what she was looking for. It didn't have to be a certain way or a certain distance. It just had to be a good place for her last stand.

She needed a steep cliff, the sun to her back—if it was still up by the time she found the spot—and a place deep in the forest.

Because when the moment came, she didn't want to be a sitting duck like she'd been the whole ride out here. Once hell broke loose, she couldn't risk Griffin getting a clear shot.

Or that Robbie wouldn't shoot.

And that meant trees. Close and winding, thick and protective.

"How much further?" Griffin called.

"Not far," Sarah said. "But the wagon won't make it."

Griffin rode up to see what she was seeing. The wagon road —deeply rutted and clogged with fallen trees and foliage— veered off to the south. But Sarah wasn't leading them south. She was leading them straight up the mountain.

"Bugger," Griffin swore. "You better be telling the truth. Ladies, out of the wagon!"

Mary and Moira climbed down and looked at Robbie and Griffin with confusion.

"We all need to walk now," Sarah said.

"Bull shite," Griffin said. "I am not walking up the side of some bloody mountain."

"It's too steep for the horses," Robbie said, riding up alongside them. "We'll leave them here."

Griffin cursed again but he dismounted and pulled his rifle out of its sheath.

Sarah forced herself not to get eye contact with Gavin to share the victory. To get this close only to blow it with a little premature celebration would hurt worse than failing.

Fifteen minutes later, after watching Griffin eat an MRE that he had in his saddlebag, they began their trek through the bushes and up the side of the mountain.

꙳ꙮ꙳ꙮ꙳

John stood in the middle of the pasture and looked around in all directions. It was colder by several degrees since they'd left the castle.

Unless that was just his imagination.

It's always colder on your own.

Aibreann jogged over to him, her right arm looped through Terry's bow.

"This is a crap place to camp for the night," she said flatly.

"Good thing I wasn't thinking of camping here then," John said without looking at her.

"Then what are you doing out here?"

"Just taking a moment to think."

"Bloody lot of good that'll do," she snorted.

John glanced at her and envied her ability to compartmentalize what had happened to them. In her mind, first they were prisoners and now they weren't so life was presently in the plus column.

He wondered what it would be like to think like that.

He wondered what it would be like to think that they'd taken a step forward in their situations instead of thinking that he'd screwed up the leadership of the castle so badly that fifteen people were now wandering the countryside cold and hungry.

And while he was relieved not to have a mutilated woman on his conscience—because Kyla's near calamity was definitely on him—he still wasn't feeling too good about himself.

"Terry and Jill have got a fire started down the rise on the other side of the meadow," Aibreann said, clearly reluctant to leave John. He appreciated her concern—as clumsy and stiff as it was.

Kyla herself had spent literally the whole eight-mile hike from the castle thanking John over and over again. He'd never have thought any of the archers could be so ebullient—let alone grateful—and he was surprised at how uncomfortable it had made him.

There was nothing to be thanking him for! He'd gotten them all kicked out of the castle!

Talk about a vacancy in leadership—McCree was right about that at least. This would never have happened if his mother or Mike had been in charge.

"Oy, John," Aibreann said.

"Right. Coming," he said, but he didn't move.

"It's not your fault, mate," Aibreann said.

Somehow hearing her say it just made it worse.

"Thanks, Aibreann," he said and turned with her to head back to where the others were.

The sputtering fire was a welcoming sight and John saw that someone had shot a rabbit because it was already on a spit over the fire. The aroma of roasting meat was a palpable welcome to him as he approached.

It was also nowhere near enough to feed fifteen people.

The light was fully gone from the sky as he and Aibreann made their way to the fire. John was surprised to see an extra person there.

Nuala sat between Jill and Terry warming her hands by the fire. She was wrapped in a heavy jacket and sipping from a cup that she must have brought herself.

"Nuala!" he said and hugged her.

"Sure you scared the bejesus out of me back there," Nuala said. "I thought for sure you were a dead man, John Woodson. And what would ye have me tell your poor mother?"

"Yeah, sorry," John said seating himself by the fire. "Oh, wow." He spotted the basket of cold corn bread that Nuala had obviously brought. "Thanks, Nuala."

"Pshaw. Tis 'nae to be thanking me, lad. I'm just that sorry it all went down like this."

"Well, at least Kyla's in one piece," John said. "Thanks to Jill and Terry. Totally Rambo, you guys." He turned back to Nuala. "The kids okay?"

"They're grand, John, so they are," Nuala said but her face was pinched and wan. "But we have a problem."

John spread out his hands. "You're telling me. We're camping out with no food, no sleeping bags and no weapons."

"Fiona's in trouble," Nuala said.

John's heart raced. He should have known this was coming. "Tell me."

Nuala hesitated. "She's got on the bad side of Himself, so she has," she said haltingly.

John felt a wash of exhaustion.

"Don't try to protect me, Nuala. We're already talking about sneaking back to grab the twins and Shivvy. We'll just add Fiona and Ciara to the list. Will she come willingly? Last time I talked to her she was pretty full from all the Kool-Aid she'd been drinking."

"She's in the dungeon," Jill said.

"Crap," John said. "I thought she just got engaged to the bastard? Okay, well, we'll just bust her out of the—" He stopped and looked at the solemn faces of Nuala, Jill and Terry and realized he was still short important information. "What are you not telling me?" he asked.

Before Nuala could answer him Aibreann and Hannah settled down by the fire and offered them pieces of rabbit. They all declined.

"Those tossers burned up all our bows and arrows," Aibreann said. "We need weapons."

"We were just talking about that," John said. "I say we go back to the castle in the middle of the night, break Fi out of the dungeon, grab the kiddies—"

"You can't do that," Nuala said.

John frowned. "Why the hell not? Mike never used McGoldrick or O'Meary for night watch for a reason. They're useless. Always falling asleep. I could play a transistor radio and get past both of them on guard. No problem."

"You can't do it by sneak attack," Nuala said. "We have to...*take* the community back. We have to attack and take control."

"Why the hell would we bother?" John said. "I mean, screw 'em. If this is what the community wants...if they want this McCree a-hole, then fine, it's their funeral. I mean the castle is gone anyway. There's really just a big campsite left now."

"More like a bog than a campsite," Hannah said, wrinkling her nose.

"We *can't*, John," Nuala said. "We have to take the community back."

"Give me one good reason why."

"Because McCree wants the girl children."

John's stomach lurched.

"I've seen the way he looks at them," Nuala said. "And he's tried several times to get Ciara into his tent alone. Right now I've got Liddy guarding our children with a rifle but the other children in the camp…"

"God," John said, shaking his head.

"So ye can't just slip in and get out," Nuala said. "Because we can't leave the children in danger."

A vein in John's forehead began to pulse. "A frontal attack to take back the castle?" he said. "It's impossible. We've got eight bullets and two bows against fifty people with thirty-two automatic weapons." John's shoulders slumped. "It's friggin' impossible."

No one spoke for a moment as they all looked into the fire.

"We have to kill McCree," Terry said, his eyes glittering as he gazed into the fire. "We have to kill him and take the castle back."

"Aye," Nuala said sadly. "Sure that's exactly what we need to do."

26

Sarah knew the answer to the question of whether she would live or die was waiting for her at the end of this hike. Either they came out on the other side or they all died.

If it went bad she'd never see Mike again. Or John. Or Siobhan.

She pushed the dark thoughts from her mind and steeled herself for what was to come. The problem with her plan was that she wouldn't really know what it looked like until it happened. She prayed she'd recognize the opportunity when she saw it and that she'd act in time.

Griffin was the one who'd doubted her every step of the way. He'd seen through her lies and her stalling. She needed him to want the prize badly enough to believe her now.

He had to believe her for this to work and for any of her group to walk away from this day.

The rain was still coming down hard but the treetops took most of the onslaught. Every step was mush and mud. Sarah's shoes had long stopped protecting her feet from the wet and cold.

As they climbed higher, the firs grew scarcer and the forest gave over to open grassy patches and outcrops of boulder covered with dark lichen.

Sarah led the way with Robbie behind her. Griffin brought up the rear. As antsy as he was, she was sure that the long trek to the tunnel must be agony for him. But there was no question now that Robbie was the wild card.

Even Griffin knew enough not to trust that Robbie was totally on his side.

No one spoke as they walked. Sarah was grateful that Gavin seemed to be keeping up, although she was sure the effort was costing him as he walked behind Robbie.

Sarah had never thought of Ireland as mountainous and since she'd lived here she'd never been near any. But as her group climbed in single file, she felt like she was back in the north Georgia mountains of her childhood.

Only with treachery and imminent threat of death in every step, she thought.

"How much longer?" Griffin yelled from behind.

"Not long!" Sarah answered—as she had the last two times he'd asked. She needed to find her spot soon or Griffin would pick his own time and the showdown would happen on his terms—not hers.

They came upon a field of boulders and Sarah's heart began to beat more quickly. She led the group between the larger rocks and jumped on and over the smaller ones until they came to the other side of the field where the path picked up again.

The path was steeper now as it headed up and around the mountain. As Sarah turned the first corner she saw what she'd been looking for. Her heart pounded with excitement.

The path wound up and around the mountain on a ledge several feet wide beside a sheer drop of thousands of feet. With Robbie close behind, she focused on putting one foot in front of the other and used her left hand to hold onto the rock face beside her.

"Tell everyone to watch their step," she said over her shoulder to Robbie. "This is the tricky part."

"Watch yer step!" Robbie yelled behind him.

A scream from behind her made Sarah stop. Robbie had turned around with his back to her and for a moment Sarah wondered if this was her moment.

"What is it?" Robbie yelled.

"Bugger all!" Griffin yelled back. "Daft bitch looked down and nearly lost her balance."

At his words, Sarah impulsively glanced down and felt her stomach muscles constrict. She felt a sheen of sweat on her face and forced down the nausea that was clawing up her throat.

"Missus Donovan?" Robbie said. "Are ye ill?"

"I'm fine," she managed to say.

"Take a deep breath," Robbie said with a look of concern.

Sarah took several long breaths until the moment passed.

The wind had picked up. Had it been the height or the sheer drop or the fact that she knew she was moments from the end of her life that had made her panic?

Stiffening her spine, she turned to continue up the ledge.

And that's when she saw it.

The ledge was wider here—about five feet—and on the rock face that rimmed it was a tangle of fir branches that looked like the broken limbs of a fallen tree. But there was a cleft in the rock that began above the fallen branches.

It was easy to imagine the branches were hiding the mouth of a small cave or tunnel in the mountainside.

Sarah pointed to the obstruction.

"There it is!" she said. "I told you I'd find it!"

"We got it, Bran!" Robbie yelled with delight. "She found it! Good on ye, Missus!"

Sarah took in another long breath to steady herself and then braced herself against the rock face. There was plenty of room for both her and another person to stand on the ledge. But she was counting on Griffin not being able to wait.

There was no way he'd let Robbie into the tunnel before himself.

Sarah was counting on it.

"Out of my way!" Griffin yelled as he stepped past Mary and Moira. Sarah prayed that nobody went over the side as Griffin made his way to head of the line. She turned her head to see Gavin flattening himself against the rock face of the ledge.

Focus on the tunnel, Sarah reminded herself. *This only works if he thinks you believe it.*

She beamed at Griffin as he reached her.

"I'll be happy to go in first if you like," she said. "I've been dying for a real cup of coffee for only about nine years now."

167

He looked at her uncertainly and then grunted. She pointed to the branch covered opening.

"There it is. We just need to strip away the camouflage. The portal isn't fifty yards down."

Griffin narrowed his eyes as he examined the thick tangle of branches. His eyes were mad with expectation and anticipation. The moment Sarah stepped toward the camouflage, so did Griffin.

Now all he could see was the end of the hunt. It was nearly within reach. So close he could taste the foaming pints of lager on his tongue.

Sarah brought her arm out straight into the side of Griffin's head with the grapefruit-sized rock she'd found beside the ledge.

Griffin made a stunned hissing sound at the impact. Before he could recover Sarah ran at him, both arms extended, and rammed him to the edge of the cliff.

"Arghhh!" Griffin windmilled his arms to try to keep his balance and for one terrible moment, Sarah thought he might. But the lip of the ledge crumbled under his heavy boots and he grappled at air, his eyes stark with terror, as he plunged over.

"Gavin, now!" Sarah screamed. She turned to face Robbie but Gavin had already tackled him, bringing them both to their knees.

Sarah jumped back to avoid being pushed over the side of the cliff and tried to see where Robbie's gun was…when it went off.

The sound echoed up and down the mountainside. Sarah stared in horror as Robbie pulled away from Gavin.

And she saw the fist-sized hole in Gavin's abdomen.

27

Gavin gasped and clutched his gut as blood seeped from between his fingers. Sarah ran to him, wrenched the handgun from Robbie's loose grip and knelt by Gavin.

Sarah's mouth went dry and her mind raced as she tried to think what to do. Gavin's skin was cold and wet and he was breathing rapidly. He was quickly going into shock.

"I didn't meant to! It was an accident!" Robbie cried.

Mary ran to where Sarah knelt by Gavin.

"Is he hurt bad? Can you help him, Sarah?"

"I don't know," Sarah said. She felt light-headed as she tried to think.

Robbie pulled off his jacket and dropped it to his feet. He stripped off his shirt and ripped it in half. He edged Sarah aside and gently slipped one end of the shirt strip under Gavin who had passed out. He began tying the ends snugly around Gavin's wound.

Sarah rocked back on her heels and felt a wave of nausea cascade over her.

"We need the wagon," she said.

"We'll never get it past the rock field," Mary said, wringing her hands and watching Gavin's face grow whiter by the minute.

Sarah grabbed Mary's arm and forced her to look at her.

"Go back to where the horses are," Sarah said. "There's a sign hidden by the trees off the main drive that said it was a logging road. It should bring you close. Go as far as you can. Leave Moira with the wagon and come the rest of the way on foot leading one of the horses as close as you can."

"Sarah," Robbie said. "Please. Let me help."

"Mary!" Sarah barked. "Do you understand?"

"I...I..." Mary looked at Gavin and her lips trembled.

"You can do this, Mary," Sarah said. "Now go!"

Mary stumbled backward to where Moira stood open-mouthed with her back against the rock face.

"Is he...is Griffin really dead?" Moira said in a hushed voice.

"Go!" Sarah yelled. "Now!"

Both women turned and ran back down the ledge and disappeared around the mountain. Sarah tried to remember how long it had taken them to climb to this point. The horses couldn't be a full thirty minutes away. She'd been dragging her feet on the way up. And Mary and Moira were going downhill. They could be back in fifteen minutes.

"Sarah, please," Robbie said with tears streaming down his cheeks. "I didn't want any of this to happen."

Sarah picked up Gavin's wrist. His pulse was weak. She looked at the bandage Robbie had put on him. There wasn't much blood. Or was that her imagination? Because there was certainly blood. Was it too much? Was Gavin bleeding out?

"You made your choice, Robbie," Sarah said, "and you'll pay the price for it. I can't trust you going forward."

"But ye can, Missus! Sure I promise ye on me old granny's grave!"

"I can't forgive you for sending Killoran after my son. You shot Gavin. He may be dying because of you. And last night Moira was raped while you sat and listened."

Robbie shook his head. "I'm that sorry for all of it."

"And I will believe you, Robby, if you do one simple thing for me."

He looked at her with hope and eagerness in his eyes. "Anything."

She pointed to the side of the cliff. "Join your buddy."

He looked at the edge of the ledge in confusion and then at Sarah.

She pointed the gun at him. "I don't think it's a lot to ask. It doesn't make up for what you did, but I'd appreciate it if you don't make me shoot you."

He looked at her, his eyes wide with disbelief. "Ye want me to k-k-kill myself? But, I was *helping* you!"

"Ever hear the phrase *too little too late*? I've got two dead bodies with your name on them. *Three* if Gavin dies. *Four* if that maniac hurts my child. Now why don't you help *yourself* by doing what I ask so at least you don't die a total tool?"

Robbie looked at her and then at the cliff's edge. He stood up, towering over Sarah, then he turned and walked to the edge.

"Robbie, stop," Sarah said.

He turned to look at her. The expression on his face was stricken but resolute. Sarah felt a fissure of shame for her cruelty. A part of her hadn't been able to help herself. She wanted to hurt Robbie, to inflict pain on him for all the pain he'd caused her.

"I didn't mean it," she said, waving him away from the edge. "We'll deal with you later once all this is sorted out."

Robbie smiled sadly. "Tell Nuala I loved her," he said.

"Robbie, no!"

He turned and stepped out into space. Sarah heard the distant thump of his body hitting the rocks below. She felt her gorge rise but fought it down at the thought of what John might be dealing with this very minute because of Robbie.

It was done. And if it wasn't quite justice, it was at least fair.

She leaned over and kissed Gavin on the cheek. His face was cold. She grabbed Robbie's jacket and covered Gavin with it.

This was the first moment she'd had to take inventory of what was happening without needing to fight sheer panic at the same time.

Gavin may or may not die but that was out of her hands. The only thing she could do was get him proper medical care as quickly as possible.

David and his *secret island* was around here somewhere. She knew they were close. Gavin's only hope—if indeed he had any—was for them to find David's compound.

Even if they made it back to the castle—a big if—the castle clinic had only rudimentary supplies. If Gavin needed anything more than stitches, he would die.

She put her hand to Gavin's cheek. This was Mike's boy. His only child. She would do everything in her power to bring him back to his father in one piece.

And that means not going to the castle to help John.

Just the thought of moving east in the opposite direction of where John was made Sarah want to vomit. Every molecule in her being screamed at her to go to her child.

But John stood at least a chance of withstanding Killoran.

Gavin would surely die if they didn't go forward.

Twice in the next thirty minutes Sarah ran down the path to where she guessed the logging road might empty out. She called to Mary and Moira, hoping to hear their voices or the jingle of the horse's harness.

Each time she went she cut branches down with the knife she'd found in Robbie's jacket.

The final time she came back to where Gavin was and finished the rudimentary sled she had fashioned out of the branches. Gavin was a stout lad and there was no way three women would be able to carry him down the path and across the field of boulders where the wagon would be.

When she'd finished lacing together the sapling branches using both her and Gavin's shoelaces, his eyes opened.

"Water?" he said, his eyes glazed and distant.

"Soon, sweetheart," Sarah said softly. She watched the sun begin to drop in the sky and was surprised to realize that it was only mid to late afternoon. It felt as if she'd been on this ledge for days.

Finally, she heard voices.

Thank God!

Sarah jumped up and ran down the ledge wall to see the wagon coming up the hill. The horse was laboring with white foam flecking his mouth. Mary was driving him and Moira rode one of the horses bareback while leading the other.

"Over here!" Sarah called. "I've made a stretcher. Help me get him on it and we'll drag him to the wagon."

Mary stopped the wagon and jumped down. Moira tied both horses to the wagon and hurried with her until they reached where Gavin lay.

"How is he?" Mary asked breathlessly as Sarah positioned the sled next to him.

"He's alive," Sarah said. "Moira, you and I'll take his shoulders. Mary, you take his feet."

Both women got in position.

"How long do you think it'll take us to get him back to the castle?" Mary asked.

"We're not going back to the castle," Sarah said. "Everyone heave on three but gently!"

Gavin groaned as they manhandled him on top of the branches. Sarah checked his pulse. It was weak and his bandage was wet.

"What do you mean we're not going back to the castle?" Mary said, her voice rising and bouncing off the stone walls that surrounded them.

"We can't," Sarah said. "Gavin wouldn't survive the trip."

"We're going to the island, aren't we?" Moira said. Her eyes glittered as she spoke.

"No!" Mary said, standing up, her hands on her hips. "That's a fairy tale and ye know it well, Sarah Donovan! We need to go back to the castle!"

"Moira," Sarah said, "go get one of the horses. Hurry!" But Moira didn't move.

"I won't let ye endanger Gavin like this!" Mary said, her voice bordering on the hysterical.

Sarah felt her energy and strength failing her. To have come so far only to have to still fight every step of the way forward…

"Let's get Gavin in the wagon, Mary," Sarah said. "We'll discuss it then."

"Oh, that we are *not* going to do," Moira said, taking a step back. It was then that Sarah saw that Moira was holding Robbie's gun.

And was pointing it at her.

Susan Kiernan-Lewis

28

Fiona stood at the back window and stared out at the ocean. The sun had dropped steadily until there was only a wash of dark orange hovering where the sea met the sky. Her left eye was swollen shut and her lips were split and cracked but her body had only bruises. Lorcan hadn't used his fists on her but had pummeled her with hard slaps and shoves.

She watched an osprey swoop down in the distance but it fell from sight and she couldn't see if it caught the fish it had been after.

She'd like to think she'd come to her senses *before* the first blow fell but she knew that was giving herself too much credit. After all, she hadn't come to his office—*to Mike's office*—to break their engagement or even to confront Lorcan with her terrible discovery of his sexual preference for young children.

No, Fiona had only wanted to see if there was a way to mitigate the crime that *she* had committed against Sarah—her dearest of sisters—when John got thrown out of the community.

So all in all the beating felt right to Fiona.

Oh, she knew Lorcan was handing it out for his own mad, narcissistic reasons. But Fiona deserved it. That was why she hadn't fought back. During the beating, she'd actually seen Sarah's face instead of Lorcan's. Not because Sarah could ever do such a thing but because it was exactly what Fiona deserved at her hands.

I'm losing me fecking mind, Fiona thought as she turned away from the ocean.

What does it say about this evil place we've called home that the only thing left of it is the bleeding dungeons?

The outside door to the hall clanged open and the noise echoed against the stone walls. Fiona tensed. She'd been in here all day and was hungry and cold. She knew Nuala would mind Ciara for her but after what Nuala had told her about Lorcan, Fiona felt a strong drive to hold her little lass in her own protective arms.

Aodhan O'Dorchaidhe and Sean Dolan came to the jail cell. They weren't visibly armed and for one moment Fiona thought they were here to let her out—perhaps even with an apology for how McCree had treated her.

But while they didn't have their guns out, neither would they look her in the eye.

Aodhan swung the cell door open wide.

"Ye'll be needing to come along now, Missus Cooper," he said.

Aodhan and Regan had sometimes been together as a couple, although nobody had ever thought it was serious, least of all Regan. Still, Fiona had served Aodhan at her dinner table more than once with Regan.

"What's happening, Aodhan?" Fiona asked, her swollen lips muffling her words.

"We're not to talk with ye, Missus," Sean said, stepping in and gently taking Fiona by the shoulders and turning her away from him.

She was surprised to feel him pull her hands behind her back to tie them and she fought down a burgeoning panic.

"I need to talk to Lorcan," she said breathlessly.

"Aye, Missus," Aodhan said. "He'll be out directly to talk with ye."

"Out? Out where?" Fiona asked as they pulled her from the cell.

But the two men didn't respond and so Fiona came along between them, bewildered and afraid. It was dark when they emerged from the underground section of the castle where the dungeons were located.

With Aodhan on one side and Sean on the other holding her arms, Fiona had no chance of falling or tripping over the rubble.

Or of escaping.

She stumbled along with them through the courtyard and looked up to see the light on in Mike's den. Through the broken wall she could see shadows moving about up there. And on the night air she heard a woman's laughter drifting down.

Fiona turned away, surprised she didn't care what Lorcan did or with whom. It had all been a sham and Fiona had been too stupid and desperate not to fall for it.

Mike would be horrified, she thought.

As the two men walked her across the courtyard and through the large gap in the castle wall where the portcullis and gates used to be, Fiona knew where they were taking her.

It had only been a few hours earlier that she'd watched the archers marched to this very spot.

The stage was still there. The stage where just a few hours earlier Fiona had been fine with allowing Kyla to lose her hand.

Fiona didn't slow her steps as they approached or resist when the men stopped and hoisted her onto the stage. Next to the tree stump, was a long wooden dowel that had been driven into the middle of the stage.

Aodhan and Sean walked her to the dowel and turned her so her back was against it.

"You're really doing this?" Fiona whispered, her voice shaking.

"I'm sorry, Missus," Aodhan said in a low voice. "It's orders."

"What's to be done to me?" she asked as Sean tied her to the post. "Am I to be burned alive?"

"No, Missus," Aodhan said. "Not that."

When they were finished Aodhan ran off the stage and disappeared into the darkness but Sean went to the edge of the stage and crossed his arms, his eyes watching for anyone who might try to interfere. Fiona realized she hadn't been gagged because that was part of the show, if she should choose to scream or beg.

"Am I to be shot, Sean?" she called out.

At first she didn't think he would answer but finally, he cleared his throat.

"No, Missus. Stoned. By the community."

Fiona blanched and held back a scream. *Stoned!* She tried to imagine the feeling of rocks hitting her face, her arms, her legs —and no place to run. She swallowed.

"My…my crime?"

"Sure twill be read to ye tomorrow at dawn, Missus."

At dawn. So she was to stay here all night in anticipation of her upcoming execution. She shook her head in disbelief.

The moments crept by and Fiona felt her legs weaken. She was able to lower herself at the base of the dowel and her head sagged forward in exhaustion. She had no real hope that she might sleep to shorten the endless night. Her mind was too full of the sins she'd committed in her life, the people she'd let down, all the reasons she deserved to die like this.

Little Maeve, the orphan she'd promised the dying Brigid she would love like her own, died on her watch, drowned alone in the surf not fifty yards from where Fiona sat. Fiona's own unborn son had been sacrificed so that the women of the rape camp might escape. And Declan? Hadn't Fiona let him down when he'd needed her most?

It didn't matter. She would see them all soon. Declan, her parents. Perhaps even Mike.

It occurred to Fiona that now she wouldn't have to face Sarah after all for what she had done to her son John.

Coward that I am, she thought as sleep claimed her, *I deserve whatever happens to me tomorrow.*

⚜ ⚜ ⚜ ⚜ ⚜

Sarah stared at Moira, her mouth agape. She glanced on the ground next to Gavin where Sarah had left the gun.

"What are you doing?" Sarah said.

"Isn't it obvious?" Moira said.

"You…you were with them all along?" Mary said her voice rising in pitch. "How can that be?"

"Well, I was and I wasn't, if ye know what I mean. Last night's little performance by that ape Griffin was the final straw for me. I told him so, too, in no uncertain terms. I don't suppose ye saw the bruise under his eye this morning?"

Moira smirked. "If ye hadn't tossed him off the side of the mountain, Missus, he would've come to a dirtier end at my hands, on that ye can be sure."

"So you're as crazy as they are," Mary said, shaking her head in disbelief.

"I'll thank ye not to calling me names, Mary," Moira said with a glower. "Ye'll not be putting me in the same bag with those two. I was planning on killing all of them when I had a chance, so I was."

"We need to get Gavin in the wagon," Sarah said. "Otherwise I won't take you to the compound. That's the deal. You might as well shoot us all right here."

"Well you're partially right," Moira said. "But I don't need to shoot ye both."

Gavin groaned.

"I thought I might save the lad a lot of pain by ending his trials right here," Moira said, glancing at Gavin on the sled.

"If you do," Sarah said, "why would I take you anywhere after that?"

"I don't know, maybe in the hope of seeing your little girl again someday? Mary told me all about her. Sounds a grand little lass. Or your son? Or maybe your husband? Trust me, Sarah, the worst thing about having all these fecking loved ones is that they hold you back when you really need to be free to survive." She motioned to Gavin. "Case in fecking point."

"I swear if you hurt him I'll die before I help you."

"Really?" Moira turned and pointed the gun at Mary. "How does this work for ye, Sarah? Feeling any more helpful?"

Mary turned and ran down the trail as Sarah launched herself at Moira.

Moira spun to face Sarah, bringing her arm around to correct her aim. But Sarah pivoted and the sound of the gunshot ricocheted off the granite walls, spitting shards like shrapnel in all directions.

Sarah felt something bite into her forearm as she dove behind a small outcropping of stones. She searched the ground frantically for rocks but there were none.

"Stop this, Sarah!" Moira said. "Let me remove the boat anchor around all our necks and I'll let you and Mary live. Fair play?"

"You kill him and I'll never take you to the compound!" Sarah shouted, hoping Moira was still capable of rational thought.

"Well, here's me thinking ye will," Moira said. She turned and pointed the gun at Gavin.

"No!" Sarah jumped up and lunged for Moira, knowing she'd never reach her in time to block the shot.

She was still three steps away when the gunshot exploded in front of her.

29

Moira stood frozen for a moment and then wavered. Her arm dropped to her side, the gun tumbling out of her fingers before it skittered off the ledge and into the abyss.

Sarah had covered the remaining three steps between them and caught Moira as she collapsed to her knees, blood pouring out of her neck. Sarah collapsed under the weight of the woman and Moira's head sagged backward against Sarah's chest.

Her eyes stared at Sarah, but they saw nothing.

Sarah looked up at Mary who was staring at Moira with fear and confusion.

"Sarah?" Mary said tentatively.

Sarah pushed Moira off her. She didn't need to check her pulse to know the woman was dead. The blood from the neck wound was coating the ground…that and the single shaft arrow that was lodged firmly in Moira's neck told her that.

Sarah stood up on shaking legs and looked up at the line of thick holly bushes growing forty feet above them on the mountainside.

"Hello?" Sarah called out. "Who's there?"

"Jaysus Mary and Joseph!" Mary said as she ran to Sarah. "What happened?"

Remembering it was the gunshot that made Sarah think Moira had discharged her weapon, Sarah quickly went to where Gavin lay still unconscious on the branches. Moira hadn't shot him.

Relief coursed through Sarah.

But they weren't out of the woods yet.

"How did you do this?" Mary asked in a hushed voice as she stared at Moira's body.

"I didn't," Sarah said scanning the bushes, the cliff top, the path ahead and behind in bewilderment and growing fear.

"No, *I* did," a voice said from the center of the bush directly above Mary and Sarah.

Both women held each other and stared in astonishment as a figure separated from the bushes and stood up.

"Holy saints be praised," Mary said in an awed whisper. "Sure it's a miracle."

"By God," Sarah said, shaking her head. A disorienting dizziness swept over her when she saw the face of their mystery savior.

"I think you're right," she said.

⚜ ⚜ ⚜ ⚜ ⚜

Regan crawled down the ridge through the thick bushes and nearly fell at Sarah's feet.

It was all Sarah could do not to gather the girl up in her arms and squeeze the life out of her. The bulge under Regan's jacket reminded Sarah that Regan was injured.

"How is it you're not dead?" Mary said as Sarah eased Regan into a sitting position next to Gavin.

"Sorry to disappoint ye, ye old hag," Regan said with a grin. "But in a way I'm alive because of you."

Mary glanced at Sarah as if this must be a joke.

"Sure, aye," Regan said. "It was because of the duct tape, ye see." Regan pulled back her jacket to show how she'd wrapped the tape across her shoulder to keep her gunshot wound closed. "Hurts like shite," she said with a shrug, which made her wince. "But it did the trick."

Mary shook her head. "You're a tough one Regan Murdoch, and make no mistake."

"Rest for a moment, Regan," Sarah said. "We want to hear your story but we need to get on the road as soon as possible."

The three women were able to drag Gavin on the sled of branches down the mountain to where the horse was tied.

Once the sled was attached to the saddle, Mary took the horse's bridle and led it slowly back down the path while Sarah and Regan walked behind on either side of the sled.

"Who did this to him?" Regan asked as they walked.

Sarah could see in the dying light that Regan's face had paled. Regardless of her tough words, she was seriously weakened and in discomfort. The sooner they got to the wagon the better for all of them.

"You won't believe me when I tell you," Sarah said. She winced at the thought of having to tell Regan about Jordie. They weren't particularly good friends but everybody was fond of the boy. He'd been as harmless and gentle as they come.

"It was that wanker, Robbie Murphy," Mary said over her shoulder. "He was with *them*."

"Robbie?" Regan said. "Go on with you! Never!"

"It's true," Sarah said, her head beginning to ache with the whirl of all the things that had happened in the last several hours.

"And so you two fought off those bastards without a weapon? Is that the truth of it?" Regan said as she looked around. "Oy! Where's Jordie?"

Sarah spoke hurriedly before Mary could blurt out the truth.

"First tell us about you. How is it you're alive? We all saw your body!"

"Sure and please God I do not know," Regan said, shaking her head. "I remember being on watch and thinking I heard something and then moving out of my hiding place to see, when boom! That was all I remembered."

"You made it back to camp," Sarah said. "You staggered in and collapsed."

"I don't remember that. All I know is I woke up in a ditch. I was thirsty and my arm was on fire. When I sat up I saw I was alone and then I remembered I'd been shot."

The wagon was just beyond the field of boulders and for the next ten minutes both Mary and Sarah focused on getting the branch sled over the rougher spots.

Gavin didn't regain consciousness and while Sarah was grateful for that, several times she feared they'd lost him for good.

When they finally got to the wagon, Sarah let Gavin rest while Mary pulled out a packet of MREs she'd found in Griffin's backpack. She added water from the canteen and handed the food concoction in a plastic bowl to Regan.

Sarah switched out the wagon horse and put one of the other horses in the harness, which took longer than she liked but it had to be done. The wagon horse was spent. While she worked, Regan ate and drank a little whiskey from a flask they'd found in Robbie's saddlebag.

"Sure how did you find us after all this time?" Mary asked Regan as she handed her a canteen of water.

Regan shrugged. "The blighters weren't worried about covering their trail," she said. "I started walking and just followed the signs."

"How bad is your shoulder?" Sarah asked.

"I think it went straight through."

"You've got all the luck, so ye do, Regan Murdoch," Mary said, shaking her head.

Regan grinned sleepily and handed the whiskey flask back to Mary.

"Anyway, you were easy to track so I just kept walking. I rested when I couldn't go any further, found some berries that didn't look too deadly. Once I caught up with ye, I couldn't imagine why ye'd leave behind the horses and the wagon. Truly, it hurt me brain to try to understand it."

"The men were trying to find the tunnel that led to David Woodson's compound," Sarah said.

"This was all about them wanting barbecue and cable?" Regan asked in astonishment.

"Pretty much."

"So how did you get on the ridge on top of us?" Mary asked.

"When I found the wagon, I was so tired, I just crawled in the back. I found some jerky and some water and fell asleep."

"Weren't you afraid the bad guys were coming back?"

"Not at-tall. I wasn't exactly defenseless, ye ken. I'd lost me gun when I was shot but I found me bow and arrows in the bushes. Anyway, I woke up as Mary started driving the wagon. I could hear there was another woman with her. And since I didn't know where the hell everyone else was, I hid under the blankets until I knew what was what."

Regan let out a long shuddering sigh and Sarah could see she was flagging.

"The wagon finally stopped and both of ye took off on foot," Regan continued, "so I followed you. I was a little slower and by the time I got to the ledge I heard arguing. I quickly backtracked to find a better vantage point. I climbed to the bush line on top of the ledge and when I saw Gavin lying on a bed of sticks and that crazy cow threatening to shoot him, I notched me bow and took the shot."

"That ye did," Mary said with open admiration. "That ye bloody well did."

"Okay, guys," Sarah said. "We need to get on the road but first we need to get Gavin loaded into the back of the wagon. Regan, stand back."

"I can help."

"I don't want you busting your duct tape. Mary and I have this. Mary?"

Mary had prepared a pallet of blankets in the back of the wagon. She and Sarah struggled to get Gavin, now dead weight, onto it. After a few close calls, they finally managed but they were all perspiring when they'd finished, especially Regan who ended up helping after all.

Once Gavin was settled in the back, Mary gave him a dose of the morphine they'd brought and he was quiet. Sarah instructed Regan to lie down beside him.

For once she didn't argue.

Mary unwound the shirt Robbie had wrapped around Gavin and secured the wound shut using the duct tape that Regan still had with her. Then she checked Regan's wound, binding it with a clean shirt and more duct tape.

When she finished she gave Regan two Tramadols that Sarah had brought for her own injuries from the castle attack. Gavin was out cold. When Mary got Regan settled, she sat next to Sarah on the wagon seat but her hands were shaking.

"Sure it's a miracle," Mary said breathlessly. "There's no denying that."

Not sure which part of today Mary was referring to, and not supposing it mattered, Sarah urged the horse forward down the logging road toward the intersecting park road heading due east and out of the park.

Toward Ballingeary.

If her guess was correct, Ballingeary was an hour away. She prayed Gavin and Regan could hold on that long.

When it seemed that the two in the back were both asleep, Mary turned to Sarah and said in a low voice.

"You know I wouldn't judge ye, Sarah, not for me life, and I hope ye know that, but can I ask what happened to young Robbie?"

Sarah felt a wave of guilt that she strove to tamp down.

"He committed suicide," Sarah said.

"Suicide?" Regan said sleepily from the back.

"Go back to sleep, Regan," Sarah said. "Your body needs to rest."

"Sure it's only fitting," Mary said to Regan. "It's because of him you were shot in the first place, as well as Gavin, and poor Jordie killed."

"Aw, no," Regan said in a small voice. "The bastards killed wee Jordie?"

"I'm sorry, Regan," Sarah said. "Now try to sleep. It's going to be a long night."

Mary and Sarah rode in companionable silence for a while. There was more of a moon tonight and that was a help. The horse moved confidently as though he'd come down this trail many times before.

Both Sarah and Mary couldn't help turning around frequently to check on their sleeping charges.

"I know how hard this is for you, Sarah," Mary said quietly, "going east when your lad is west. I'm that sorry I made it any harder on you back there with Moira. I don't know what I was thinking."

"That's okay," Sarah said. "One way or the other we're all going in the right direction now."

"Do you think…" Mary let the sentence hang but Sarah knew she was referring to their precious cargo. It was anyone's guess how badly injured either Gavin or Regan were or if they'd make it to David's in time.

That at least, Sarah realized, was out of her hands.

Susan Kiernan-Lewis

30

After Nuala left to go back to the castle, John sat with Aibreann and Terry. Darby, Jill and the other archers had laid down near the fire to try to get a few hours sleep.

The only thing John knew for sure was that this was probably his last night on earth.

They had no plan to take the castle back beyond a direct assault. Even if they were to sneak up on the community, how could they possibly spirit away twenty-one children? And if by some miracle they'd managed that, they'd be on the raw end of a witch-hunt by an enraged community—all armed with automatic weapons.

"I say we sneak up on three sides," Terry said. "If they're planning on killing Fiona at dawn like Nuala said, that's our time to strike."

"Sure no," Aibreann said. "That's when they'll expect us to come."

Terry poked the fire with a stick and said nothing.

"We need to take out McCree, right?" John said. The other two nodded. "Then I say we sneak up and set three snipers to take the best shot. Once we kill McCree, everyone else should fold."

"I wouldn't count on it, lad," Terry said. "That bastard O'Meara has been waiting for this for awhile now."

"Okay, then we save a bullet for him," John said, wincing at his own words.

"Are ye forgetting we have only eight bullets and six arrows?" Aibreann said. "And those are divided between only two archers? If we're lucky and they don't get to us as soon as we start shooting, that's only fourteen tries. There's nine men back at the castle who'll be armed and ready for us."

"Got any better ideas, Aibreann?" John asked tightly.

She looked at the fire and John had a feeling she was thinking of her little boy, Bill. Nuala had told her that he'd been placed with one of the families when she was arrested yesterday. A part of her must be very keen to get back to that castle.

No matter the cost.

"Who's your best shot?" Terry asked Aibreann. "Hannah?"

She nodded.

"Then we need to make sure she's got the clearest shot at McCree. The rest of us will watch the others."

John agreed. "We'll need to hold our fire unless someone does something stupid."

"They're all going to do something stupid," Aibreann said, staring into the fire.

"Yeah, well, more stupid than usual."

Like pick up a stone to hurl at Fiona.

"Make sure there's at least two archers with Hannah," John said. "Make them your next best shots." *To pick up her bow if she falls.*

Aibreann nodded again. "Aye. That'll be Tilly and Jenna."

"I don't want Darby to come with us in the morning," Terry said. "Or Jill."

"Jill's a good shot," Aibreann said.

"We don't have a rifle for her," John reminded her.

"Besides," Terry said, "if things go rotten, I don't want Darby to be…on his own."

How John longed to reassure Terry about their odds of pulling off the day. But even he knew the limits of blarney you could feed an Irishman. They were significantly outnumbered and outgunned and very likely they would not have the element of surprise.

Not with Fiona due to be stoned at dawn. The entire community knew exactly when John and his group would likely come to try to free her.

And if it all went miraculously their way and Fiona was saved and the community put down their arms and welcomed them back as if nothing had happened—a pretty outrageous *if*—it still meant that John or someone was going to have to assassinate a man.

Execution without trial.

John was amazed to realize he was perfectly fine with that.

✻⸙ ✻⸙ ✻⸙ ✻⸙ ✻⸙

Two hours later, they said goodbye to Darby and Jill and headed toward the castle. Jill was tearful but Darby was angry at being left behind. There was a moon for which John was grateful. Everyone was quiet and if John thought for a moment that the archers were reflecting on the harrowing prospect before them, he chided himself.

They were weary and hungry and cold. The only thing that kept them putting one step in front of the other—besides Aibreann's prodding—was that they were also pissed off.

The only weapons most of the archers had were the rocks they picked up on their way back to the castle.

John was the best shot with the rifle so the task of taking out McCree would fall to him and Hannah.

They needed to arrive unseen and take cover around the stage where they assumed McCree would be holding court. After that, it just came down to taking the cleanest kill shot and hoping it didn't trigger a barrage of firepower raining down on them.

Terry walked beside John. It had been hard watching him say goodbye to his wife and son. All three knew the odds of meeting up again in this lifetime were not good. John thought of Tommy, Terry's older boy, who'd gone back to the MPC compound with John's father. John tried to block out the image of Tommy finding out what had happened to his father.

He's bound to wonder how the hell I could have cocked things up so bad, John thought miserably.

And then John thought of his mother and the look on her face when she heard what happened to him. He shook himself out of the thoughts.

What was it old Archie used to say? *If it's not helping, it's hurting. Yeah, old Archie had a saying for every occasion.*

Even dying.

"It's right around the bend," Terry whispered. "Everyone ready?"

"As we'll ever be," Aibreann said tensely.

"Hannah," John said, "stay low and get to the collapsed clock tower."

Hannah nodded.

"Jenna, you and Tilly go with her," Aibreann said. "You know what to do. When you see the bastard, take the shot. If you have to use every arrow in your quiver—"

"I'll get him," Hannah said grimly.

"The rest of you," John said, looking at the other archers, "spread out. When it all starts going to hell, see if you can grab someone's gun in the crowd. Use your best judgment, I guess."

Even Aibreann raised an eyebrow at that. The archers were not known for anything remotely having to do with good judgment.

Terry held the other bow. He'd hand crafted every bow and arrow in the castle and had taught most of the archers their skill.

"You know what to do, Mr. Donaghue?" John asked.

"Lad, I'm that sure ye can probably call me by me Christian name today," Terry said wryly, his face pinched into a grimace of a smile. "Aye. I know what to do. Line up the bastard in me sights and make sure he doesn't live to see his dinner tonight."

John nodded.

"Nobody do anything until McCree shows up," John said. "Got it? If we're discovered or if we start wasting arrows and bullets before—"

"We've got it, lad," Terry said. He turned to the others. "Quiet as mice, eh? Nobody does anything until McCree shows his face."

They all nodded and then turned to infiltrate the castle from different sides. Hannah and her two back-up archers would enter from the south along the oceanside to take up their positions on the ruined clock tower. The pile of rubble would afford a good vantage point of the stage.

Terry and four of the other archers—armed with rocks— would come at the castle from the north across the parking lot and via the moat. Because Terry would need height to shoot down from, he would split with the archers and make his way to the damaged northern wall where the nuns' makeshift convent used to be. From there he too would have a good sightline on the stage.

That left Aibreann and John. Aibreann was tall and well known by the community. There was no way she could mingle or lose herself in the crowd. The plan for the two of them was that they come at the castle straight on, hide in the bushes and abandoned vehicles by the entrance, and rely on the fact that everybody would be too fascinated with the prospect of stoning a woman to death to notice them.

This meant that John and his rifle would have the clearest shot at McCree.

"You good?" he said to Aibreann just before they parted to find their own paths.

"I will be soon," she said with determination as she hefted the rock in her hand.

As soon as they rounded the corner to the main drive, the moon was no longer their friend. Everybody instantly melted into the ditches and tall grasses by the drive.

John took in a long breath and felt the comfort of his rifle in his hands.

It was do or die time.

Susan Kiernan-Lewis

31

Nuala didn't sleep a wink that night. She held the .22 in her lap. Her thoughts were thick and sluggish, the product of her weariness and her fear.

She was not entirely sure how things had gotten to this point. When she left John's campfire last night the only thing she knew for sure was that whatever John and Terry planned was going to end in disaster.

Terry hadn't looked directly at her when he'd said someone needed to kill McCree but she felt like he was speaking only to her.

Who else could do it? Who else could get close enough? Who else wouldn't be suspected until it was too late?

She wiped a hand across her face and wasn't surprised to draw it away wet with sweat.

What would happen to her if she did this? If she succeeded in killing McCree, would the community kill her? Exile her? Take her children away?

She swallowed hard and hefted the gun in her hands. She wondered who she would be after she killed him. Would she still be able to sing to her children or would the words stick in her throat? Would she be able to kiss them good night or would they be able to tell that their mother was a murderer?

She thought of her sister Abbie and how afraid she'd always been unless Nuala was by her side. Nuala squeezed her eyes tight against the memory of how Abbie had died—alone and terrified.

And then, just so she covered every possible base that needed contemplation, she allowed herself to think what would happen if she tried but *didn't* kill him.

Was there something worse than being stoned to death?

Because surely McCree would order it for her.

Earlier this evening she'd caught a brief glimpse of Fiona on the stage with Liddy and Sophia. Thank God for those two. Even though Sophia was on McCree's radar because she was foreign, she didn't let that stop her from doing what was right.

And when you have a child to protect, that's never an easy thing to do, Nuala thought as she allowed her mind to drift back to the image of her own three children as they slept in Liddy O'Malley's tent.

Please God let me see my dear little ones again and let it not be as someone is pulling a noose over me head.

It was getting light and she knew the time was coming. She said a quick prayer for her safety—not believing she had the right to ask for success in her mission—and for the safety of her children.

Then she stood up and put on the heavy denim smock she wore when she was doing the wash. It had big pockets in front. She buttoned it up to her chin and slipped the handgun into the right side pocket.

She debated practicing drawing it out like some sort of cowboy at the OK Corral and decided that practicing would just make her more nervous.

Either I do it or I don't.

She slipped silently out of her tent, noting that there was nobody about. If John and the rest of them had already come into camp, they were well hidden because Nuala didn't see anything unusual.

She walked straight to McCree's tent—Sarah and Mike's old tent—and stepped into the shadows. She knew McCree would start his day in Mike's study as he had yesterday and the day before.

There was something about that ruined room that drew him. Usually Fiona brought him tea there so someone else would do that today or he'd go without. In any case, the point that mattered was that he would be alone.

Nuala watched his tent for a few moments before realizing it was vacant.

He'd already gone to the study in the castle.

Silently cursing her bad luck, she turned and picked her way toward the castle hoping she wasn't too far behind him. She should have spent the night in the shadows watching his tent not cowering in her own wondering if she was going to hell for contemplating murder.

Now she would pray she wasn't too late to do the unthinkable.

John focused on approaching the castle without being seen. He was aware that there should be guards on duty but he couldn't rely on the fact that they were normally asleep on their watch.

He kept to the long ditch on the north side of the main drive and worked his way as quietly as he could toward the front of the castle which, even broken and tumbled down, loomed ominously in the distance. He remembered the first time he saw Henredon Castle and how safe it had seemed to him then.

That seemed like a long time ago.

At this time of the early morning there were very few people moving about and so he would be much more noticeable. He watched the encampment from the safety of the bend in the road leading to the front drive for several minutes until he was sure there was nobody moving about who might see him.

He crouched and moved stealthily to one of the abandoned cars that marked the beginning of the first line of tents. He was able to stand to one side and remain out of anyone's sight if they happened to come out of their tents.

The stage was fifty yards ahead and it was there he saw the only motion in the camp. He crept around the rusting car to get a closer view and saw that there were people on the stage. At first John couldn't figure out what they could possibly be doing.

He spied Jill and Terry's tent and hesitated. If it were uninhabited, it would provide the perfect spot—once he cut a slit in the back—for observing everything that happened on the stage. Would someone have moved into it in the few hours since Jill and Terry left?

Deciding to risk it, he stepped down the narrow pathway that wound around the tents. Crouching low and with a quick look over his shoulder to confirm that there was nobody around, he flipped back the tent opening.

It was empty.

He was surprised it was still standing since people had already stripped the interior of the bedding, clothing and personal effects.

He moved to the back of the tent, estimated the height he would need to hold his rifle to get his shot, and got out his skinning knife to make the slit. When he did, he pulled the slit open and was able to see clearly everything that was happening on the stage.

The three figures he'd seen were women which accounted for why they were so quiet.

He instantly recognized Liddy O'Malley and Sophia Donovan administering to the third figure who stood rigidly—awkwardly—in the middle of the stage.

Fiona.

She was tied to a thick wooden dowel that was jammed into the center of the stage. Her head and shoulders hung limply forward. For one terrible moment, John thought she was dead. Then he heard her moan and speak a few soft, unintelligible words.

Liddy was holding a bottle of water to Fiona's lips while Sophia wiped her face.

It was all John could do not to go storming to McCree's tent that minute and murder him while he slept.

John pushed away his outrage and tried to think. Did it matter *how* the bastard died? Did he really need to die in front of everyone? Was that going to be helpful in some way to regaining control of the community?

If John went to McCree's tent, surely he'd be guarded. Probably by McGoldrick and O'Meara. John would have to kill anyone who stood in his way before he got to McCree.

There went the element of surprise.

No, as much as he would like to deal with the monster this minute for what he'd done to Fiona, it was best to stick to the plan.

Thirty minutes later, as the sun peeked out over the horizon, people began to gather and mill about in front of the stage. Dawn came and went, and while more people gathered, McCree had yet to show up.

John began to feel antsy. With the daylight, he could see that Fiona was in bad shape. Her left eye was swollen shut. Her lips were blistered.

He watched the crowd as they gathered at the foot of the stage. He recognized every single face. He'd celebrated Christmas with these people, toasted the births of their children, sat next to them at dinner in the great hall—and now here they were—at best to witness a friend of theirs be stoned to death and at worst to help kill her themselves.

How could he ever forgive any of them?

He looked at the faces of the women in the crowd. Every single one of them was exhausted and afraid. They looked like robots with no thoughts but only dull acceptance of one more terrible experience to endure on top of all the others that had made up the last eight years of their lives.

When had that happened? Was it the loss of the castle walls? When one day they were cozy and protected inside against the horrors of the world and the next they were throwing rocks at wolves to keep them from snatching their dinner from the campfire?

Even John knew the devastating feeling of vulnerability because of the loss of the castle. They'd made light of it and rallied around Mike and his promises to rebuild and make it stronger, bigger, better. But really? Did anyone really believe that?

Was it any wonder the community had latched on to the first person who seemed like he knew what he was doing? The first person who said outloud the things they'd all been thinking? That camping out here in the open was a very precarious, very dangerous way to live?

These people were afraid, John thought. *We never really processed what happened when the bombs came down, when good men died and women and children ran screaming for their lives. Somehow we all just pitched a few tents and went forward.*

And that's not how humans operate.

And then they lost Mike. And then Sarah.

It's no wonder they reached out for this lunatic.

They'd lost their home and both their leaders within days of each other.

Out of the corner of his eye John noticed the Mother Superior and her nuns moving toward the stage. Clearly they expected a repeat of yesterday's success with Kyla. John was fairly sure McCree didn't respect anything the Mother Superior stood for.

If she thought she'd prevent this travesty with stern words and a moral admonishment to do the right thing, she was going to be severely disappointed.

Sophia gave Fiona a kiss on the cheek and climbed down from the stage. Liddy stayed a few moments longer and talked quietly to Fiona who never lifted her head and then she too left when the Sisters mounted the platform.

At the same time, John saw a flicker of light hitting metal from above and beyond the stage and because he knew where to look, he picked out the motion that had to be Hannah. She was in place. He felt a rush of relief.

At least she hadn't been caught. From where he was John couldn't see if Terry had made it but since all was quiet, he assumed he had.

Danny McGoldrick and Riley O'Meara passed the tent where John hid and stood with their backs to him as they surveyed the stage. For one moment, John contemplated putting two bullets in their backs where they stood.

He wasn't sure how the crowd—which seemed ambivalent at the moment—would take that. It was possible it would galvanize them in a way that would not be in John's favor.

Best to stay with the plan.

John watched a group of children run around the stage. Some had rocks in their hands and they pretended to throw them at each other. The sight made him sick. He recognized at least three children who Fiona had nursed when they were sick.

He held his rifle at his waist, ready to stick it through the ripped opening the minute he spotted McCree.

But the sun climbed higher and higher and the crowd grew and still McCree was nowhere to be seen.

John bit his lip and tried to think what to do. Should they just wait? What else could they do unless they wanted to start a battle with the people milling about the stage?

There was no way John could communicate with the archers or Terry to change the plan. *All they know is to do nothing until they see McCree.* There was never any contingency plan.

And in the mean time we don't have enough arrows or bullets to take out everyone who tries to throw a stone at Fiona.

Would they start stoning her before McCree showed up?

Where the hell is he?

Suddenly, John saw both McGoldrick and O'Meara sprint into the crowd. A couple of women screamed and the nuns ran to the edge of the stage to get a look at what was happening. As John watched in horror, McGoldrick returned to the stage with Aibreann.

"Might as well be a show of two for one!" he laughed.

Aibreann turned and spat in his face. Without hesitation, he turned his rifle butt to her and slammed it into her face. A woman screamed. Aibreann lay on the ground as O'Meara pulled back his boot and slammed it into her ribs.

John brought his rifle to his shoulder and shoved it through the slit, lining up O'Meara's head in his sights.

Suddenly his rifle jerked upright and was wrenched out of his hands from the outside.

John turned to dart out the front of the tent but before he'd taken two steps, the tent flap opened. Two men stood with rifles pointed at him.

Sean Dolan aimed his gun at John's head.

"Nice 'n easy, Yank. Sure we don't want to hurt you before time."

Susan Kiernan-Lewis

32

Nuala crept up the open stairwell to the second floor of the castle. She was surprised McCree felt so comfortable going about the castle without a guard and then she reminded herself of the man's arrogance. And the fact that he would surely be armed.

As she reached the second floor she had a birds-eye view of the stage and the surrounding tents. It was lighter now and the crowd was growing.

Her stomach churned and suddenly she felt very cold. She just wanted this over with! She felt so exposed on the open stairs. Any one of the people down there could look up at any time and see her—it was certainly light enough to see a shadowy figure moving about.

She felt the heavy gun in her pocket to give herself courage —but it only made her more nervous.

Was she really going to be able to do this?

She reached the door of Mike's study, her heart pounding so loudly she was sure McCree could hear her approach.

Suddenly a shout made her snap her attention back toward the stage. She couldn't see what was going on but she saw that there were several figures on the stage moving about. Nuala realized it must be the Sisters.

But who shouted?

More shouts meant something was happening down there.

Had they found John's group?

Nuala knew she had to move *now*.

Without stopping to think any further about it, she pushed open the heavy door and entered the room. McCree sat at Mike's large oak desk and looked up as she entered. Not in alarm or even curiosity. But annoyance.

"What are you doing here?" he asked peevishly.

He had two handguns on the desk before him and Nuala tried to swallow the lump in her throat.

"I…I came to ask ye for mercy for Fiona," she said, not knowing what else to say. If she tried to pull her gun out, he could easily shoot her a half dozen times before it ever cleared her pocket.

This isn't going to work.

"Mercy?" He looked at her oddly and cocked his head as if a thought just came to him. "Sure ye'll have been working with her to create her devilish concoctions, won't you? Why didn't I think of that before?"

Nuala licked her lips and tried not to look at the guns on the desk.

"I suppose that would make it easier for you to kill us both," Nuala said, hating the tremor that she heard in her voice.

"Not a matter of *easy*, ye stupid woman," McCree said. "Only a matter of protecting my people."

"They're not your people."

"And whose else would they be? Yours?" He grinned.

"I've lived with them for six years. They're more mine than yours."

"Is that a fact?" He was definitely enjoying himself now. Nuala wasn't sure if that was a good or bad sign. "Hands where I can see them, please." He picked up one of the guns from the desk and pointed it at her.

Her stomach erupted in acrobatic butterflies, her muscles tensed and contracted.

"You…you intend to just shoot me?" she stuttered, forcing herself not to think of her poor orphaned children. "Do you think *your people* will accept you gunning down the nanny they all send their children to? In cold blood?"

He shrugged. "I'll say you attacked me. You were distraught about your friend's impending execution and you attacked me."

This Nuala never expected. She thought they would talk and she would pick her moment to take him by surprise.

She never expected he would just shoot her! She felt a slow tightening in her chest.

There was no way she could get her gun out in time.

She was a fool for underestimating him.

Dennis and Damian and little Darcie would never see their mother again.

I have lost everything.

Susan Kiernan-Lewis

33

John stood next to Fiona on the stage and watched, sickened as the men of the castle lined up the archers and Terry. Sean Dolan and a few other men were breaking the last of the bows into pieces on the ground.

There was no way any of them could expect mercy now.

Sister Ambrose knelt by Aibreann and was trying to clean the blood from her face. Aibreann's nose was broken and bleeding but her eyes searched the crowd. John got a sick feeling that she was hoping to look on the face of her little lad one more time.

"So we tried ta exile ye and that didn't work!" Danny McGoldrick said strutting in front of the stage. His eyes were glazed with fervor as they raked the archers—every one of them insolent and unafraid.

"So now we'll execute ye one by one," McGoldrick said, leaning into the face of Hannah who didn't blink.

McGoldrick turned to Terry. "Where's your boy, Donaghue? We'll be needing to exterminate him first and foremost. Sean, go find Lorcan. He should be here for this."

One woman cried out from the crowd, "I won't be party to this! This is murder!"

"Are ye planning on wandering the countryside with the wolves then, Annie?" Sean Dolan sneered.

"If I have to!"

"Aye, me too!" another woman said. John saw several of the women pulling their children away from the stage toward their tents.

Suddenly Jill emerged from the crowd. In her hand she held a large stick and nothing more.

"Bugger this!" she yelled, waving the stick over her head. "You've all lost your minds!" She made it all the way to the stage and began to untie Fiona. Instantly, the nuns moved to create a shield in front of her and John and Fiona.

John could see the men were hesitant to shoot the nuns. But one man seemed to have no problem putting Jill firmly in his sights.

"Look out!" John shouted as the sound of a gunshot echoed in the air.

The man howled and grabbed his arm which was gushing blood from between his fingers.

Sophia stood alone with a rifle in her hands—its barrel smoking—and little Maggie clutching her leg.

"The next shot I aim better," she said in a shaky voice.

Nuala appeared from behind Sean Dolan and pointed her pistol to his head.

"Everybody put your guns down. *Now*," she said calmly. The men turned to stare at her in surprise. Nobody moved.

"Bugger I hate it when men act like men," Nuala said in frustration, cocking her gun. "But sure it's up to you. I've just shot and killed Lorcan McCree." A gasp rose up from the crowd. "So I'm on a bit of a roll here."

Sean lowered his gun.

"Archers!" Nuala called out. "Collect their weapons!"

Darby appeared from behind Nuala and ran to his mother Jill to help untie John.

When Hannah approached McGoldrick to take his rifle, he jerked it away, refusing to give it up. Nuala aimed her gun at him and shot him in the foot.

He screamed and dropped his rifle which Hannah scooped up.

"Pity we couldn't do this the easy way," Nuala said, curling her lip. "Typical man."

She turned to address the crowd and raised her voice. "All right here's how this goes and please don't try me. As I've said I've just killed a man so I don't think killing a few more will add much to my prayer list tonight. Do what I say and kindly save me the agro."

The crowd murmured as Jill and the nuns helped Fiona into a sitting position on the stage. One of the nuns draped a blanket over Fiona's shoulders while another moved to where McGoldrick lay writhing on the ground.

John stood by Fiona with his reclaimed rifle in his hands. Everyone was looking at Nuala.

"This *community* is officially dissolved," Nuala said loudly. "I don't care if you started out with Mike and Sarah eight years ago or whether you just joined us last month, the community's gone."

The crowd talked amongst themselves, looking around in agitation and confusion.

"Are ye throwing us off the castle grounds then, Nuala?" one woman called out.

"Nay, Jenny, not at-tall," Nuala said. "I'm reorganizing us, so I am. Every woman and child is to step over to the stage with Fiona and the good sisters. Quickly, if you please."

The group didn't move. Separating the women from the men sent shock waves through the whole group. The men more than anyone knew that didn't bode well.

"I had nothing to do with this!" a man yelled out.

"If ye did nothing to stop it, you were a part of it," one of the Sisters called back and then slapped her hand to her mouth, her eyes startled at her own outburst.

"Well said, Sister," Nuala said, nodding. "And me own sentiments exactly. Ladies, if ye don't mind? I promise I'll not be mowing down your lads once you do."

Slowly the crowd separated as the women scooped up babies and grabbed the hands of children and moved to where Fiona sat trembling on the stage, her head down. Mother Angelina kept a soothing hand on Fiona's shoulder.

Once the women were in position near the stage, eight men stood alone. McGoldrick was still thrashing around on the ground, his shattered foot bleeding into the dirt.

Sister Alphonse, the castle's healer, was attempting to get his boot off. The man who Sophia had wounded sat on the ground beside him while another nun was busy packing his shirt with padding to provide pressure for the wound.

John and Terry, now both armed, stood on either side of Nuala. The archers, also armed, stood one step behind her, and glared at the men.

"Now, you lot," Nuala said standing in front of the eight men. "Here's how this is going down. Jimmy and Danny there will stay where they are until they're treated by the good Sisters. Riley O'Meara, you'll wait with them."

O'Meara's head shot up and he gave Nuala a nervous look. Everyone knew why the other two were separated out. But why was he? He rubbed his hand against his pant leg and licked his lips.

"Riley!" his wife called to him. He put up a hand to reassure her.

"Nay, lass. I'll be fine."

"The rest of you lot," Nuala said nodding to the remaining five, "will leave today."

A gasp emitted from the crowd and a few women cried out. "No!"

Nuala turned to the women.

"Sure you're welcome to go with your men and nobody will fault you if you do—unless you have children because of course the bairns will be safer in a group." She turned back to the men, who were now staring at her with their mouths open.

"For not standing up and trying to stop this—you are exiled from this community. You'll leave with no weapons except your pocket knives since I don't trust you not to use them against us. As for your women and children I won't keep them against their will. But if you truly care for them, you'll urge them to stay with the community where they'll be safe and you'll go your own way in peace."

"For...for how long?" one man asked plaintively.

"Until I decide that this place is no longer a good place to be," Nuala said. "Once I leave—if I do—you're welcome to come back to it."

"You can't do this, Nuala O'Connell!" one of the women screamed.

"You're welcome to go with your husband, Colleen," Nuala replied without looking at her. They'd been friends. Once. A thousand years ago.

"What about the other three?" another woman called out. "My Jimmy's been hurt!"

"Once he's treated, he'll be turned out with the others," Nuala said firmly.

Riley O'Meara stepped toward Nuala and both John and Terry raised their rifles.

"And myself?" he said to Nuala. "It sounds like you have something special for me and Danny, do ye?"

"Oh, aye, Mr. O'Meara," Nuala said, her face hardening. That this smirking devil would put her in this position in the first place made it easier for her to do what she needed to do.

Not easy, mind. But it helped.

"You and Mr. McGoldrick will be executed within the hour," Nuala said.

The women exploded in screams of horror.

"For the pain you've caused," Nuala said, "And for the attempted murder of Fiona Donovan Cooper."

The wives of both O'Meara and McGoldrick ran to Nuala pleading and weeping. The archers placed themselves bodily between them and Nuala. The Mother Superior pushed past the archers.

"Nuala O'Connell," Mother Angelina said, her eyes flashing. "I'll not be allowing this."

"Sorry, Mother," Nuala said, her eyes on O'Meara. "You've got no say in it."

"This makes you no better than McCree."

"So be it," Nuala said but she would not look at the nun.

"This is vengeance, pure and simple," Mother said firmly. "I'll not let you stain your soul with the murder of those two devils."

The nun crossed her arms and resolutely stared Nuala down.

An hour later, Liddy had gotten the main cookfire going with a pot of stew bubbling over it and nearly the whole community, including the men who were preparing to leave, were eating the first communal meal they'd had since the castle was bombed.

Many of the women were still saying goodbye to their men. The good Sisters had succeeded in obtaining Nuala's mercy for the two ringleaders of the near-coup. Riley O'Meara would leave with the other men and McGoldrick would leave as soon as he could walk again.

Nuala had also relented in allowing the men to take a rifle each. She knew none of the men had it in them to attack the castle. They'd already proven themselves spineless in that regard when they'd stood by and allowed evil to happen.

Now Nuala sat by the fire with her three children and watched the archers as they restlessly patrolled the perimeter of the camp. They would ensure that the men left—and with nothing more than had been allowed.

Terry had said he'd get busy creating more bows and arrows but Nuala wasn't sure that was the best use of his time. Without a castle wall to fire down upon, her feeling was that bows and arrows had seen their day. Better that the archers became proficient with firearms now.

Fiona sat next to John across from the cookfire. She was shaken but her injuries would heal. Healing her mind was another thing altogether. Nuala would be surprised if Fiona was ever the same again.

Cor, I wouldn't be, Nuala thought, shaking her head.

Darby stood with some of his friends by the stage. It pleased Nuala to see him the center of attention for a change. Yes, he was different. But he was also a hero and these days they needed as many of those as they could have.

It seemed that Darby had *not* stayed back at camp as he'd been instructed but followed John and his father to the castle. When Jill saw he was missing, she raced after him and slipped unnoticed into the crowd while she searched for the others.

Since Darby knew that the major problem his group faced was lack of weapons, he went straight to Mike's study where he knew Mike kept a stash of rifles. The minute he showed up, he heard McCree himself coming down the hall.

Darby dove under the big oaken desk where he hid hoping McCree wouldn't stay long.

To his horror McCree actually sat down at the desk forcing Darby to scoot back to the furthest corner under the desk. Just as he was sure McCree would hear his panicked breathing or his heart pounding, Nuala came in. Darby listened to the two of them talking and when he realized McCree was about to shoot Nuala—not knowing what else to do—Darby reached up and pinched McCree on the thigh.

The man squawked in surprise and dropped his gun.

The gunshot Darby heard next was the sound of Nuala shooting McCree between the eyes.

"It was a team effort, so it was," Nuala said to Terry and Jill as they all sat by the cookfire. "We wouldn't any of us be sitting here eating stew if it weren't for Darby disobeying orders so I hope you'll take that into account when you call him to task later."

Terry nodded, his eyes going to where Darby was laughing with his friends.

"Aye," he said. "I'm that proud of the lad."

"Now what?" Jill asked. "You know you're our de facto leader, don't you?"

"Maybe. But the leader of what?" Nuala said with a laugh.

Aibreann came over to where they were sitting. She squatted down with her toddler Bill in her arms.

"I'd say you're the leader of sixty-two women and children," she said.

Nuala looked at her with surprise. "None of the women are leaving with their men?"

"Not a one."

"It's like I said," John said as he joined them by the fire. "We're a matriarchy."

Nuala turned to Aibreann.

"Tell the archers," Nuala said, "that from this day forward no strangers will be allowed into the camp. We will have a guard at all times on all sides except the ocean. *Everyone* will be turned away. If they don't go, your lot has orders to shoot *to kill.* Until Regan returns you and the other archers answer to me. Is that clear?"

Aibreann nodded and grinned. "Guess this means we'll be needing a new camp child minder," she said.

As Aibreann turned away, the archer Tilly jogged over to Nuala with her rifle loose in her hands.

"Yo, Chief. Unknown rider coming up the drive."

34

The dark settled in, and a cloying fog crept in around the wagon wheels just as Sarah and Mary were emerging from the forest park. It had been a cold and slow trip. Sarah hadn't wanted to take any blankets from the back where Gavin and Regan slept so she and Mary shivered violently as their bodies tried to keep warm.

The only sound in the forest was the rattle of the horse's harness and the creaking of the wheels over the overgrown access road.

Mist clung to the trees obliterating any chance of being able to read a road sign until they were right on top of it. They passed the exit signage of the park and Sarah heard Mary sigh with relief.

Sarah wished she could feel as confident that the worst was over.

She only knew roughly where David's compound was. She was still seriously thinking of running around and waving her arms hoping to be picked up by surveillance.

Except the fog definitely put a damper on that plan.

"How long?" Mary asked in a low whisper.

Sarah was grateful Mary had held off asking that question for as long as she had but it was still too soon. How nice it must be to think someone else had everything under control, she thought. That you can just settle back for the ride and ask them where and when things would happen.

"An hour," Sarah said not at all sure.

The ground sloped downward and the fog thickened as Sarah drove the wagon and watched the fog pool around the horse's legs.

"He'll be okay," Mary said quietly.

Sarah didn't know whether Mary meant John or Mike or Gavin. Or for that matter Robbie. Sarah had thought back more than a few times to the moment when Robbie had thrown himself off the cliff—*because she'd goaded him into it.*

She tried not to remember the image of him disappearing before her eyes—just like she tried not to remember the moment Robbie and Gavin separated to reveal Gavin's terrible wound. She dragged a hand across her face and felt the exhaustion of the day bear down on her.

"Would ye like me to drive, Sarah?"

Sarah shook her head and then glanced at Mary.

"I was wrong about you, Mary. I'm sorry about that."

Mary was silent for a moment.

"Nay, ye weren't," she said finally. "But I'm better now."

"What will you do when we get back to the castle?"

"Start over, I suppose. If the others will forgive me. If not, I'll go away."

"With Liddy and Roysen?" Mary's sister and small niece were all the family Mary had left now.

Mary shook her head.

"Nay. They're safer in a group. I'd not take that from them."

Sarah put her hand on Mary's.

"I'll speak up for you. And I'm sure Regan will too."

"Thank you, Sarah." Mary stiffened her back as she visualized the long road ahead to get the castle people to trust her and accept her. As far as Sarah was concerned, if they didn't want to live with Mary they could all bugger off.

Mary had more than proven her worth and made up for her crimes.

They rode again in silence for several more miles. Every now and then Sarah thought she heard a distinctive sound. At first she chalked it up to the forest but when she thought about it, the sound was mechanical. Man-made.

As she drove through the fog she couldn't help but think of John. Would he be okay? Would he realize who Killoran was— a liar and an opportunist—or would he fall for Killoran's lies?

Without the protection of the castle walls, everyone there was totally exposed to whoever turned up to threaten them. What if Killoran took one of the children and put a gun to its head?

What could John possibly do then?

She pressed her lips together and banished the image of John being led away from friends and family as a hostage of Laith Killoran.

Suddenly Mary grabbed Sarah's arm.

"Up ahead," she said. "People."

Susan Kiernan-Lewis

35

John had not allowed the stranger, a man named Killoran, to approach closer than the edge of the camp. After speaking with him, he left two archers behind with their rifles pointed at Killoran's chest.

As he walked away, John heard the man protest, "Not even a bed for the night or a bowl of food?"

John heard the answer in the form of a loud click as one of the archers cocked her rifle.

There's a new sheriff in town, John thought.

Nuala met him in front of his tent, her boy Damian by her side. Her face was grim and her hair was in a loose braid down her back. He could see she wasn't the same woman she'd been two weeks ago. Her eyes were sharp and mistrusting as she stared over John's shoulder at the stranger in the road.

"What does he want?" she asked.

"He says my mother sent him. And I'm to go with him."

"Why didn't Robbie come back instead? Or Gavin?"

"He said they're still searching for Mike. But my mother's hurt and she needs me to help find my father's compound."

Nuala frowned. "Can you do that?"

John nodded. "I think so."

"How badly is she hurt?"

John turned to glance towards Killoran, who held himself stiffly as he faced the archers. There was an arrogance that rolled off him. John had met men like him. The ones he'd known were always bad news.

"I don't know," he said.

"I don't like it," Nuala said. "Does he have proof he's sent from Sarah? Or that she's even alive?"

John agreed with Nuala that something about the guy didn't feel right. But the thought of his mother hurt or dying didn't allow for any other answer.

"I don't like it either. But I have to go."

❧❧❧❧❧

Fiona sat with her arms around Ciara and watched the bustling activity about her. Everyone was just a blur of faces—and none of them looking at her. Was it because they couldn't bear the censure they might find there?

Fiona didn't hold any of it against any of them. How could she? They'd just wanted what she wanted. To be safe. To keep their children safe.

"Mummy, too tight," Ciara said and pulled away from Fiona's grip.

She has no idea how close she came to losing me.

"Fi?" Nuala knelt by Fiona and gave her arm a squeeze. "Are ye all right then?"

Fiona forced herself to nod. "I'm grand," she whispered.

Behind Nuala three archers stood with rifles in hand, their eyes roaming the crowd to spy out trouble or danger. Beyond them, Fiona could see the banished group of men as they gave their wives and children farewell embraces.

There had been no resistance among the women to Nuala's order. Fiona had to think that was because on some level the women knew Nuala was right.

"Sophia's taking over the bairns now," Nuala said. "Will ye let her have Ciara?"

Fiona could see that Sophia had materialized at Nuala's elbow. Sophia held wee Maggie in one arm and Sarah's Siobhan clung to the hem of her tunic. Sweet, maternal Sophia had stood against her community and put a bullet in a man who'd threatened to harm John and Fiona.

A tear trickled down Fiona's cheek. *Such a brave, fearless lass*, she thought. But no, that wasn't it. Being fearless had nothing to do with it. Of course Sophia had been afraid.

And she'd stepped forward anyway.

"Fi?" Nuala said.

Fiona looked at her and this time she was able to smile as Ciara ran to Sophia.

"Aye," Fiona said. "Sophia, thank you."

Sophia gave her a quick smile and then backed away with Ciara in tow.

Fiona could see that the other archers had moved to establish a defensive grid around the tents. Nuala was speaking to her but something was nagging at Fiona in the back of her brain. Something from before Lorcan and the madness that had overtaken her. Fiona watched Terry's lad Darby walk by leading one of their few remaining horses.

The horse was fully tacked. Fiona could see the saddlebags. *Someone was leaving.*

"What's happening?" she asked.

Nuala stood up, evidently satisfied that Ciara was in good hands and whatever Fiona needed for healing would be done in Fiona's own time.

"Sarah's sent for John," Nuala said.

Fiona turned her head to look at Nuala. "Sarah?"

"Aye. She's sent someone to say John's needed. He's leaving now."

"Who? Who came back?"

"A stranger. Nobody we know."

"Is…is Sarah hurt?"

"The stranger says she is," Nuala said. "But we don't know for a fact."

Fiona stood up. "I'm going with them."

🎇 🎇 🎇 🎇 🎇

Killoran was still standing in the distance but could see Sarah's son and a small woman both saddling horses. A tall older man stood beside a horse in earnest conference with young Woodson.

Killoran didn't worry about what the old bastard might be saying. Nor did he worry about the handgun visible in the boy's holster.

Nothing trumped the card Killoran had. Killoran had the lad's mum, so he did, and no wise words of caution or prudence, no gun, *nothing* was more powerful than that.

When the two bonny little archer lasses had stopped him at the perimeter and none too gently insisted he not come any closer, he'd itched to show them he wasn't just anybody to be trifled with—*especially lasses!*—but he held back.

He knew that if they all thought they were on the same team, it would make things easier in the long run.

He'd be able to travel with Sarah's son without worrying about needing to tie anyone up or that someone was pointing a knife at his back. They'd ride at least as far as the west side of the park—probably reach it by late afternoon.

Then on the pretense of resting the horses he'd stop and explain to the lad the full monty.

Ye'll be taking me to yer da's lair or ye'll watch me skin yer mother alive before yer very eyes.

Killoran watched John and the woman who was coming with him say goodbye to the tall redheaded woman.

And then just to show young Woodson that he wasn't given to exaggeration, Killoran would put a bullet between the eyes of the small woman.

Killoran felt a warmth radiate throughout his body.

That ought to work a charm.

36

Sarah stopped the wagon in the middle of the road and listened to the noise coming toward them down the road. They only had the combat knife she had taken from Robbie's jacket and a Ruger semi-automatic pistol with just enough ammunition for eight shots.

"Friend?" Mary asked in a quiet, shaky voice.

"I guess we'll find out."

A long scream in the distance rent the air and made Mary grab for Sarah's hand. Sarah licked her lips and tried to see into the fog. Slowly, shapes began to form. The sound of engines grew louder.

Vehicles! Gas-powered vehicles.

"I think it's David's people," Sarah said.

It had to be! They were in the right area. Who else would be driving *trucks*?

A moan from the back of the wagon snagged Mary's attention and she crawled back to check on Gavin and Regan. Sarah continued to stare up the road until she saw the ghostly yellow beams of twin headlights pierce the fog before her.

She held her breath as the beams grew closer and the dark form of a large truck emerged. Now she heard voices under the vibrating rumble of the truck's motor.

But beyond that there was something else.

Further away, under the sound of the truck and the rumble of men's voices, she heard…wailing. Soft weeping and keening came to her as if the truck had torn a hole in the silence that had surrounded them up until then.

The horse shied and whinnied shrilly and Sarah tightened her grip on the reins to steady him.

As the truck barreled down the road toward them, it occurred to Sarah that it might not stop. She had no idea who was in that truck. They might easily decide to mow down a horse-drawn wagon in their way.

She'd known more than a few people in the last several years who would've done exactly that.

Eyeing the verge off to the side, Sarah slapped the reins against the horse's rump to move him. But the horse wasn't used to pulling a wagon—or responding to driving commands —and the sharp movement made him scream and rear up.

Realizing the horse was about to charge down the road into the path of the truck while dragging the wagon and the two tied horses behind it—Sarah screamed for Mary. Then she tossed the reins down and launched herself over the wooden breeching strap onto the terrified beast's back.

The leather harness prevented her from getting her legs around him to control him astride and her sudden pressure on his back triggered him into a gallop straight toward the truck.

"Grab the reins!" Sarah screamed to Mary as she dug her fingers into the horse's mane and clawed until she found where the reins connected to the bit.

The animal shied violently then and Sarah was nearly dislodged, only catching herself at the last minute from slipping off the horse collar and heavy traces. She wrapped her arms tightly around his neck and spoke into his ear, trying to be heard over his panic, "Whoa, whoa, boy! Settle down, now."

She'd ridden Blue many times. The horse knew her. His ears pricked backward and he downshifted to a canter. She pushed the advantage—all the while watching the truck grow larger and larger before them.

She pulled on the right side of the horse's neck rein and was relieved to see Blue move his head in that direction.

"There you go, boy," Sarah said soothingly. "Let's let the big bad truck have the right of way."

The horse slowed to a trot and followed Sarah's lead as she directed him toward the shoulder.

As soon as they were on the side of the dirt road, the horse's haunches twitched violently and then he settled, snorting and eyeing the truck as it pulled up beside them, only twenty feet away.

The driver of the truck was wearing a military uniform. He spoke into a handheld communications device and Sarah felt her heart lift.

It had to be David's group! Nobody else in post-apocalyptic Ireland had communications!

"Excuse me," she called to him. "We need your help!"

"Turn around," the driver said to her. "This is a restricted area."

Sarah saw the back of the truck was full of men. She could hear the weeping louder now.

"I have people in the wagon who need help," Sarah said, sliding off the horse and beginning to approach the driver.

He drew a pistol and pointed it at her. Behind him in the truck cabin Sarah heard the unmistakable sound of a rifle cocking.

"Turn around," he said. "While you still can."

☆ ☆ ☆ ☆ ☆

John and Fiona rode silently behind Killoran. At first Killoran kept up a steady patter of conversation but John wasn't in the mood to talk and not surprisingly, neither was Fiona. John still couldn't believe that she wanted to come with him.

After what she had been through, John would have thought she'd want to spend the next several days in bed. But with the determination and grit that he knew was his aunt Fiona, she'd packed up a case of herbs and medicinal salves that hadn't been destroyed by McCree and his men and insisted on coming.

John knew she was trying to make amends to him in the only way she knew how. But he also knew she felt she'd betrayed Sarah, her dearest friend, and in some way—leaving the safety of the castle behind and her little daughter Ciara—and coming with him was a matter of recompense.

John wasn't sure whether he was happy to have her along or worried she'd end up being one more thing to have to deal with.

When Killoran finally gave up the attempt at conversation, they all fell into an almost comforting silence, each with their own thoughts and concerns.

Was it possible that his mother really would have trusted this guy to come back for him? Was his mother really injured? Why didn't he believe this dude? What were he and Fiona walking into?

Once they left the main drive and then the highway leading south, they passed an old pine forest that swept up a hill. The rocky ground gave way to soft, moist earth covered in a layer of pine needles.

John kept his eyes peeled for any sign that his mother—and her wagon—had come this way but it had rained too many times since she'd left and there was no trace of them.

All John could do was trust that this guy was leading him to her.

They rode most of the day under dark clouds threatening rain the whole way. The terrain was getting rougher and less familiar by the hour.

Finally they came to a pasture. Fog was moving in as they crossed the pasture and followed Killoran down a steep ravine. John's horse slipped on the mossy stones but caught itself. John looked over to see how Fiona was handling all this, but her face was closed and unreadable.

The temperature had dropped as the shadows grew and flitted behind the trees.

"We'll need to rest the horses," Killoran said, pulling his horse to a stop. "The ground is uneven going forward and they'll need their strength."

There was something about the way he said it that made John tense up. It was a forced jollity when there was no need for it.

John scanned the darkened clearing to see if anyone was waiting there for them. And then he looked at Killoran already on the ground.

There was nobody waiting to ambush them.

There was only Killoran.

And he was reaching for the rifle in his saddle's scabbard.

37

Sarah grabbed the horse's bridle and turned the wagon around. Her heart was pounding, knowing how easy it would be for the driver to just shoot her.

The truck disgorged a stream of men, all in uniform, all with the emblem *MPC*—which stood for *Meliores Priores Consortium*—clearly visible on their sleeves.

So, definitely David's men.

The soldiers began to erect a checkpoint. Twin tripods appeared on each side of the road—each fitted with an auto-cannon machine gun.

Sarah hadn't felt comfortable evoking David's name to the driver. There was something about the deadness in his eyes that told Sarah he'd be just as happy to shoot them all and roll their wagon into the nearest ditch.

Once she had the wagon turned around, Sarah climbed back into the driver's bench and took the reins from Mary.

"Where are we?" Regan said in a weak voice laced with pain before falling silent again.

Mary turned to watch the men working in the road behind them.

"What are we going to do now?" Mary said. "You know they'll both die before we get back to the castle."

"I know."

They rode in silence back down the road they'd come and Sarah knew Mary was feeling the same hopelessness she was. To be retracing their steps—going *away* from help—was agony.

As soon as they were out of sight of the truck, Sarah drove the wagon off the road and into a clearing hidden behind a copse of fir trees and stopped.

The quiet of the forest assailed them. Only the creaking of the harness and the toss of one of the horse's heads broke the silence. Listening, Sarah heard the hooting of an owl and far away, buffered by the line of trees, and the sounds of the men working on the roadblock.

After a moment, Sarah handed the reins to Mary.

"Wait here." She jumped down and ran to the back of the wagon and pulled the reins free from her horse. Quickly, she tightened his girth and checked his feet for rocks. Then she led him around to the front of the wagon.

"Sarah, what are ye about?"

"I have to find David."

"What? No! You can't leave me!" Mary clasped her hands to her chest. "It's dark! I have no weapon!"

"There's a gun under the seat. Take it out now."

"No! I don't know how to use it! I was a Kindergarten teacher before the bomb dropped!"

"And now you're an angel of vengeance," Sarah said, mounting her horse.

"Sarah, please."

"There are eight rounds in the gun. Use every one of them if you have to. Protect those two, Mary. Protect yourself. I will be back with help. I promise."

"Sarah, no. I can't do this," Mary said and sank down on the seat.

"Mary, you have to. If someone tries to take the extra horse, let them. If they try to take anything else, shoot them."

Sarah leaned over and squeezed the older woman's arm. "Mary, you can do this. I know you can."

Mary took a deep breath. She straightened her shoulders and reached under the seat and pulled out the gun.

"Keep your eyes open," Sarah said, then turned her horse away and into the woods.

❧❧❧❧❧

"Take your hand off the rifle," John said evenly to Killoran. Killoran turned to him, his face an open expression of surprise.

"Sure no. What could ye mean, lad?"

That's when John knew he should have already drawn his pistol. That's when he knew he should have drawn it five miles ago.

But he hadn't.

Killoran had his rifle in his hands now, his smile expansive and expectant. He pointed it at John.

"Hands away from your pistol, laddie. Nobody needs to get hurt. Missus, I'll ask ye to dismount and step over toward me."

"Don't do it, Fiona," John said, his hand on his pistol.

"Sure no, *Fiona*," Killoran said. "Don't do it as the lad says and I'll kill him where he sits."

"He won't, Fi," John said. "He needs me to take him to the compound."

But Fiona had already dismounted.

"Now if ye'll kindly step away from the horse," Killoran said to Fiona, waving the barrel of his gun to indicate where.

Before Fiona could comply, John vaulted off his horse, drawing his pistol at the same time.

John heard the rifle go off as he hit the dirt and rolled under his horse's feet. The horse reared and screamed in terror as a divot of dirt and grass blew up next to him as the second rifle blast punched the air.

Susan Kiernan-Lewis

38

The horse wheeled away from the gunshots as John rolled onto his stomach, both hands holding his gun. Not bothering to aim, he pulled the trigger in Killoran's direction.

The first shot hit Killoran in the groin. John squeezed off two more shots, higher, both hitting the man in the stomach.

The smoke from John's firearm's discharge puffed in a smoky wreath around him. He leapt to his feet and ran to Killoran who lay squirming in agony on the ground. John snatched up the rifle.

He turned to look behind him.

Fiona lay by a silver birch tree. She held a hand to her stomach. A hand coated in gore.

With a cry of anguish, John ran to her and dropped to one knee. Killoran's shot had been intended for Fiona.

But why?

"Fi!" John said. Her eyes fluttered open and the faintest of smiles appeared on her face before she closed them again. John looked around but all the horses had run off when the shots were fired.

John gently removed the knapsack of herbs from Fiona's shoulder. He could tell she was still breathing shallowly.

He had difficulty swallowing as he tore open the knapsack and saw small jars of unguents and other liquids. There was an ache in the back of his throat.

This can't be happening. Dear God. This can't be happening.

John glanced around the clearing. Killoran had stopped twitching.

John tried to think, to imagine what he could do. Fiona needed help. She probably needed a level one trauma center. There was no way he could get her back to the castle and all he had was homeopathic salves and ointments.

She was going to die here.

He sat back on his heels and looked at her, his heart breaking into a thousand pieces.

They were in the middle of nowhere. He had no idea where his mother was or where his father's compound was from here.

He took a deep breath and set about dressing Fiona's wound the best he could, applying salve and then binding it with his t-shirt, praying it was clean enough but knowing in the end it didn't matter. It was all he had.

When he finished, he positioned her as comfortably as he could and built a small campfire.

They had no food and no blankets. John felt the exhaustion of his emotions and the day overwhelm him as he lay down beside his unconscious aunt and fell asleep.

❈❈❈❈❈

Sarah blessed the moonlight as she and her horse picked their way through the woods. She knew nothing of navigating by the stars and she didn't have a compass so she was using her best guess that she was still traveling east—which had to be the general direction of the moonrise.

Her plan was to circle around the soldiers on the main road and either find someone willing to talk to her—or start waving her arms for the surveillance cameras.

She hadn't wanted to tell Mary just how desperate it all was. In fact, while she felt buoyed by the action she'd taken—at least she had a plan—she also was aware that she'd just abandoned not only Mary but two critically ill people.

If it weren't for the absolute knowledge that a return to the castle—their only other option—was a death sentence for both Gavin and Regan, Sarah would have turned back.

The thick forest of tall firs eventually gave way to open meadows and Sarah knew she was out of the park once more. She prayed she was nearly to Ballingeary.

Several times she tried to hear beyond the sounds her horse's hooves made crunching through the leaves and broken twigs on the forest floor. A few times she thought she heard wailing and each time she did she turned in that direction.

Where there are people there is hope.

The layer of pine needles on the forest floor beneath her began to give way to a firmer, rockier ground. As the trees dissipated and the ground became more stone than dirt, the noises became clearer.

She stood in her stirrups to try to see through the darkness. She had no idea how long it was until morning and she reminded herself that for now the night was her friend. She moved on relentlessly forward until the wails became louder and louder.

What in the world has happened?

Whatever it was, it was something terrible.

A snap of a stick sounded in the stillness of the woods and Sarah froze. She slid from her saddle leaving the reins looped on the horse's neck. If her horse should bolt, she didn't want him killing himself tripping on his reins.

She moved on foot as silently as she could to the nearest stand of trees but her shoes crackled loudly on the twigs underfoot with every step.

A man slumped against a large tree, his knees drawn to his chest.

The second Sarah saw him, her hand went to her waist where she'd tucked Robbie's knife. It wouldn't help against a gun but it gave her courage.

She quickly saw that she needn't have bothered. The man was beyond wanting to attack anyone.

What had happened here?

Sarah skirted the dead man and pressed on, faster now on foot, her eyes probing the shadows and the darkness.

She *must* be to Ballingeary by now! She didn't expect to see any lights of course, but there should be *some* sign that the town was near!

She stopped to catch her breath and try to think. She was so determined to get help back to Mary and the rest of them as fast as she could that she hadn't really been thinking, she'd just been moving. But what was she moving into?

She took another step and froze. He was laid out flat on the rocky ground, his head twisted to one side, blood congealed down his jaw. She smelled a strong scent of iron and realized she'd smelled it for several minutes now.

A battle, she thought. *That's what's happened here.*

Now she saw the bodies lying on the ground. Three. Four. Six.

A chill clutched her spine as she moved.

Who did this? The men in the trucks? Were they the victors?

Why did they kill these people?

Was it to protect David's compound? Did David's men do this?

Sarah stopped and felt her heart pounding in her throat. She had no idea of what was waiting for her if she continued on.

She took another step and then stopped. Immediately she heard the unmistakable sound of a rifle's slide action dropping its cartridge in the breech and then a loud *thunk* as the bolt slammed closed.

39

The sound of helicopter rotors was a sound that John had reason to know well. When he'd gone to school in Oxford, he'd been taken to the United Kingdom and returned by helicopter more than once. Now he seemed to hear them in his dreams, and always when he was worried or afraid.

Which was most nights.

The sounds became louder and John woke with a start before realizing it wasn't a dream. There was a helicopter overhead.

And that could only mean one thing.

He went to Fiona, holding his breath for what he was afraid to find. The fire had died out in the night and she was trembling in the early morning chill—but she had survived the night.

John checked her bandage to see that it had not bled more in the night. Whatever damage the bullet had done it must not have hit anything major. She was alive and there was a helicopter.

He ran to the edge of the clearing but the tall trees blocked any view of the surrounding sky. Forget trying to signal the helicopter. He briefly considered shooting his gun to tell them where he was but didn't want to risk hitting the helicopter.

This was his dad. He just knew it.

Running back to Fiona, he suddenly felt vibrations underfoot and then heard a steady rumble of a motor-powered vehicle, and felt a rush of terror mixed with joy. He stood, trying to process what it was.

The minute he realized it must be a large caravan of motor-powered vehicles, he pulled off his jacket and draped it over Fiona to give her some warmth. Then he sprinted up the hill toward the road they'd traveled down. The closer he got to it, the louder the noise got until John saw two trucks coming his way.

He held up a hand and three men jumped from the back of the truck—assault rifles held at chest level as they ran toward him.

Whatever happened now, happened, John thought as he waited for the men to reach him.

"John Woodson?" one of the uniformed men barked at him. All three weapons were pointed at John.

John nodded, his hands limp at his side. If these men meant him harm, the two bullets left in his gun would do little to protect him or Fiona.

The man stopped in front of John and reached for the radio by his collar while the other man stood and pointed his gun at John.

"We got him," the man said and then quickly gave their coordinates. Then he reached forward and disarmed John and pushed him off the road and into the ditch that bordered the road.

John's legs felt weak as he staggered into the ditch. He'd read that this was what the Nazis used to do to people they were about to execute.

He stood in the ditch with the one man's gun pointed at him and waited.

The he felt an adrenaline rush as he heard the sound of the rotors grow louder and he realized why they had needed to get out of the road.

The helicopter was landing on the road.

Despite the gun on him, John began to climb out of the ditch. He watched as the helicopter cleared the nearby treetops and touched down. The door opened immediately.

His father stepped out and waved to the soldiers, a relieved grin on his face as he walked over to John.

"I got your message," his father said as he hugged John tightly.

The tracker John had used last night before falling asleep had been the one piece of technology his father had recovered during his brief time before the castle was bombed. He'd given it to John when they parted in case John ever needed him.

Weeks later when anyone who found out he'd had the device all along asked him why he hadn't called his father earlier, John would only say that until Fiona lay dying in his arms, he had never really believed that things weren't manageable.

Last night things had finally gotten out of hand.

"Fiona's hurt," John said, gesturing toward the clearing. "Can you get her to a medic or something? She was shot in the stomach."

David turned toward his sergeant and spoke to him. The man went to the helicopter and came back with a stretcher. He and another man ran across to where John had spent the night. John and David moved quickly behind them.

"What happened?" David asked as they ran.

"A guy came to the castle yesterday morning," John said. "He said that Mom was hurt and that I needed to get her to your place."

"He knew about my place?"

"He did, yeah."

"But you didn't tell him?"

"No, Dad," John said with annoyance. "I kind of shot him a bunch of times after he tried to kill me and Fiona."

They reached the campsite and John saw that one of the men had already started an IV on Fiona while the other one prepared to put her on the stretcher.

"How does she look?" John asked.

They didn't answer but just loaded her up and ran with her across the clearing to the waiting helicopter.

"Where are they taking her?" John asked. "I need to go with her."

"No, son," David said. "They know what they're doing."

John stood with his father and watched the helicopter lift up and fade into the cloud of fog hovering over them. The trucks full of soldiers remained on high alert as they stood in the road.

"We've got to find Mom," John said. "She's out here somewhere hurt."

"Your mother's not hurt," David said, looking at his watch.

That's when John heard the sound of the second helicopter and within seconds saw another helicopter appear from the mist

The sounds of the rotors made it impossible for John to ask his father anything more.

And when the helicopter landed near them and the door opened, John realized there was nothing more he needed to ask.

Because his mother was the first person off the helicopter.

40

Sarah recognized David as the helicopter began to land. He stood in the clearing talking with his men. Two hours earlier, after she'd been stopped by ground troops of David's organization she'd been allowed to speak to David on a communicator. Moments later, a helicopter had arrived to take her to where she'd left Mary and the wagon.

She and Mary had watched with joy and relief as both Gavin and Regan were transferred to the helicopter and flown away. They stayed in the wagon surrounded by a dozen soldiers until another helicopter arrived to take them away.

Sarah almost didn't care what happened next. Gavin and Regan were getting the treatment they needed and for now that was all that mattered.

She and Mary were flown back over the Killarney National Park.

Because of the mist and fog, Sarah could see little of the terrain below until they were nearly touching down. And then the sudden vortex of debris from loose rocks and dirt from the rotor wash made it impossible to see where they were or who was waiting for them.

When the helicopter landed, Sarah was the first one out. Without even knowing what she was looking for, her eyes went directly to where John stood. She emitted an involuntary gasp of joy as she ran to him.

Sarah clung to her son, the relief and exhilaration coursed through her. There had been so many moments in the last few days when she was sure she'd never see him again. Her thoughts were too scattered to pin down. She just held him and lost herself in the physical fact of him.

It was John who pulled away first. Sarah held his face in her hands and looked into his eyes. Whatever had happened with Killoran had left her son untouched.

At least physically.

"Did Killoran bring you here?" she asked.

"I *knew* you hadn't sent him. I just knew it. But I couldn't take the chance. I had to go with him."

That of course was exactly what Killoran had been counting on.

"I know. Where is he now?"

John shook his head. "It's was horrible, Mom. It's my fault Fiona got hurt."

"Fiona?" Sarah looked around. "Fiona is with you?"

"*Was.* Dad had her airlifted to the medical facility at his compound."

"How bad?"

"I don't know, Mom," John said, his eyes filling with tears. "She never woke up."

David approached them and put a hand on John.

"It's all right, son," he said. "They're doing everything they can for Fiona and so far so good."

John nodded and wiped his eyes. He looked over Sarah's shoulder and smiled. "Hey, Mrs. O'Malley."

Sarah turned to see Mary standing by the helicopter. Sarah walked quickly to her and led her back to John and David.

"Where is everyone?" John asked them. "Robbie? Gavin? Regan?"

Mary began to shake and Sarah put an arm around her but turned to address David.

"Are we leaving right now or can we sit for a bit?"

A few minutes later the soldiers laid out blankets and MREs. After they'd eaten, Sarah sat with Mary and John and warmed her hands by the fire the soldiers had built.

It was unbelievable to Sarah that things had worked out as they had.

But she still had so many questions.

"Well, you'll tell *us*, John Woodson!" Mary said sharply and Sarah was glad to see some of the woman's spunk return.

"Nuala killed him," John said flatly. "And if she hadn't not only would Fiona have been killed but me too and probably all the archers. He was a friggin' lunatic."

"I can't believe this," Sarah said, shaking her head. "So who's in charge now? Terry?"

"Oh!" Mary said, with a quick intake of breath. "I think the lad's saying *Nuala's* in charge!"

Sarah nodded. "I can see that." She was watching David as he talked to his men. The helicopters still hadn't returned and she guessed they would probably spend the night right where they were. She'd ask him to take John and Mary back to the castle without her.

"Hey, Sarah," David called. "Can you come here a minute?"

Mary lay down by the fire and John wrapped himself up in a blanket and leaned against a nearby tree. Sarah stood up and instantly felt the chill in the air as she stepped away from the fire.

David held a flashlight in one hand and a walkie-talkie in the other. It occurred to her that this would be a good time to ask him about Mike while they were away from the others.

As she reached him, David startled her by taking her hand. It had been so long since she'd had any physical connection with him that she was surprised at how familiar and comforting it felt. But when she looked into his eyes, her comfort faded.

"What is it?" she asked, tense and alarmed now as she searched his face.

"It's Gavin," he said gently. "I'm sorry, Sarah. He didn't make it."

Susan Kiernan-Lewis

41

Sarah's legs gave out and David shot a hand out to support her. He quickly led her to the far side of the lead cargo truck where he sat her down on the front step.

Her vision blurred and she felt her body grow cold. After everything they'd been through she'd been so sure that they'd beat the odds and come out on the other side. She shook her head as tears streamed down her face.

"I am so, so sorry, Sarah," David said softly. "But Fiona and Regan are doing well. My people say they should both fully recover."

Oh, poor Sophia, Sarah thought, her throat closing up as tears blinded her. *Poor little fatherless Maggie.*

And Mike. This will kill him. To lose his only child, his only son.

She buried her face in her hands and let the sobs, guttural and primal, come up from her diaphragm. She felt David kneeling beside her, his arms around her. Sarah wept in raw gulps until she had no tears left.

After all they'd been through, after so many moments that she thought might be her last, to have lost him now—brave, sweet Gavin. It was too much to bear!

As she drew a ragged breath and tried to compose herself, she reminded herself of all she still had. John was alive and unharmed. Regan and Fiona would survive. The castle community was whole.

It was only Gavin and Mike who were lost to her.

All she could think of was the shock of thick red hair that was Gavin's trademark. She saw him in her mind's eye returning to camp with his lovely Sophia after being chased off by Regan and the Druids.

She saw the hundreds of times that Mike would gaze on him as only a fond father can. And the many, many times over the years when Gavin was the good older brother that John wanted and needed.

John will never be the same after losing Gavin.

"Sarah, I'm so sorry. I know you were close."

"How am I going to tell Mike?" Sarah asked brokenly. "How am I going to tell him his boy is dead?" Her face crumpled again.

"Do you know where he is?"

Sarah looked at him and wiped her face with her sleeve. Instantly, David produced a handkerchief and she blew her nose and took a long breath.

"I was kind of hoping *you* knew where he was."

He pulled away from her and narrowed his eyes. "You think I had something to do with Mike's disappearance?"

She took another long breath and felt the dejection and disappointment of what was coming.

If David doesn't know where he is, how am I ever going to find him?

"I didn't take him. I'm sorry, Sarah."

She nodded and stared at her hands.

"Can you help me find him?"

He held her hands and kissed her on the cheek. When she looked at him she could tell he was struggling to tell her something. She tensed in preparation for the worst once more.

"If I tell you what I know, Sarah, you have to believe me when I tell you I just found out today. Okay?"

"Found out what?"

"I swear on the head of our child that I had nothing to do with Mike leaving your camp four days ago. Do you believe me?"

"Okay," she said, watching his eyes carefully. "*But*?"

"But I know where he is."

42

It hadn't taken David's men long the next morning to locate and wrap Jordie's body as well as Moira's for the return trip to the castle. They'd tried to recover Robbie's body too but it was inaccessible on the mountainside. They did report that he was not alive. They also reported spotting Griffin's body a few yards away. The fall appeared to have decapitated him.

Sarah stood by the dying fire as David's men made preparations for them all to leave. Mary and John would return with the bodies in the truck caravan, and Sarah would leave with David on the helicopter that was even now waiting for them on the road.

David had been careful not to reveal exactly where Mike was, saying only that all Sarah needed to know was that he was able to take her to him. Her heart pounded with excitement at the thought of seeing Mike again.

There were so many questions to be answered—and the way David had gone silent after telling her about Gavin, it was clear *he* was not willing to be the one to answer them.

Sarah watched John solemnly walk beside the stretcher that carried Jordie's body. She could not bring herself to tell him about Gavin. Not yet. He had so much to process, she wanted to spare him this for a little while longer. Sarah couldn't bring herself to tell Mary either.

It didn't seem like such a crime to give these two a few extra hours without the stress and pain they'd had to endure for the last three weeks.

Sarah walked hand in hand with Mary to the lead truck.

"Sure what do I tell Nuala?" Mary asked. "When she asks about Robbie?"

"Tell her the truth," Sarah said. "That he and Jordie were killed by two men trying to get information on the location of David's compound."

"So I'm not to tell her what a lying, low-down backstabber he was then?" Mary said with a frown.

"Is there a point to that, Mary?"

"Sure Regan is bound to tell her some day."

"Not if we ask her not to."

"I don't have to say he died a hero, do I?"

"Well, in a way, he did, Mary. And I'd prefer it if you could bring yourself to say so. It would be a kindness."

"I see that," Mary said with a frown.

Mary had changed in these last four days. Sarah saw it and hoped very much that the people in the castle would see it too.

"If anyone gives you any trouble at all—" Sarah started to say.

"They won't," John said firmly as he came to stand with them. "Because when it comes to heroes, Mary O'Malley is one of my personal favorites." And he wasn't smiling when he said it. Sarah leaned over and hugged him and so did Mary.

"I'll see you soon," Sarah said to John. "I just can't wait even another half day. I have to find Mike."

"I know, Mom. Bring him back as soon as you can. Just don't you go disappearing too or I'll send Dad after you."

Sarah kissed him on the cheek. "I'll be back. Count on it."

❀❀❀❀❀

It was raining by the time the caravan of trucks began to drive away. Sarah and David stood side by side and Sarah waved but it was all she could do not to march over to the helicopter and hop in.

David finally turned to her. "Ready?"

Sarah walked to the helicopter and climbed on board. Her mind was buzzing with questions.

How does David know where Mike was? Is Mike a hostage? Why hadn't Mike tried to come home?

As the helicopter lifted off in the rain, Sarah could see the trucks heading north on the winding road. She was sure that John and Mary could probably hear and see them as well.

She pushed away the image of poor Eliza Barrett with the body of her son, and of Nuala receiving the devastating news of the fate of her fiancé.

Sarah further pushed away the heartbreaking hope that John and Mary would give Sophia about Gavin when that hope was such a lie.

Sarah turned to the window and focused on the ground below. It was too noisy in the cockpit for speaking and so she concentrated on the post-apocalyptic landscape.

This was her first birds-eye view of Ireland in the eight years since she and David had come to this country for a stress-relieving holiday and ended up fighting to stay alive.

She could see a series of what looked like shanty slums grouped along a long creek—mostly dry except for a thin ribbon of water.

A few miles away she saw several fires that appeared to be cottages with their thatched roofs ablaze. She'd hoped to get a view of the battlefield to see if the carnage was as extensive as she'd believed. But she saw nothing below that resembled what she'd seen.

When she'd asked David about it, he'd pretended not to know what she was talking about.

Susan Kiernan-Lewis

43

David tried not to watch Sarah's face. He had to keep reminding himself that she was several years behind where he was in wrapping her head around the devastation that was the new Ireland—in fact all of Europe for that matter.

When you're stuck in your own little world that doesn't extend a total of ten miles across, it's easy to think that life is a certain way because that's all you see.

Many people would find that kind of ignorance comforting.

But for David, the concept was truly inconceivable.

Sarah was so excited to see Mike again that it occurred to David it might be wise to take advantage of her present happy state to let her know what needed to happen next. With any luck, after thinking about it, she would agree with him about the next move.

He didn't want to have to coerce her if he didn't have to.

He would, certainly, if necessary. But he'd rather not.

He tapped her on the shoulder and when she turned he pointed to the headset on a hook by her window. They both put them on. Now they could hear each other.

"Looks pretty different from up here, doesn't it?" he said.

"How much further?"

"Not much. Listen, there's a good news bad news element to you seeing Mike again."

She frowned. "What are you talking about?"

Might as well just tell her. If she goes ape, she can't do too much damage at five thousand feet up.

"Once I take you to where he is, you won't be allowed to return to the castle afterward."

She turned fully to face him. "What are you talking about?"

"This…place where we're going….it belongs to MCP. Once you go there, well, there's no leaving."

Her mouth fell open but before she could speak he quickly said, "I've got no problem bringing John to you—and anybody else you want. There's plenty of room. You'll see that. But this is a one-way ticket, Sarah. No going back."

A muscle flinched in Sarah's jaw.

"You're saying I can have my husband or my home but not both."

"Is that pile of rubble really so dear to you? Isn't home where your *family* is?"

"So I won't be able to talk to Nuala?"

"Look, I can take you to the castle right now. You can stay as long as you want. But when you get back in this helicopter to go to Mike—you're not coming back."

"Why?"

"It doesn't matter why! It's just the way it is! Accept it or live without him!"

"You know I can't!"

"Fine. Then here's my one-time offer to you. I'll bring you to Mike *and* allow you to leave again on one condition."

"I loathe you, David. For you to even say those words…"

"*One condition*. You must take John, Mike, Siobhan, Fiona —whoever you want—but definitely John, and go back to the US."

"What? Why?"

He hesitated. "Something's coming. Something bad."

Sarah waved at the window where the raging fires were visible. "Worse than this?!"

"Trust me. Yes. Do you agree? Otherwise, no Mike."

"Fine. I…I…yes, I guess I have to."

"I'm serious, Sarah. I'll hold you to your promise."

"I said yes." She ripped the headphones off and tossed them on the floor.

David took in a long breath. Now he would give her the time she needed to sort it out, to think through it.

After a moment, Sarah reached down and jammed her headset back on but didn't speak.

Twenty minutes later, the helicopter broke free of the cloud bank and flew out over the sea. Sarah turned to look at him with her mouth open in wonder.

"One of the Blasket Islands?" she asked.

David was surprised she even knew about the Blasket Islands. They weren't well known outside the United Kingdom.

"I thought you said your island wasn't really an island," Sarah said.

"Mike isn't with me," David said, his eye on the dark shape on the water coming closer and closer. "He really *is* on an island. In fact one of the most remote in the UK. So remote that few people have ever been there."

"It looks like...like..."

"A dead body, I know. In fact, that's one of its names. In Irish the island is called *An Fear Marbh*, or *the dead man*. It has no harbor, no beach, no bridge, no airstrip. It's completely inaccessible."

"Unless you have a helicopter."

Sarah was shaking her head and David could only imagine how confused she must be wondering how in the world Mike had gotten to this forgotten lonely island in the middle of the North Atlantic Ocean.

They flew closer until the island's jagged cliffs and crumbling monastic ruins came into view. It was only late afternoon but already the sun had dropped beneath the horizon and David knew it would be dark soon enough. He preferred not to spend the night if he could help it.

The helicopter landed on the helipad built by MCP.

Sarah was leaning forward excitedly as the helicopter set down. As she disengaged her seatbelt, David reached over to stop her from opening the door herself.

"Remember your promise," he said. "I brought you to him. So you'll go back to the States with John."

"I told you I would. Now you tell me why Mike is here on an island clearly run by your organization."

"Because he's injured, Sarah. I'm sure I told you that. He was involved in...a battle the day before yesterday."

Sarah slumped against her seat as the rotors slowed to a stop. She gaped at him in horror.

"The battle that your men fought," she said, her eyes widening. "Mike was fighting *your* men? How in the world—?"

"That's a long story and believe me I'll let him tell you about it. The point is, he's been treated at our compound and now he's convalescing."

Sarah turned to stare out the window as a uniformed soldier ran to open the door. She could see the wind was whipping the hood of his jacket around his face.

"What are his injuries?" Sarah asked.

"He took a bullet to the shoulder, but it's healing. Some shrapnel."

Sarah turned to look at him as the soldier jerked open the door.

"Shrapnel? Where?"

"You'll see soon enough."

✻✻✻✻✻

The wind cut through Sarah as she stepped out of the helicopter onto the tarmac. From the air, the island had looked largely uninhabited except for some construction built into the side of a cliff.

She followed David and two soldiers to the building. As soon as they stepped through the door, Sarah saw flickering gaslight sconces lined the hallway.

So no electricity, she thought.

In spite of what David had said, she'd half expected this to be his complex. But it was clear that while the building had been built to accommodate specific needs, there was nothing else—besides the helipad—to show it was anything but strictly post-apocalyptic.

As they walked down the darkened hall with its flickering lighting, Sarah could smell onions and garlic frying— something she had not smelled since before she'd left the States.

Even without electric lights, this place has things that are nowhere else in Ireland nowadays.

Sarah felt her excitement ramping up as they walked. Her worry warred with her elation to see Mike again. She had already decided that she would hold off telling him about Gavin —at least until she'd had a chance to see how badly hurt he was —and to hold him and rejoice in having found him again.

They paused before a heavy wooden door. David said a few words to the soldiers. They nodded curtly and left them.

"This is the clinic," David said. He hesitated but Sarah grabbed the doorknob.

"If you tell me one more time to remember my promise, I will punch you in the nose," she said, her excitement and anticipation rippling off her in palpable waves. She pushed the door open.

The gas lights in the room flickered but there were enough of them to easily see that the room was a large infirmary with separate rooms curtained off, holding individual beds.

"First bed on the left," David said from behind her.

Sarah ran to the curtain and pulled it back. Instantly she gasped.

There in the semi dark was the familiar form of the man she knew as well as her own reflection.

Mike was sitting up in bed with a book in his lap. His head was wrapped in heavy white bandages and his right shoulder was also heavily bandaged.

Mindful of his bandaged shoulder, Sarah wrapped her arms around him, feeling the solid strength of him, and in spite of the medicinal air surrounding him, his familiar scent. She pulled back, her eyes wet with tears to look into his dear face.

"I can't believe it's really you," she murmured, a lump in her throat.

His eyes, soft and brown, regarded her.

It was clear he had no idea who she was.

Susan Kiernan-Lewis

44

"Mike?" Sarah said, her lips trembling. "It's me. Sarah."

Mike shook his head wearily and closed the book on his lap.

"Are ye one of the nurses then? I'm sorry if we've spoken before but I can't remember."

The horror of what he was saying flooded through Sarah. She felt David's hand on her back but she shrugged it off.

"You…you don't know me?" she asked, stunned.

"I'm sorry, I—"

"Stop apologizing!" Sarah said. "I'm your *wife*! You don't know me? I've gone through hell and murder to find you… and…and how the hell did you end up here! Can you at least tell me that?"

Mike frowned and his eyes darted behind her to David. He gave a helpless gesture with his hand. David grabbed Sarah by the arm and pulled her away.

"Give him some space, Sarah," David said.

A woman in a starched white uniform hurried down the hall toward them.

"What is all the shouting about, please?" she said sternly.

Sarah looked at her and then back at Mike who was now regarding the nurse with a hopeful expression as if she might be able to get this crazy woman away from him.

"I can't believe this," Sarah said, shaking her head as David pulled her away from the bed. "I can't believe he doesn't know me."

"Sarah, please," David said. "Let's go to the—"

She whirled on him.

"You knew this all along, didn't you?"

"Mr. Woodson!" the nurse said sharply, "would you *please* take this woman out of the ward? She's upsetting the other patients."

Sarah pushed past David and ran out the door.

✥❀✥❀✥❀✥❀✥

Fifteen minutes later, Sarah sat with David at a small cafeteria. A woman stood behind a wooden counter in front of a rudimentary kitchen. The scent of brewing coffee filled the room.

"I didn't know for sure *what* he'd remember," David said over his steaming mug of coffee.

"You didn't know he had amnesia?" Sarah asked sharply. "You didn't know he wouldn't know me from Adam's house cat?"

David gestured helplessly. "I wasn't sure."

"How? How did he get like that?"

"I told you. He was in a battle. He got shot."

"He was shot in the shoulder. Shoulder wounds don't make you forget your wife!"

"There was some shrapnel. That's the head injury."

"I can't believe this. I can't believe any of this. Why the hell was he fighting you?"

"He was attempting to find my compound for—"

"I do not believe that!" Sarah said, nearly shouting. "You're expecting me to believe that my husband kisses me goodnight, then gets up in the middle of the night without his damn shoes and decides to go find your compound? That's bull!"

David inhaled deeply and exhaled audibly.

"It's the truth, Sarah. He was with a group of people who were attempting to locate the entrance to our underground facility. We intercepted them when they got too close."

"And then what? You just decided to use your automatic weapons to mow down a handful of people in rags coming at you with Swiss Army knives and peashooters?"

"They were much better armed than that."

"I don't care! It was an effing massacre, David! I saw it! I was there!"

"Okay, yes, things got out of hand. I wish I could impress upon you how important the work is we're doing and how compromised it would be if we were discovered!"

"Well, baby, I think you succeeded in adequately *impressing upon* the poor bastards you left lying in their own gore back at Ballingeary!"

David shook his head and held his tongue with effort. Silence formed between the two and Sarah tried to remember how it had felt to be married to this man. Had she ever really known him at all?

The waitress came over and poured fresh coffee in their mugs, then set down a plate of Irish soda bread. Sarah touched the bread. It was warm. It had obviously just been pulled out of the oven.

Clearly whatever was happening on this island, baking over campfires or peat ovens wasn't a part of the picture. They might not have electricity, but they were better off than just about any place Sarah had seen in Ireland in the last eight years.

"How many people are on this island?" she asked quietly, trying to blot out the picture in her mind of Mike looking at her as if she were some mad woman who had nothing to do with him.

"About a hundred. There are cottages on the island."

"And who are the people who live here?"

"What do you mean?"

"I mean, David, the woman who just served us. Was she born here? Shipwrecked? Is this her job? Does she work in the canteen? Is she on somebody's payroll? Because where I come from, nobody has a job unless you count trying to stay alive."

David ran a hand across his face but didn't answer.

"Does this island belong to your organization?" Sarah persisted.

"We created it, yes."

"But this isn't where *you* live, is it?"

"This isn't the compound, Sarah. This isn't where MPC is based, if that's what you're asking. It really is just a lonely island out in the middle of nowhere."

"I thought that was the definition of where your compound was."

"No. My organization's headquarters is nowhere near here. Look, Sarah, you do know how essential secrecy is to the success of my organization, right? I mean, we are attempting to preserve the most important discoveries of our world's civilization—knowledge that will take centuries to relearn if it's lost!"

"Please spare me the sales pitch," Sarah said. "*Why* are these people here on this island? Why is my husband here?"

"Mike showed up near Ballingeary two days ago with an army of some very desperate people," David said.

"I just don't believe that."

"He and these other men demanded entrance to our compound and when denied, they were repulsed by force. Most were regrettably killed."

"I don't believe any of this!"

"Is that or is that not your husband in there?" David pointed in the direction of the clinic. "Because I'm telling you Mike Donovan and a few other people who weren't killed outright were picked up after the battle, treated at our medical facility near Ballingeary for their injuries, and then transferred here. End of story."

"Well, I need the *middle* of the story!" Sarah shouted.

"In that case, maybe I can help," a woman's voice said.

Sarah turned to see a woman who had silently entered the canteen. There was something very familiar about how she held herself.

But it wasn't until she had entered fully into the flickering kerosene lamplight afforded by the tabletops that Sarah saw with astonishment who she was.

45

Aideen Malone stood before Sarah, her hands in the pockets of her rain jacket, her eyes regarding Sarah sadly.

"Aideen," Sarah said before turning to look at David who shrugged.

"May I?" Aideen said, pulling out a chair at their table. "I heard you'd come and that you'd seen Mike. Sure I figured you'd have questions."

Aideen's face was more harshly lined than when Sarah had last seen her. In truth, a part of Sarah was surprised that Aideen was still alive. Aideen had left their community five years earlier on her own steam but it had been a blessing to all when she'd agreed to go. Aideen had met Mike during that terrible time when Sarah was lost in the Welsh National Forest trying to find her way home. Aideen had hoped to have him for her own.

"What do you know about why Mike is here?" Sarah asked.

"He's here because of me. Or rather, because of Taffy."

Taffy was Aideen's daughter. Sarah guessed she must be twelve by now.

"Perhaps you could start at the beginning?" David said. He waved to the woman in the kitchen to bring another coffee.

"It was you, wasn't it?" Sarah said. "*You* lured Mike away from the castle that night."

Aideen smiled. "You flatter me, Sarah, so ye do, that I could lure Mike to do anything. Nay, 'twasn't me. But I'll be telling ye the truth of it if ye'll let me."

Sarah's stomach gurgled in agony at the thought that Mike was not twenty feet from her but still as lost to her as he'd been five days ago when he'd vanished into thin air.

"Please," Sarah said tersely. "I'm all for hearing the truth."

Aideen leaned back in her chair and gathered her thoughts.

"After I left Ameriland, five years ago, Taffy and I found a home with a group south of Tralee. They were perhaps not quite as organized as your lot but in time we grew to care about each other and protected each other. I met a man named Conor Hayes."

Here, Aideen stopped and her eyes filled with tears.

Sarah glanced over at David but he was looking at his hands.

"Conor was a lot like Mike," Aideen said. "He treated me grand and I loved him something fierce. For whatever reason, I never got with child with Conor but sure he loved my Taffy like his own."

Sarah forced herself not to drum her fingers on the table but her impatience must have been apparent. Aideen narrowed her eyes at her.

"I always knew where Mike was," Aideen said. "Ye didn't need to live within a hundred kilometers to know about the castle community governed by Mike Donovan. And sure I told Conor all about him too. Everything was fine, so it was. But then two things happened." Aideen looked at David. "We heard about the man who lived in a hidden community with electricity and computers and modern medical facilities."

David swore and looked away.

"We heard this man was an American and the first husband of Mike Donovan's wife. I realized then that your first husband must not have died after all."

"Okay, so you wanted to go and live in the magic kingdom like everyone else who's ever heard of it," Sarah said.

Aideen turned cold eyes on Sarah. "Not at-tall, Sarah. But when Taffy came down with scarlet fever I knew I was going to lose her if I didn't get a miracle. My Conor made sure that miracle happened." Tears streamed down Aideen's face and then Sarah knew for sure that Conor must have been one of the casualties of the battle.

"So you went looking for the compound to find help for Taffy," Sarah said quietly. "And Mike? How did he end up with your group?"

Aideen wiped her eyes and smiled thinly at Sarah's word choice.

"Conor and his mates came to your castle. We'd all heard it had come down and there were no more walls between you and the elements. Or your neighbors come to that."

"They came at night?" Sarah said, her jaw tense with anger.

"Aye, so they did," Aideen said, her expression refusing to apologize for it. "Conor knew which one Mike was. Hard not to know, being so big and all. When Mike left your tent and walked to the bogs just outside the camp, Conor and his men intercepted him."

"Assaulted him, you mean."

Aideen shrugged. "He wouldn't have come willingly. So he came the only way he would. Unconscious and half naked."

Sarah's fury seemed to emanate from her fingertips. That Mike had been accosted and forced from the camp was something she'd always known must have happened, but to hear it told so blandly was almost too much to bear.

"He was brought back to our camp and I don't need to tell you, he was so angry he was practically mental, so he was. At first I didn't think he'd help us but when he learned it was for Taffy—to save her life—he soon settled down. He wanted to return to the castle and tell you but we couldn't wait. He agreed to take us to where he believed the secret compound was—where medical facilities were that would save the life of me child."

"And did it?" Sarah asked. "Save Taffy's life?"

Aideen's face cleared and she nodded at David. "Sure it was a hard price to pay, but she was treated at your husband's compound and she sleeps this very night in a warm bed not a hundred feet from where we're sitting."

"Glad everything worked out for you," Sarah said coldly.

"Mike sent you a message saying where he'd gone," Aideen said.

"I never got it."

Aideen shrugged. "These are uncertain times. Anything could have happened to it."

Sarah turned to David.

"So she's here because she's seen your secret compound?"

David nodded. "Basically, yes. Nobody's who's been there can be allowed to just wander the countryside. Our mission is too vitally important to—"

Sarah held up a hand. "Stop. For the love of God, just stop." She turned to Aideen. "And you don't mind being held here on this rock in the middle of the ocean?"

Aideen shook her head. "Sure it's nicer than any place I've lived since the first EMP destroyed everything. We're safe here, we have enough to eat. Until you showed up, everything was fine."

"What is *that* supposed to mean?"

"It means, you've only been on the island less than an hour and already you're causing problems. Mike was very upset to see you."

"He was upset because he was starting to recognize me!" Sarah said.

"No, Sarah," Aideen said. "He has a *brain* injury. He was upset because he's very vulnerable right now and a woman burst into his room shouting at him. I'd hoped that you'd have changed since I last saw you but it's clear you haven't. You're still insisting on having everything your own way—regardless of who you hurt in the process. Even if that's someone you claim to love."

Sarah stood up, knocking over her chair.

"You kidnapped my husband and you got a lot of people killed to get what *you* want, including your own husband it sounds like. So I'd be careful about who you're accusing of getting her own way at any cost. Mike's *brain injury* is because of *you*. It's a miracle he wasn't killed. So you can stow the lectures. Besides I won't be around long."

Aideen stood up.

"Good," she said. "I just needed to hear it from your own lips. I won't apologize for what I did. You would have done the same, so you would. Any mother would."

Then she turned and left the room.

Sarah turned on David.

"You knew about this all along. You knew about Aideen. About Mike's amnesia."

"Look, Sarah. I think the thing to remember here is that I had nothing to do with any of this. If anything, I cleaned up a very big mess that somebody else started. You're welcome."

"You're unbelievable."

"It doesn't matter what I am. *You* promised that if I took you to Mike you would take John and leave Ireland and I'm holding you to that. Something is coming, Sarah. Something bad, and I'll not have our son anywhere near here when it does. If you love him, you wouldn't want it either."

Sarah felt the exhaustion and confusion of her long day roll through her body in waves. She wanted to cry. She'd been so excited to see Mike again. She felt like he'd literally just been dangled in front of her only to be snatched away again.

"Tomorrow the helicopter will pick up John," David said. "Along with Siobhan, Sophia, Maggie, the two twins Matt and Mac and anybody else you want to come with you—no matter how many trips it takes. They will bring them here to the island. You'll all have a couple of days before the ship is ready to sail to the States."

"We're going by ship? What about Fiona and Regan?"

"They'll be taken to the US when they're recovered. Unless they don't want to go in which case they'll be brought to this island where they will stay until they die of old age. We make food drops monthly. They'll survive."

"What about this mysterious thing that's coming? Will they survive that?"

David hesitated. "I honestly don't know. With luck." He stood up and checked his watch. "In any case, it's late and we're both tired. I'll show you where the visitors' quarters are."

"I need to see Mike again."

"Sarah, he's under a regime of medication. I'm sure he's asleep by now. He's trying to *heal*. Especially if we put him through a sea voyage in a couple of days, he'll need all the rest he can get."

"What are you saying?" Sarah said with frustration. "Mike won't want to come with me. He doesn't even know me!"

"We can bring him by force. My suggestion is you take him with you to the States and in time, maybe he…"

265

"Maybe he what?" Sarah looked around the room in bewilderment. "Maybe he decides not to hate me for abducting him? Maybe he agrees to live with me as man and wife because he's just so happy living in an American subdivision watching cable TV? Are you crazy? I can't take him against his will!"

"Well, you might have to. You promised me that you'd take John back to the US before this thing—"

"I need more time! If I'm going to help Mike remember me, I'm going to have to spend time with him to try to jog his memory. At the very least, we'll need to move him into my room or the one next to mine."

"That's probably not a good idea."

"How is he going to remember me if I don't see him?"

"Look, Sarah, I wasn't sure how to tell you—"

"Tell me what?"

"You know he was brought here with Aideen, right?"

"So?"

"It's just…well, it seems…"

"Spit it out!"

"Right now Mike believes he's Aideen's husband."

If you want to see how everything works out for Sarah and Mike, be sure to check out *White Out, Book 10 of the Irish End Games* which will be published in the Summer of 2017.

Author's Note:
The island of Inishtooskert where I have plopped our hapless crew is famous for its strong Irish culture and the fact that it does indeed resemble a dead body or sleeping giant out in the middle of the North Atlantic.

ABOUT THE AUTHOR

Susan Kiernan-Lewis lives in North Florida and writes mysteries and dystopian adventure. Like many authors, Susan depends on the reviews and word of mouth referrals of her readers. If you enjoyed *Dead On*, please leave a review saying so on Amazon.com, Barnesandnoble.com or Goodreads.com.

Check out Susan's blog at susankiernanlewis.com and feel free to contact her at sanmarcopress@me.com.